FIRST CONTACT!

I stared, amazed, at this object which had injected sounds into my head. Fascinated, I picked it up and listened again.

Warbling as before. Then scanning. Mutual scanning. A light touch sweeping across my mind, my own touch sweeping across another mind. An utterly alien mind! I was in direct contact, but with what? A kaleidoscope of images, then the familiar image of Earth seen from space. A long hull glowing as it entered atmosphere. An impression that the hull contained the other mind.

High above the Pacific Ocean a small silver ovoid, like the one I held, shot out from the hull. The hull continued its downward course and splashed into the sea. The picture blanked. The other had shown me what it was and how it had arrived.

Unless this was some complex scam, the thing on my desk was an extension of the mind I had scanned. A mind in a spaceship that now rested somewhere under the Pacific Ocean!

EDWARD LLEWELLYN
in DAW editions:

THE DOUGLAS CONVOLUTION
THE BRIGHT COMPANION
PRELUDE TO CHAOS
SALVAGE AND DESTROY
FUGITIVE IN TRANSIT
WORD-BRINGER

WORD-BRINGER

EDWARD LLEWELLYN

DAW BOOKS, INC.
DONALD A. WOLLHEIM, PUBLISHER

1633 Broadway, New York, NY 10019

DAW Collectors Book No. 679.

First Printing, July 1986

1 2 3 4 5 6 7 8 9

PRINTED IN U.S.A.

PROLOGUE

WORD-BRINGER SPIRALED in toward Earth, released its probe as it entered atmosphere, and splashed down in the Pacific almost a thousand kilometers south of the Aleutians. It sank slowly to the ocean floor while its probe, attracted by signals from the coast, swooped toward Oregon. A small silver ovoid, it landed in a clump of trees within a fenced compound near the cliffs and was soon covered by drifting leaves. It lay hidden, singing softly, while its master settled into the Pacific ooze.

A girl of nine, her head filled with sorrows and dreams, wandered alone among the trees. She heard the singing nobody else had heard. She dug the egg out of its nest of leaves and put it to her ear, listening in delight, seeing visions of fairyland.

I learned all this later, but you need to know it now if you are to understand the story I am about to tell. You may regard me as what literary academics call an "untrustworthy narrator." I am a patent-lawyer who writes an occasional popular-science article so I lack a novelist's ominiscience and can only relate events as I saw them then.

1

THE VIEW FROM the penthouse offices of Ebermann and Haskard was inspiring—the kind that inspires vultures. Washington, in all its rich promise, lay shimmering in the noon heat as though the tension endemic to the city were distorting the air itself. In the distance the dome of the Capitol gleamed in the sunshine. Away, across the Potomac, a chopper was angling down toward the Pentagon. Around us rose the towers of Washington's only industry— the processing and manipulation of words. An industry which spun off sufficient wealth to support powerful organizations such as E&H, Inc., Industrial Consultants, and individual attorneys, such as myself.

Below to my left were the gray colonnades of the Commerce Department, the old home of the US Patent Office. Patent Art is my special skill. Wisdom was insisting that I stay within its safe boundaries; curiosity was urging me to learn more about the proposition the partners had just made. Curiosity won. I turned toward Harold Ebermann, hunched behind his vast desk. "Let's get this straight. What I just heard sounded crazy."

"It is a long shot, Richard," said Adam Haskard, leaning against the far wall of his partner's office. "But we're willing to gamble on your talent."

"You'll pay me to listen to some professor read a paper I won't understand, hoping that I'll spot where he's covering up?"

"You knew enough chemistry to blackmail our client last year." Ebermann scowled.

"Conray Chemicals? I didn't need much chemistry to finger that bit of crooked incompetence."

"Richard, you picked out the one flaw in an otherwise excellent patent application." Adam moved across the

7

office so I had to turn to face him. Negotiating with Ebermann and Haskard was like rallying after your partner has dropped his racket. "You sensed their planted diversion. Nobody else did. Or could."

"Conray deserved what they got."

"What you got," grunted Ebermann.

"We bear no ill will." Adam smiled as a vulture might be expected to smile. "In fact it was your success then which prompted us to invite you here now. Why we're proposing this joint adventure in trade."

"Sounds more like industrial espionage. These days I'm strictly a patent attorney."

"You haven't written up a patent in years," growled Ebermann. "You live by looting other people's."

The insult diverted me, as he doubtless intended. "A patent's an open description—by definition. A 'secret patent' is a contradiction in terms. Anyone who tries to get patent protection without making full disclosure is a crook."

"And you're a public benefactor! Some people don't see you that way."

"Management doesn't like being challenged by one guy working for himself."

"What they don't like," Adam broke in, "is having a master patent placed in jeopardy by threat of incomplete disclosure." He smiled his vulture smile. "I admit you usually mention the flaws to the management concerned, rather than to the courts or a competitor."

"For a price," muttered Ebermann.

"A very small percentage of the patent's value." Adam lit a cheroot. "You could almost regard such payments as fines levied against an offender. After all, an unofficial guardian of the public weal is entitled to some private reward. The bounty hunter is a traditional figure in·our society."

"I don't go after some poor devil of an inventor!" I was stung by his analogy. "I go after corporations. D'you know why? Because they're easy meat. They're problem crushers. They've got squads of experts. But a corporation has no soul and no insight."

"While you have. Insight at any rate. I know—I've watched you work. Richard, what's your secret?"

"He doesn't know," growled Ebermann. "He doesn't know any more than a hog knows how it smells truffles."

"Your success still irritates Harold. But seriously—I'm interested—how do you see things that aren't there? ESP?"

"ESP's bunk. Psych snakeoil! Parapsych's as fake as astrology." I was irritated by Adam's suggestion that I had some occult method for detecting deceit. What I did have was an acute sense of the bogus, a sensitivity for statements that are off-key. The sensitivity which allows a conductor to bawl out a fourth violin for a half-tone error in a grace note. Duplicity, in speech or writing, shrieks at me like a wild discord. All my life I have been sensitive to the counterfeit, a talent which has left me with no close friends and a number of enemies; especially in high-tech corporations which hold questionable master patents and dislike litigation.

A patent application is an art form. A good application, like any good art, only reveals its hidden meanings to the informed and dedicated eye. The creative patent lawyer, like the creative goldsmith, works with valuable materials, the products of high-tech R and D. The patent attorneys of large corporations are skilled at crafting the outputs of research laboratories into their final form—the issued patents.

Their skill lies in claiming the widest of ends while divulging the narrowest of means; in steering between the Scylla of incomplete disclosure which will invalidate the patent if it is challenged in court, and the Charybdis of including detail which will devalue it in practice. My art lay in identifying incomplete disclosure, but I was sensitive to suggestions that there was something psychic about my methods. "Adam, you hanker after mystical explanations for things you don't understand. Do you wheel and deal by the stars?"

Adam shrugged. "More people do than you'd think. Astrologers earn a lot more than astronomers. And there's more of 'em." He laughed. "Sure—I read 'What the Stars Foretell' after I read the market reports. Enough people trade by the stars to tip a sensitive market. Also by who wins the Superbowl. Or the length of women's skirts. But you, Richard, how do you read the corporate mind?"

"I can't read anybody's mind. I'm good at spotting incongruities. When experts cover their trail they leave clues behind."

"The bird with a broken wing?"

"Eh?" said Ebermann. He was basically a statistician, and real-world metaphors were not his forte.

"A mother bird may mimic a broken wing to divert attention from her nest," explained Adam, who was educated as a lawyer but had literary ambitions. "A predator with experience in such tactics—plus a sharp nose—may backtrack to a meal."

"Their tricks tend to be typical," I agreed. "If they try to divert attention from something in a patent, it's often worth finding. But in scientific papers, like the one you're suggesting I monitor, if an author is devious he's usually only trying to disguise his ignorance."

"There's more psychic than logic about you, Ryan," growled Ebermann.

"Some of the people you've tangled with think you can read minds," said Adam, smiling.

"People who think that can't have minds worth reading."

"Our client's sure you can." Ebermann scowled at me. "That's why you're here. They're insisting we retain you to scan this professor. If they weren't insisting—!" His gesture said that I wouldn't have been invited to any kind of joint adventure in their peculiar trade.

"I think they're right," said Adam. "This is a job nobody else can do. And—for you—there's more in it than money. You're an artist in your way. Every artist enjoys an audience. Your very success denies you one."

"If they knew what you're up to in the Patent Office," added Ebermann, "you'd be as popular as a pimp in a rival whorehouse." When he did attempt metaphor he was apt to be crude.

"Do I detect a threat?"

"Of course not," cut in Adam. "Richard, we're offering you more than profit. We're offering you the chance to perform under the admiring eyes of the only two people in Washington who can appreciate your quality."

By the rules of our game, if I sought to learn more than they had chosen to tell me already it would imply an element of commitment. "This job you're suggesting—it's bizarre. I'll probably find nothing."

"That's our risk."

"And it's strictly a term deal? A sure thing for me—a long shot for you?"

"That's the gamble we're taking. After all—" Ebermann shrugged. "You'll be a bona fide consultant." A tax deduction—the US taxpayer would be taking most of the gamble.

"Is it legal?"

"It's better than legal—it's ethical. The Feds may be trying to grab a monopoly. Blocking that kind of creeping socialism is the most ethical act I can think of." Ebermann probably did think that.

"I haven't used an on-line approach for years. I scan documents—not people." I turned back to the window, considering what the partners were suggesting. E&H were my antithesis—a firm that used all the fashionable methodologies of management studies, operations research, and industrial engineering, all the sophisticated techniques of mathematical models and computer simulation, to bring aid and comfort to organizations in trouble from government, labor, or their own inefficiency. But Adam's particular delight was industrial espionage; it satisfied something in his psyche as well as his lust for abnormal profits. He and Ebermann, between them, had more than their share of brains and determination but, lacking my insight, they had to use the methods of massed technological attack. And this project evidently demanded insight.

"Action in real time. People—not paper. Good sport and a sure profit." Adam was tempting me with that entrapping myth, a risk-free gain.

"A sure profit for you, Ryan," Ebermann reminded me. "A gamble for us."

"Who? Where? When? I'll not take you up on anything until I think there's a chance I won't let you down." I saw Ebermann glance at Adam and added, "Honest dealing."

"Honest dealing—of course." Adam moved to perch on his partner's desk and I dropped into a chair. From now on whatever I learned I would forget if we did not close the deal. As they would forget we had met. Commercial trust is an absolute prerequisite when dealing in information, even more vital than when dealing in hog-belly futures. "The target is a Doctor Edgar Slipe, Granard Professor of Chemistry at Cornell. He's scheduled to give the keynote address at a meeting of the Federated Chemical Societies in Baltimore next week."

"The keynote address? That's the slot where they put

some elderly prof on his way out. Gives the oldster a last
chance to misremember the past and misread the future.
And who ever says anything of value at Federation meetings? They're academic orgies—an excuse to enjoy travel
grants.''

"Slipe is a Past-President of the Federation. And he
fixed it with the program committee to give the keynote
address. We have inside information that he's planning to
say something of value to our client.''

"Something of value? In the keynote address at a public
meeting?''

"If we thought Slipe was liable to make an open claim
our client wouldn't have told us to hire you—not at the
fees you charge.'' Ebermann scowled at me. "But Slipe's
the kind who wants credit as well as cash. He wants it
more than most. He's also part paranoid. Afraid some rival
will grab whatever he's got if he doesn't establish prece-
dence. Our client thinks Slipe's onto something good and
he'll use this meeting to take out insurance. Drop ambigu-
ous remarks into the record. Remarks he'll be able to
resurrect later when he claims priority. You know the
strategy, Ryan.''

"He wants to talk but he's not yet ready to publish or
patent,'' added Adam. "Probably trying for an end-run
round Cornell's patent policy while he closes some industrial deal. Slipe's one of those guys who should be in *this*
business—not in academe. Our guess is that he plans to
bury markers, and he'll go easy round the places where he
plants 'em.''

I nodded. That did make a kind of sense. Dated and
witnessed notebooks are good evidence of priority in a
patent application but they don't carry the same conviction
in court as do statements made at a public meeting and
recorded in the proceedings. But it certainly required a
taste for publicity and a component of paranoia to use a
keynote address for such a purpose. "And you think I'll be
able to spot where he's covering up?''

"We're prepared to bet on your clairvoyance.''

"Not clairvoyance—experience.'' I said irritably. I am
always astounded by the way that even intelligent executives become suckers for the paranormal. How fortune
tellers, or psychics as they prefer to call themselves, can

extract money from otherwise tough-minded businessmen by claiming to tell the future. There are psychics in Washington who make more money than I do.

"Experience—if that's what you prefer. We're betting on your knack for spotting deception."

"Even if I don't understand what Slipe's talking about?"

"You knew enough about polycrystalline silicon to milk Conray Chemicals last year," growled Ebermann.

My knowledge of polycrystalline silicon had been superficial, but my insight into the thinking of Conray's patent department had been deep. "Is that going to be Slipe's subject?"

"Our client thinks he's onto a new method of purifying polysilicon—the stuff they make microchips from." Ebermann pulled a heavy manila envelope from his desk drawer. "Here's the dirt on Slipe. His CV, publications, et cetera et cetera. Read this and you'll know enough to scan him."

"You expect me to read what he's published, listen to him lecture, then tell you where he's laid smoke?"

"That's the general idea," said Adam, with a smile. "We're backing your intuition, Richard."

"Intuition based on ignorance produces bullshit. Expensive bullshit."

"Ryan," growled Ebermann, "you often produce shocks. But seldom bull. I'll grant you that."

"A week's consulting fees. Plus expenses. Probably with a nil return. You two are after big game."

"We're still casting about." Adam again smiled his vulture smile. "If you flush a bird you may care to join the action."

He was asking me to play hound to his hawk. I don't know much about falconry, but I doubt if it's the dogs who make the killing. I temporized. "Fee for service. And no residual constraints?"

"Only the usual."

"I listen to Slipe talk. Record him on tape. Analyze the tape along with any clues I pick up from him direct. Then give you a transcript along with where I think he's using camouflage?"

"If that's how you want to do it."

"After that—finish?"

"Finish—if you choose it that way. Or if you get nothing of value. But if you strike pay dirt I hope you'll want to join the digging."

"And if I want to excavate alone?"

"You'd be unwise." Ebermann hunched farther forward across his desk. "But the only enforceable clause is that you'd give us first refusal on anything you turn up."

"You're being generous, Harold."

"I don't enjoy it. It's not our usual way of doing business. But we always seem to be generous when we do business with you." He pushed the manila envelope toward me.

Slipe's background was the bait. If E&H were being generous there was something very valuable beyond that envelope. And they needed my talent to reach through to it. I hesitated—and was hooked. "I'll give it a try. It sounds crazy to me—but I'll do my best."

"You always do, Richard." Adam smiled. "Only, this time, we're your clients."

I stood up, weighing the package in my hands. "Feels like there's a hell of a lot in here."

"Then you'd better get going." Our deal was closed. Ebermann saw no further need for even his brand of courtesy.

"Good hunting, Richard," said Adam as he walked with me to the elevator.

Hunting what? As the doors of the elevator closed I felt a shiver of the strange—a warning to throw Slipe's dossier back at Harold Ebermann. To stick to the skinning of fat corporate cats. This had the smell of more lethal game.

2

THE FEDERATED CHEMICAL Societies were meeting at the Stromberg-Hilton, a hotel of such blatant opulence that no sensible person would choose to stay there were he paying the bill out of his own pocket. As I was not paying out of mine I had reserved one of the more expensive suites and then failed to exploit its luxuries by spending most of another night studying Slipe's publications. They did not read like the work of a man about to produce a finding of commercial value. They did suggest an acute mind—a mind acute enough to exploit the findings of others. I woke from a few hours' sleep with a headache and no desire to hear Slipe expound in person. I drank coffee as I shaved, lit my first cigarette of the day, pinned on my name tag, and went to the Grand Ballroom where Slipe was due to give his keynote address after the mid-morning break.

The final speaker of the first session was still in full incoherent flow. I selected a seat half-hidden by a pillar, from which I would be able to get a good view of Slipe without his seeing me. Then I studied the audience.

It was sparse. Mostly ambitious graduate students and duty-bound colleagues of the speaker, by the look of them. Not surprising. If anything of importance is said at a large scientific meeting it is said in the bars or bedrooms. Modern science and technology are so fragmented that only a few specialists can hope to understand what a speaker is saying while he is actually saying it. Nor is even the most distinguished of modern researchers likely to reveal his latest discovery to a general audience. New ideas do not spring fully formed from the head of some genius, nor did they ever. Ohm lost his university appointment after propounding his law. To us now it is self-evident, but to his academic contemporaries it seemed absurd. If you care to read his original paper you will understand why—even when translated into English from the original German it evades comprehension. Flemming described the action of an enzyme released by penicillin notatum to the Royal Society in 1927 while his audience slept, thinking it was only old Ambrose still talking about lysozymes.

Science and engineering are even more compartmentalized today than they were then. The leaders in one field are usually naive in the next. A researcher may not realize what he has really discovered until a colleague explains it to him later. Anything new is revealed in small closed symposia where everybody knows, understands, and suspects everybody else. Intensive exchanges of information in an atmosphere of admiration, envy, and informed argument. The definitive paper, published months or years later, is, by then, old stuff to the cognoscenti. Large meetings, such as the one I was attending, are scientific clambakes. Some new knowledge is doubtless bartered within the separate specialist cliques, but it is seldom mentioned in the papers on the official program.

You might accuse me of envy or arrogance in these criticisms of the science elite. You may be right. I am no scientist and I have never had an original scientific idea in my life. But my talent for sensing bogus is paired with an ability to recognize the genuine. An ability to appreciate what creative minds are trying to say while they are floundering in their own words.

It was, in fact, my lack of originality that steered me into my present career. I graduated from MIT in Engineering Science, a high-prestige course which produces neither engineers nor scientists. Most of my classmates headed for graduate school and academe. I could not face a further prolongation of adolescence and opted for industry, where my inability to think creatively became obvious, at least to myself.

Creation is the essence of engineering. A noncreative engineer, if he has any pride in his profession, is condemned to a lifetime of frustration. I rejected the temptation to shift sideways into sales or middle management and quit to use what I had discovered to be my true talent—my ability to appreciate originality in others. I set out to become a science writer.

Time ran out as did my money while I was still learning the tricks of the writing trade—a free-lance journalist inhabits the modern equivalent of Grub Street—and the Defense Intelligence Agency silenced me. In one of my few published articles I described recent developments in negative radar imaging more fully than it was supposed to be described in the open literature. After harassing me for months, the DIA was finally convinced that I had used nothing more than my own insight. By that time my name was mud to editors.

But the experience introduced me to the art of scientific deception and showed me a rich field ripe for harvesting. I managed to obtain a law degree and served my time in the Patent Office. Patent law was then one of the few legal specialties, although the lawyers were already starting to ape the doctors and divide the cake among high-priced protected specialists. With my paper credentials complete, I set up in private practice as a patent attorney.

The practice prospered. Partly for reasons mentioned by Adam Haskard, but more through my insight into the psychology of scientists, engineers, lawyers, and corporation executives. In the process I added to my engineering education an extensive and peculiar knowledge of high-tech applied science. Nothing patentable is entirely foreign to me. But, until that morning, I had restricted my interests to patents of commercial value. This was my first open-ended interaction for years. I adjusted my tape recorder and waited for Slipe.

The current speaker's concluding remarks had to compete with an obligato of clattering china from the foyer as waiters unloaded coffee urns and set out cups and saucers. He faded into silence and peered down from the rostrum. The chairman tried to stimulate some discussion, failed, thanked the speaker, and terminated the session. Most of the audience headed for relief and coffee. I lounged back behind my pillar, smoking a forbidden cigarette and glancing at the people starting to drift back into the Grand Ballroom.

Slipe was collecting a larger audience than I would have expected for a keynote address. There were, of course, the usual mandarins attending from courtesy to a senior colleague. But there were also younger intense-looking men and women of the assistant professor variety. If they came to keynote addresses at all, they came only to sneer at their seniors. Plus a sprinkling of hard-nosed citizens, the representatives of scientific management, who seldom attend addresses of any kind. Conray Chemicals was not the only firm hunting Doctor Slipe. A number of others evidently believed that he was liable to say something relevant to their special interests.

A woman in spectacles and a badly tailored gray suit came down the aisle to sit three rows ahead of me—an unremarkable woman who would be lost in a crowd of ten. But the man who had been saving her a seat carried more muscle and looked more formidable than most men in the audience. And her profile teased my memory. She glanced around, as though sensing my scrutiny, before reaching into her handbag and adjusting a tape recorder.

A new chairman appeared on the platform and exhorted the various gossiping groups to take their seats. People began to settle down. The Grand Ballroom was full and latecomers were standing crowded at the back of the hall. This indeed promised to be an unusual keynote address. The chairman hinted at it when he announced the title, which was not in the printed program. "Some Critical Factors Affecting Polycrystalline Purification," by Professor Edgar Slipe, Granard Professor of Chemistry and Past-President of the Federation.

Slipe emerged from the shadows like a plump Polonius entering from the wings. There was a patter of polite applause. Slipe smiled, shook hands with the chairman, and accepted the speaker's microphone, which he hung round his neck with the air of a priest donning a vestment. Then he moved to the lectern, dropped his notes upon it with a gesture that said he, at any rate, was not going to read a prepared speech, and looked out over his audience. He paused until satisfied that he had their attention, then launched into what sounded like an extemporaneous talk on the problems involved in the purification of the chlorinated derivatives of silane gas.

Had I not recognized him from his photograph I would have known him by his style. He was delivering a carefully prepared address with such skill that most of his audience would accept it as spontaneous. Within a few minutes he had established the impression he was a modest researcher leading us along a comprehensible path through a thicket of complex scientisms. He spoke as he wrote, with a clarity not found in the abominable prose and worse rhetoric which most scientists adopt when they try to emphasize the importance of their work. And his skill cloaked the fact that most of his speech had previously appeared in his published papers. Some of it even turned out to be quotations from other people's papers.

He moved confidently through his presentation. I allowed his meaning to flow over me while I concentrated on detecting the surface eddies which would mark subsurface snags. My pocket recorder was running, my finger was on the cue switch. Later I would review what he said; now I must sense *how* he was saying it. Concentrate on his eyes, his mouth, the rise and fall of his voice, the emphasis he laid on certain words—and his attempts to deemphasize others. I strained for the subliminal clues distributed through his presentation that signaled he was starting to pick his way across treacherous ground.

The first came after about five minutes; the momentary pause a man makes when he enters an area of hidden danger—the care of a soldier considering each step when returning through a minefield he himself has laid. I pressed the cue switch to mark my tape, relishing this reassurance that I could still detect patterns of deceit while a speaker was weaving them.

There were a number of such hesitations and several lapses of the tongue before Slipe concluded his address with a rhetorical recapitulation and coda. The applause which broke out immediately as he stopped speaking showed that he had seduced most of his audience. The number of eager questioners on their feet suggested that he had said something they thought important. For me he had been most informative in what he had left unsaid. He stood there, fat, self-satisfied, smiling, enjoying the kudos for which he lusted, until the clapping subsided and the chairman selected the fortunate few from the many eager to ask questions.

Slipe continued to display his command of the situation.

He dodged the first, handled the second with sophisticated brevity, and in answering the third he moved into generalities and played out the clock. The chairman closed the discussion and Slipe came down from the platform glowing like a man who knows he has performed well.

As he had. His presentation had been the equivalent of a well-written patent, a patent designed to confuse rather than reveal. He had dropped offhand comments, inserted casual phrases, so that the record contained remarks which at present seemed slight, but could, when required, be retrieved to support a claim to priority. I knew where they were though not what they implied.

The chairman thanked Professor Slipe for a memorable presentation and began to announce the title of the next. Half the people in the room headed for the exits, the other half for Slipe. He was engulfed by a knot of questioning colleagues. After a few minutes of smiling congratulations and handshakes he disengaged himself with a gracious gesture toward the next speaker who was standing at the lectern, shuffling his notes, and gazing despondently at his diminishing audience.

The woman ahead of me was standing, waiting to join the exodus. I glimpsed her full-face and my memory locked on to the photograph of a beautiful woman. That same woman, but now dressed to avoid appearing beautiful. She started to turn, as though looking for whoever was looking at her, but I was already slouching back behind my pillar. Justine Ladrich from Loucher Freres, a Paris firm of financial consultants with whom I would not wish to deal. When I ventured another glance she was disappearing up the aisle. I waited for her to clear the exit before I followed.

I was still waiting when Slipe's successor launched into a monologue on the mechanisms through which oxygen attracts metal contaminants in polycrystalline silicon. After several minutes he called for his first slide and the lights went out. When they came on again he had lost half his audience. The second time they went out he was about to lose me. I was rising to escape when a firm hand grasped my wrist. And a familiar voice ordered, "Sit down, Ryan!"

I sat. Colonel Metzler had that effect. I glanced at the axelike face lit by the reflection from the screen. "Colonel! What are you doing here?"

He overrode my question with his own. "Ryan, what are you up to?"

With Metzler, limited truth is the safest policy. "Me? I'm covering the meeting for a client. Looking for potential patents."

"Potential patents—hell! You were scanning Slipe."

"Colonel—I had no idea the DIA was interested in Slipe. If I had—I wouldn't be here."

"Then forget I was. Until I remind you. We'll be in touch." With that threat he was gone.

Before I could escape myself the lights returned, leaving me trapped among empty seats with the chairman asking for questions and the speaker peering down in search of his graduate-student claque. I left before he could fixate me.

The appearance of Justine Ladrich and Colonel Metzler had changed this trip from a profitable fishing expedition to an encounter with sharks. And had acted on me like the bell on Pavlov's dogs, flooding my mouth with a taste I had renounced. Like a single cigarette after months of abstinence, it had revived an old unhealthy hunger.

3

"SLIPE'S HIDING SOMETHING, all right," I told Ebermann the next day. "I've shown you where. I can't tell you what."

"That, we didn't expect." He continued searching through my report spread across his desk, studying sheet after sheet. Ebermann knew what he was looking for. Presently he grunted, "This sentence you've circled—where he says 'fluorinated derivatives of silane gas.' Doesn't he mean to say 'chlorinated derivatives'? As he said before?"

"There? He meant not to say 'fluorinated derivatives.' It's obvious."

"It isn't obvious."

"It is to me." I drank the coffee which Adam's secretary had just delivered and lit a cigarette. After a night of listening to Slipe on tape, of correlating his subliminals with his words, I was weary. "Whatever you're after, I'll have it marked in there. Want to bet? My fees—double or quits?"

"I suspect you'd win, Richard." Adam had come into the office. "And our accountants wouldn't allow a doubled fee as a legitimate business expense." He smiled at me. "What is silane gas anyway?"

I shrugged. "Something they use for preparing polysilicon for microchips." I had already deduced that all this excitement revolved around a new technique likely to shake Silicon Valley.

Adam strolled across the room to look over his partner's shoulder. Whatever he saw must have pleased him. "Want to stay with the hunt, Richard? Now that you've picked up a scent?"

"All I want right now is to pick up my check. And get to bed."

Ebermann shifted his bulk back in his chair and addressed his partner. "I've been trying to persuade Ryan into a joint venture. I think he's winded more than he's saying. He goes on talking about fee-for-service only." He glared at me. "Ryan—you should be a PR man for the American Medical Association."

"I work best on my own."

"It also lets you play your own game." He hunched forward. "Remember, if you find anything worth selling, you sell to us. That clause is enforceable."

"Ebermann—your background is showing."

"Ryan—you're a conceited hypocrite. And a paranoid with cause!" His anger was true indignation. "Since you acquired a cut-price part-time law degree you've been talking a lot of sanctimonious crap." Ebermann was a product of the Bronx, Columbia, and Harvard Business School; when he became heated his diction became mixed. "You're solid selfish greed."

Adam was laughing. "Richard's psyching you, Harold. We want him as a consultant."

"With Ryan's hide—he'll take a kick in the balls for a buck."

His metaphors were mixed but he was getting under my skin. "Feed me my check and I'll fade."

Ebermann scowled and touched a button. Another lovely secretary appeared, smiled at me, and laid a check on his desk. I smiled at her. Despite weariness I again envied Adam's ability to recruit staff who are both ornamental and efficient. Cooperative too, I had reason to believe. The secretarial agency I use rarely sends me a woman with all three assets.

"At your prices, Ryan," grumbled Ebermann as he signed, "we've paid for the privilege of my saying what I think."

I examined the check, then put it in my wallet. "You're both satisfied that I've performed as per contract?"

"Sure—sure," muttered Ebermann impatiently. "You're an Irish wunderkind. You've sniffed out the truffles."

"You're the artist I said you were," Adam said, smiling.

"Then maybe you'll want to buy some more news."

Both partners looked up from my report and neither was smiling.

"Points noticed in passing," I added quickly. "Not in Slipe's presentation."

"What's the price?" asked Ebermann with slow menace.

"Whatever value you put on it. Not cash. Just an info credit."

"Done. Now give."

"For starters—the Feds are watching Slipe."

"That we knew—zero credit."

They had known but they hadn't warned me. Verging on the unethical. I did not protest, but I would remember. "Second—Metzler was there."

Ebermann glanced at Adam, who started to light a cheroot. Then he looked at me. "Colonel Metzler from DIA? Your old boss?"

"He never was my boss. I was only an occasional consultant."

"Shot in the ass while consulting? So I heard."

"You've heard more than Metzler would like you to know."

"We know enough to stay clear of him and his Unit." Ebermann stuffed tobacco into his pipe. "Okay, Ryan, you've got a small credit. Anything else?"

That exchange of glances had been worth more than a small credit. "Nothing definite. Maybe I'll contact you later. When I remember more. And after the market's risen." I yawned and stood up. "Too tired for now. I'm for Annandale—and bed."

"Does clairvoyance burn up energy?"

"Clairvoyance—shit! I've told you—there's nothing clairvoyant about me. I just see what anyone could see if they'd take the trouble to look."

"Methinks the man protesteth overmuch," said Adam to his partner.

"Eh?" Ebermann scowled. His literary education is nil. "He sure charges overmuch."

"Wait just a moment, Richard." Adam waved me back to a chair. "Here's another proposal which might interest you—as a writer."

"I'm not a writer. Not any longer. I'm a lawyer now." But I sat down.

"You're still a writer at heart. So how'd you like an

assignment to interview some top scientists for a series on their sources of inspiration?"

"I'd like it. But ever since the DIA went after me about that negative radar article I've been poison to editors. They liked my stuff but they didn't want trouble. Spineless wonders! They talk about investigative journalism, and you give them something genuine—"

"Easy, Richard, easy." Adam held up his hand. "I know how you feel. And you've a right to feel that way. But Conray Chemicals has diversified into publishing. If you're interested I think I can persuade an editor to give you an assignment. They already hold your insight in high regard. How does that proposition attract you?"

It attracted me all right. As Adam had known it would. The mere suggestion had reawakened a hunger to again see my words in print. "What editor would toss me something like that now? Even under corporate pressure?"

"I know one who'd be glad to. He still talks about that negative radar thing of yours. Come off it, Richard. It's no big deal to sell talent. And you've got talent."

However fatuous, praise is a goad to a writer's ego. "Why does Conray want me? Some message they're trying to sell? And what's in it for you?"

"For us. This would be a joint venture."

"How adventurous? I live safely these days."

"Adventure—not danger. No risks in this project. Neither physical nor financial—for you, at any rate. But rewarding—cash and fame." He leaned forward. "I've sold Syndicated Scientific on the idea of such a series already. That'll give you coast-to-coast coverage. And the basis for a book that'll make you a best-selling author."

"Adam, I know your devotion to literature. But what are you selling me?"

"Conray's own Syndicated Scientific now. And pop science boosts circulation."

"I'm not sure I'd have the time."

"I can arrange for a competent ghost to do the writing if you'll do the interviewing."

"Ghost—hell. Anything printed under my by-line will be written by me."

"Of course. But we'd provide secretarial backup, arrange for the interviews, do all those chores—should you wish."

"Tell me what and why. No commitment yet."

"Easy, Adam." growled Ebermann. "As a writer, Ryan now specializes in blackmail letters to corporations. Make him close the deal before you bring him in."

"That goes both ways." I stood up. "I'm too tired to think crooked right now. I'll come by tomorrow when I'll be bright enough to sense what you're really after."

4

ANNANDALE IS A suburb of Washington, twelve miles inside Virginia. I own a couple of houses on one of its older streets, and I have my simple law office and study on the first floor of one house and my apartment on the second floor. This is both economical and convenient, for in my type of practice the image I present to corporate opponents is more important than the impression I make on clients. The corporations with whom I come into conflict have legal departments spread through several executive levels in their head office buildings and, at first, they do not take seriously an individual who lives over his store.

One such unwary company had financed my Annandale operation. They had finally found it safer to settle my account with negotiable information rather than with traceable checks, and paid me with news of an imminent real estate deal. I had been able to acquire the block I was now on ahead of the developer, who had arranged for its rezoning through his political contacts. Neither he nor his contacts realized that the various titles held under various names were all mine until he had bought most of them. Since then his bids on my two key houses had been growing in size and desperation. One day I would doubtless surrender, but for the moment I was too well suited to move.

My two houses are inconspicuous. The real estate agent who had sold them to me had dismissed them as "basic accommodations." But in addition to their key role in the developer's plans, they have other advantages. For example, the house I occupy has a garage opening onto a back alley which most visitors do not realize exists. It also has an exit via the furnace room into the basement of the house next door. I rent that house, on very reasonable terms, to a

Mr. Wang, who runs a restaurant on the ground floor and God knows what on the second. Mr. Wang often sends me in excellent Szchewan meals and ignores occasional comings and goings through my furnace room and his storeroom. None of these facilities are really necessary in my current career, but I feel more comfortable when I can enter and leave my house unobtrusively.

Ebermann called me paranoid. If such is true it is only because my talent for sensing deceit enables me to sense it in most of the people I know. That has taught me to keep my private affairs private and my staff always temporary. I prefer fee-for-service arrangements and have current accounts with a secretarial agency, an agency that supplies housekeepers, and an organization which can produce an attractive hostess for almost any occasion or function. I pay good fees and get excellent service most of the time and, although I may envy Adam's general-purpose staff, I realize that the confusion of functions must cause him considerable trouble.

When the doorbell rang on the morning after I had delivered my report to E&H I staggered out of bed assuming that it was my secretary-of-the-week arriving an hour before she had been booked. Half-awake, lacking coffee, still recovering from sleep lost while immersed in the works of Edgar Slipe, I failed to check the video and opened the front door, prepared to blast the girl. I faced Colonel Metzler making the equivalent of a dawn attack, invading my base at the time when he knew my vitality would be at its lowest ebb.

"Morning, Ryan." He stepped past me into the hall. "We must talk." He headed toward my study.

I diverted him into my office, protesting the hour and offering him coffee.

"I don't need caffeine. And you can try thinking without it." He stared round my unimpressive workplace, then at my modest computer terminal. "Still hiding your assets, eh?" The terminal interfaced with something much more sophisticated.

I subsided behind my desk, rubbing my unshaven chin, yearning for coffee, and trying to gather my wits. "It's good to see you, Colonel. But—?"

"Good for who?" He took off his trenchcoat—the Col-

onel was in uniform even when wearing civilian clothes—
and sat down, facing me. "You know why I'm here." A
statement not a question.

"I guess it's about Slipe?" Colonel Metzler is one of a
dying and dangerous breed. A soldier with the faith, the
determination, and the brains of an old-time Jesuit. His
faith is in the United States as the last hope for civilization. His determination is to defend the Republic's security. And his brains have locked him into scientific
intelligence when he would rather be out shooting the
Republic's enemies.

"You're damned right it's about Slipe. Who sent you
after Slipe?"

I lit a cigarette, saw the Colonel stiffen at the smoke,
and felt better. "My clients thought Dr. Slipe might say
something of interest to them. They retained me for an
opinion."

"Ryan—you don't lie. But you twist truth like a looper.
You were there to psych Slipe. What put you onto him?"

"That's privileged information. But it doesn't involve
the Federal Government—or the security of the United
States. I'm strictly in the private sector now."

"I know you are. I know how much money you're
making. I know what you're doing to make it. I know this
place is a poor-folk front. The Unit keeps an eye on its
past consultants—especially on twisted talents like yours.
In case we need to consult you again."

"I'm afraid I'm booked up at the moment."

Metzler stared at me. "We've always disliked each
other, haven't we, Ryan? But we've always respected each
other."

That was true—as Colonel Metzler used the word. I lit
another cigarette. Hell, this was my office! "I was monitoring Slipe's paper for a client. Trying to pick up anything he let slip."

"Anything worth money. The private sector's a natural
for you. You always did have an eye on the main chance."

"During my time as a consultant to the Unit I never
made a buck. And you know the chances I had."

"You earned enough from the jobs I tossed you to get
through law school. Let me believe you'd join us. Instead—
you went off to make money."

"Most generals fix themselves up with good jobs before they retire."

"Most Generals—" He bit back his opinion of most generals. An opinion which had delayed his becoming one. "Ryan, if you're as smart as you think you are—and you're not—then be smart enough to cooperate. Have you any idea why your client turned you loose on Slipe?"

"Something to do with the purification of silicon. But that's only an informed guess."

"Your informed guesses are usually close to the mark. That's why I hate to see you wasting your clairvoyance— all right, your God-given insight—on commercial filth while the nation that protects you is threatened." He brooded for a moment. "Notice anything?"

"Well, Justine Ladrich was there. So I guess Loucher Freres are interested in pure silicon."

"Justine Ladrich! I didn't see her. She's an expert in staying inconspicuous. Yet you spotted her. That confirms it." He stared at me. "Do you know what that woman is?"

"She's one of Loucher's financial analysts, isn't she? I've never met her. Only seen her photograph. I've heard she's pretty smart."

"Too damned smart to be natural. She's clairvoyant. Like you."

"I'm not clairvoyant! And she can't be. There's no such thing as clairvoyance. Maybe she has the same sensitivity to subliminal clues that I have—but that's all."

The Colonel shrugged. "Call yourself what you like." He leaned forward. "Know who Loucher's main clients were once? They sure weren't our allies. That's why I want your help in this Slipe business."

"Colonel, I'm already retained—"

"Ryan, where's your patriotism?"

"I used it all up in that Chicago operation."

He softened. "You acted like a real pro."

"And got a slug in the backside! As a civilian consultant, not supposed to be involved in violence. Pity nobody told Juarez."

"There's no violence in what I'm asking now."

Metzler was trying to get me involved. When I'd only expected a warning to walk wide of Slipe. "Colonel, I'm just not available. I've got too many responsibilities as it is. I can't—"

"Listen to what I'm asking before you sound off. Slipe claims to have discovered a method of making superpure silicon. And he's able to produce specimens far purer than anybody's close to matching."

"How do you know. These academics—"

"He's been handing around samples. Looking for the highest bid. A man after your own heart, Ryan." The Colonel was back to his original self. "But a scientist capable of achieving that kind of breakthrough on his own?"

"Unlikely. He's probably pirated the work of some junior."

"Hasn't got anyone in his lab worth a damn. He hasn't done any real research in years. A dud surrounded by duds. So what's woken him up and sent him off on the right track at his age?"

I shrugged. "Shake it out of him." Old reactions were reviving under Metzler's prodding.

"Difficult. Slipe's a political animal. With powerful friends. One of the star witnesses before that damned Senate committee on the social responsibility of scientists. You heard him talk. You can imagine how he fascinated those soft-minded Senators." The Colonel brooded. "Anyway, it's not so much superpure silicon—it's where he got it from. Who fed the technique to him?"

"A leak from some high-security lab which has found things even the DIA doesn't know?"

"A leak in a big lab? Wish it was. Those leaks are easy to spot and leakers easy to throttle." He shook his head. "Slipe must have gotten it from some small private lab somewhere. Who, how, and why? That's what I need to know. And that's why the Ladrich woman was on deck. She's after the secret of Slipe's success too. And she's using her talent to find out."

I needed coffee. And there was only one way to reach it. "Come upstairs and tell me more. While I fix us both breakfast."

Surprisingly he came, and surprisingly he began to talk. And he wasn't talking to persuade or inform me. He was talking because he had to talk to somebody and, as he had remarked, we might dislike each other but we had learned to respect each other. "There's something going on, Ryan. Something that makes my skin tingle."

"In this city there's always something unhealthy happening. State and Defense between 'em keep the scares coming."

"Oh, it's not the usual stuff." He waved aside the current wars and rumors of wars.

"You mean—comets in the sky? That sort of thing?" I was laughing.

"No." He paused. "Well—maybe. It's no real secret though it's not public—but somebody, not the Russians, landed something in the Pacific awhile back. Something that came down slowly in a controlled orbit. So it wasn't a meteor. And it wasn't a missile or a drop-out space station. At least, not any station we or they know about." He sipped his coffee. "Dammit, Ryan. I always tell you more than I mean to."

"My paranormal perception doesn't reach that far. Seriously Colonel, what do you want me to do?"

"All I want is a quiet word if you pick something up. In return for classified information I've just given you. Information valuable to your client."

"I'll do that. If it doesn't conflict with my client's interests."

"Your client will probably be glad to learn the DIA is after Slipe. Of course, if you'd care to be a consultant to us, there'd be no conflict of interests."

"Me? A consultant to the Federal Government again? At the fees Defense pays its scientific consultants? No thank you."

Metzler stood up. "I could probably get you retained as a lawyer—or as an economist. They're on a better scale than scientists or engineers."

"I'd rather do what I can from patriotism alone."

He looked at me, grunted, and left.

I went to my terminal to find out more about Loucher Freres. It told me that they were a rich and powerful firm of financial consultants, based in Paris. Among other things they published the most popular of the European financial tip sheets. About Justine Ladrich it could only say she was one of their analysts.

* * *

Metzler had obviously wanted me to tell my client that the DIA was interested in Slipe. Perhaps to cool their interest. Perhaps so that they would pass on anything they discovered to him and so secure their position with Defense. I hadn't mentioned to the Colonel that my clients already knew and had not been impressed. However, I mentioned it again to Adam when I visited his office that afternoon.

"Metzler came to see you this morning, eh?" Adam was still not greatly interested and changed the subject. "Richard, have you thought over that proposition I put to you yesterday?"

"About my writing up a series of interviews with scientists? Haven't had time to think about it. Or work out why you'd want me. Does Ebermann want me, too?"

"Of course. We're partners in everything related to business. And we're hoping you'll make it a trio."

"Like I said yesterday. Tell me more before I commit."

"Richard, you're the only person we'd trust without a prior commitment."

"Thanks. I love you too." I lit a cigarette. "Okay. Clamp's on. Now—give."

"As I suggested yesterday, your part will be to interview about half a dozen scientists and write the interviews up. You'll be free to write 'em as you see 'em. And what you write will be read by millions. The only constraint is that among the scientists you interview there will be some whom we'll name."

"Slipe for one?"

He nodded.

I stared at him. "Before I buy this I want to know why." In fact, I was already sold. The hunger to see one's words in print, to feel that one is convincing others through logic in exposition and clarity in expression, is as puerile as a hunger for posthumous fame. But not a hunger easily suppressed.

"Okay. You've read Slipe's background. What strikes you as strange?"

"The fact that after he's been barren for years he suddenly pretends he's fertile. Claims to be able to produce superpure silicon. He's got samples to prove his claim."

"God!" Adam stared. "You really are psychic! How did you know that? No matter. But you're right. He's been hawking his stuff around. Looking for the highest bid. That's how Conray got involved. But a scientist capable of a major discovery? I ask you?"

"Not likely," I agreed.

"Hasn't done anything worthwhile in years. These days he's a specialist in academic politics. Scientific administration." Adam lit a cheroot. "You could tell him you're focusing your articles on the mental sources of scientific genius. That would be true and might encourage him to talk—or avoid talking. Start him radiating those signals you pick up."

"Not signals—subliminal clues. Clues about superpure silicon manufacture?"

"More about where he got the idea."

"Having scanned Slipe on the podium you now want me to scan him in person?"

"We think there's a lot to be extracted from Slipe. About his sources of inspiration. And from the others."

"What others?"

"Six revived has-beens—like Slipe. Chatting with 'em you might be able to sense what lab's leaking secrets."

So there were others. Metzler hadn't known—or hadn't told me about them. "You think there's a leaking lab?"

Adam shrugged. "What other explanation? Six sclerotics restored to thought all at once? Defies probability."

It certainly did. "If I don't find anything, do I still get published?"

"Of course."

"And I can keep what Syndicated pay for the series? I'll want to retain everything except first serial rights."

"You'll get all the cash and all the credit. We can trust you to extract the maximum of both. I'll send you a list of the scientists to interview. Jackson's the editor, and he's ready to print your stuff."

"I'll think about it."

Adam smiled. "You're going to enjoy it." He took a file from his desk. "Here's the dirt on the geriatric six. What they did years ago and what they haven't done since. At least, what they hadn't done until last year when they were all regenerated about the same time."

I took the file from him, in effect making myself a partner in the operation. Adam became enthusiastic. "This may be the biggest thing we've ever been onto. Slipe's only the tip of the iceberg. Somebody—somewhere—is making major breakthroughs and feeding them to selected academics."

"Academics only?"

Adam nodded. "Burned-out professors. None of the renewals we've identified have been in industry. Who and why? If we can get even a hint of what's leaking we'll cash in, one way or another."

"Some mad scientist? Perhaps—oh God, no!" I had been hit by a lethal thought. "Some anticommunist science underground behind the iron curtain? Dammit, Adam, I didn't sign up to tangle with the KGB."

"The leak's not from some commie lab." Adam slowly shook his head. "We're sure the source is in the US."

"What about Metzler? The DIA isn't my favorite organization either."

"Believe me, Richard, no government agency's really into this yet. Metzler was probably there because the Feds are trying to nab Slipe under the Technology Export Act. But so far he's only been showing his silicon to US companies."

"You mean only you and Harold have noticed these coincidences."

"Harold did. And only by a lucky chance. Apart from Slipe none of the others have discovered anything of military or commercial interest. For now—we're alone."

I considered mentioning Justine Ladrich, but Loucher Freres were not in the same business that we were. And therefore, I hoped, not competitors.

5

DURING THE PREVIOUS two years six elderly scientists, all in the hard sciences, had suddenly become productive after lying fallow for decades. That six academics with their reputations behind them should suddenly become fertile demanded a suspension of disbelief—or a suspicion of fertility elsewhere.

Sometimes in soft areas such as social psychology, often in art and literature, always in economics and politics, a celebrity can ride a reputation into his dotage, scattering profundities as he rides. In fields where there is no appeal to repeatable observations, a commanding presence and strong opinions substitute for demonstrable facts. But in the hard sciences a continuing reputation demands the continued production of verifiable new knowledge.

Five days later I sat in my office reading the dossiers which Ebermann had given me. I had asked, "How did you spot these retreads? A chance drop in some search program?"

"Don't worry about how I got onto 'em, Ryan. We'll operate on a need-to-know basis. And that you don't need to know."

Which had suited me. He didn't need to know about Justine Ladrich. And I preferred not to know too much about E&H's methods of discovery. I now had a contract with Syndicated Scientific News to do a series on researchers who had made major discoveries in the last two years. Back in my own office I was applying my own methods to the dossiers.

Ebermann had, of course, already searched the scientific and personal histories of the suspect six for correlations. The computers had produced a list of irrelevant coincidences—they were all elderly American scientists—none had published anything quoted in the Citation Index for years previous to their recent seminal papers—all had chaired sessions at the annual meeting of the American Association for the Advancement of Science. That kind of garbage. Nothing to stimulate insight. I had to start the interviews blind.

Slipe was my first target and easier to hit than I had expected. The promise of having his research presented in the popular press as a major scientific breakthrough made him eager to describe the wonders which would result from superpurifying silicon. Syndicated set up the interview and I sat in his comfortable office at Cornell while he ran through his curriculum vitae. "A writer with your reputation for accuracy must want to get his facts right." Dr. Edgar Slipe knew nothing about my reputation but plenty about stroking journalists.

I claimed my twin gods were accuracy and objectivity and wasted the next twenty minutes taking notes about the highlights of his career and examining photographs of himself with which to illustrate my article. He selected one designed to inspire confidence—Slipe had an instinctive sense of public relations. When I congratulated him on his address to the Federation he settled back in his chair, looking plumper and more self-satisfied than ever. "You were present, Mister Ryan?"

I nodded. "I'm not a chemist, Doctor, but I'd heard from friends who are that you'd be worth listening to. And you were. I don't understand much about purified silicon, but I know how important it is to the semiconductor industry. They'll need the purest silicon they can get for VLSI."

"Very Large Scale Integration! How those technicians love their anagrams." He laughed. "I'm afraid that the welfare of Silicon Valley—or the Japanese electronics industry—were the least of my motivations for investigating a most interesting problem in basic chemistry. If there is a spin-off from my research—well, of course I am gratified. But I must ask you to emphasize in your article that I am primarily a scientist searching for such truths as we can extract from the physical world. Knowledge for its own sake."

"I'll certainly make that clear to my readers, Doctor."
The man was a humbug of such a quality as to be almost
admirable. "As a matter of fact, the series I am writing
focuses on the act of discovery—the process through which
great scientists come by their ideas—rather than the ideas
themselves." As a shadow crossed his face I added, "For
that process to be interesting the discovery itself is of
prime importance. For me to describe the process of inspiration the scientist must be able to express himself clearly.
You and your work fulfill both those criteria, Doctor
Slipe. That's why I asked Syndicated to make you the
subject of my lead article."

He preened himself, then hesitated. "Inspiration is not
the term I would use to describe the process of discovery.
In my case the means of superpurifying silicon came only
after years of hard research. That's what lies behind all
great scientific discoveries. Years of dedicated devotion to
knowledge."

"With your collaborators, Doctor Slipe?"

"I have no collaborators. No great team of workers to
do my work for me. Ultrapure silicon is the product of my
own reasoning and research."

He had backed away from the word 'inspiration.' The
first sign that I had touched on a sensitive area. "Plus a
moment of special insight?" I suggested.

"Insight?" He hesitated. "What do you mean—insight?"

Another hint of suspicion. I pressed the point. "Well—a
sudden moment of special vision. The kind of vision Kekule
had when he sat dozing in front of the fire, wondering how
the carbon atoms joined. When the sparks suddenly seemed
to be snakes chasing their own tails and then locked into
the six-carbon ring."

"I know the myth of Kekule's dream. That's what it
is—a myth!" His vehemence was a cue. "Nothing so
romantic as dreams in my case, I can assure you."

The word "dream" had triggered another reaction, had
brought him suddenly on guard. I quickly shifted the
subject to the social benefits which might be side-effects of
his discovery. As a leading light in Physical Scientists for
Social Responsibility he was glad to expand on the rich

rewards the taxpayer was supposed to reap from a generous support of basic research. I promised to let him check the draft of my article and to get his approval before publication—a promise that professional science writers rarely give. But my sense that there was certainly something unusual about his discovery, my wish to dig deeper later, overcame my integrity as a journalist. I wanted to remain on good terms with Dr. Edgar Slipe and we parted amid mutual compliments. His reactions to some of my questions confirmed Metzler's suspicion. There was much to be suspicious about. Slipe was certainly not the originator of superpure silicon. And the term which had triggered the most alarm was the word "dream."

I told Ebermann and he was not impressed. He had developed a theory that some new psychostimulant which renewed intelligence had been discovered and was being used by an in-group of elderly scientists.

"Slipe never had much intelligence to restore."

"Intelligence improver, perhaps," snapped Ebermann. He was probably hoping for some such wonder drug to use in his own dotage.

My next target was a Professor Gossage, a theoretical physicist who had forecast something about quarks which I did not understand but which had generated excitement among applied physicists, some of whom were firing particles at nuclei with tremendous energy and at immense cost, in their attempts to destroy his theory.

In contrast to Slipe he was a charming old boy, slightly bemused at the excitement he had generated. "A flash of insight while considering a problem?" I suggested.

He shook his head. "Not that I remember. I don't think I was particularly interested in quarks at the time. In fact, I was wondering whether I should replant my day lilies when I went to bed that night."

I went to full gain. I had touched an engram in an honest scientist. "You had some kind of a dream about quarks, sir?"

"A dream? Not exactly. I remember being awakened by the telephone, then going back to sleep. I started thinking about quarks when I got up the next morning. Saw them in a different way while I was shaving. Strange, that." Again he shook his head. "Hadn't remembered much about it until you asked me." He laughed. "Better not put that in your article—or my colleagues will be convinced I'm senile."

"Nobody'll think that, sir. Not after what you've done." I hesitated. "I seem to remember you chairing a session at the Washington meeting of the AAAS?"

"You do, eh?" He looked more pleased than when I had praised his quark theory. And I had flicked another engram. "That meeting—?" He shrugged as the engram faded. "Thought that was my swan-song at the time." He walked with me to the door of his office. "Don't make too big a thing of this quark stuff when you write about it. Wouldn't have let you interview me except that the Dean said the publicity might help the University's grant applications."

"Sir—it is a big thing. Over at CERN they think it's a very big thing. You deserve great credit."

"Kind of you to say so, my boy. But somehow I'm not convinced I do. That telephone call—?" He shrugged and gently ushered me out.

He had reacted, probably without realizing it, to three things. A dream, a telephone call, and the AAAS meeting. I put aside my notes from that interview and pushed on to the next. A testy suspicious chemist on the verge of retirement who had discovered something about the diffusion of hydrogen in zirconium alloys. With him I went too fast. The words "dream" and "telephone" evoked a sharp reaction. He cut me off and threw me out before I could introduce the AAAS.

I had picked up a common thread joining these three, and decided to follow it myself. Ebermann had already done a computer search of all the other scientists who had chaired sessions at the AAAS meeting—there had been over three hundred different sessions. The New Year meeting of the AAAS is the biggest clambake of them all. Apart from the suspect six, none of the other chairmen had Citation Indices—the measure of how often a scientist's publications are quoted by others—which had suddenly shot up.

I tied my own modest terminal into E&H's giants and called for the names of the people who had chaired sessions at that meeting. When I looked through the list I noticed one who could not possibly have been there, as he was in jail at the time for trying to murder his wife. I modified the program for the names of those who had actually chaired sessions but not been named on the original program. It took the computers longer to dig out that information but eventually they named a dozen last-minute substitutes. When I called for the Citation Indices on those twelve, one name immediately stood out, an academic who was neither elderly nor eminent. In fact she was young, female and, until recently, unknown.

This might be a false trail, but the prospect of interviewing a young female—even a young female mathematician—after my sessions with three elderly males, was too tempting to let pass. Her name was Jean Grayson and at the time of the AAAS meeting she had been a graduate student of the professor scheduled to chair the session. He had been sick and she had taken over because she had been the only person available who had known enough about their abstruse area of mathematics to replace him. Since then she had completed her Ph.D., gone to Princeton as an assistant professor, and published a paper on some new property of prime numbers. A paper of such importance that soon after its publication she had been promoted to associate professor with tenure. The kind of sudden promotion which occurs only to pure mathematicians.

Dr. Jean Grayson differed from those on Adam's list in every respect except her sudden rise to obscure eminence. Differed from them also by showing surprise when I telephoned seeking an interview as the basis for an article. Her only hesitation was doubt that anybody not fascinated with prime numbers could be interested in her. After I had assured her my readers would be, she invited me to Princeton.

On the telephone she had sounded agreeable and approachable; in person she was both and more. The young woman who met me at the door of her office had a succulent mouth, gray eyes, auburn hair, and a slim figure. She was so unlike my idea of a female math professor that I took her for the departmental secretary and handed her my card. "I'm looking for Dr. Jean Grayson. She's expecting me."

"I'm Jean Grayson." She also had a delightful smile. "If you're Richard Ryan—then I am expecting you. Come on in. Let me shift this stuff so you can sit down." She moved a pile of journals from one chair to another and settled behind her desk. "Excuse the chaos. End-of-term chores."

I was still off-balance. "It's kind of you to see me at such short notice. I didn't mean to interrupt your work."

"Delighted to be interrupted. Marking Math 240 is something that shrieks to be interrupted. I gathered from what you said on the phone that you're doing a series of articles for Syndicated Scientific?"

"You know about them?"

"I always read articles under their by-line. To learn what's happening in the real world. They're usually accurate and you people write well enough for even me to understand what you're saying." She smiled. "I admire science writers—the good ones, I mean."

And she did mean it. For once my insight brought me pleasure rather than disillusion. Academics rarely show admiration for science writers. Most are patronizing or ingratiating during an interview and hurt or offended by the resulting article. They claim to be misquoted almost as often as politicians.

I showed my pleasure and hoped I could write up to her expectations in the series I was preparing. "I'm focusing on the creative process in discovery rather than on the discoveries themselves."

"I'm not sure that I've made any great discovery."

"Your Citation Index is way up. Your colleagues must think what you're saying is important. I'm only an engineer myself, so perhaps you could explain what you've done in language an engineer can understand."

She glanced at my card. "Only an engineer from MIT! Prime numbers—let me try to fascinate an engineer."

She was already doing that. And she proceeded to fascinate me further. With most pure mathematicians my claim to be an engineer would have been an invitation to condescend. Jean Grayson spoke to me as a colleague, trying to describe what she had done and what she was doing. I couldn't understand most of what she said, but I enjoyed listening to her say it. "Is that the sort of thing you want for your article?" she asked after a while.

"Well—as I mentioned—in this series I'm especially interested in moments of revelation, the instant of insight. Can you remember when you first had your new vision of primes?"

"I've been wrestling with the damned things ever since I started graduate school. There's something almost magical about prime numbers." She wrinkled her forehead. "I'm always turning their properties over in my mind—subconsciously, I guess. Relationships suddenly surface. Often when you're not expecting them. Sometimes when you're thinking of something else."

"Or when you're asleep?"

"Not asleep—" She stopped abruptly. "Half-awake, perhaps."

"Kind of daydreaming?"

She nodded slowly. "Now that you mention it, I do seem to remember a kind of half-dream." She looked up, suddenly excited. "I did wake up one night thinking about infinite primes. You know—the way you sometimes wake up thinking you've discovered the reason for human existence. And, in the morning—if you remember at all—it's nonsense."

"But yours wasn't?"

"Yes—no! It seemed garbage and I must have thrown it out because I'd forgotten about waking up until you reminded me. But now I think of it, I was dreaming much the same idea that I had days later. Stored in my subconscious, I guess."

"Do you remember what woke you?"

"Something must have. I usually sleep through the night." She shook her head. "I can't remember what."

"Maybe the telephone rang?"

"The telephone?" She put her hand to her mouth and stared at me wide-eyed. "Yes—I'd forgotten. The telephone was ringing. Do you think that had anything to do—?" She laughed. "Did somebody phone me with a new idea on primes? Sounds crazy, but I've often wondered how inspiration strikes."

"Who knows? Remember anything else about the phone? Or that half-dream?"

"Not right now." She frowned. "But I'll think it over. And tell you when I see you again."

A handsome young woman of genuine brilliance, wherever her insight into prime numbers had come from. And as frank as she was honest. Suggesting I see her again. I responded by inviting her to dinner.

6

IN DR. JEAN GRAYSON I had struck pay dirt and she was a pleasure to mine. Also easy. Eager to talk and without detectable deceit. She accepted my invitation to dinner the instant I asked.

She accepted so readily that I took it as a tribute to my charm, but when we settled down at a table in the Nassau Inn she showed that she wanted to go on chewing over the memory of a telephone call and a triggering dream, the memory revived by my questions. I tried to shift the conversation away from that enigma—I needed to think it out before we talked it over—but she continued worrying at it and stopped eating at intervals as some new memory-flash returned. Finally she put down her fork, stared at me across her steak, and announced, "Somebody did speak to me on the telephone that night. And she said something about infinite primes."

"She?"

"Good God—yes! She! A girl's voice—I remember that now."

I tensed, relaxed, and laughed. "Psyche's a female. It was probably your own psyche voicing your own ideas."

"Psyche didn't have my voice."

"What kind of a voice did she have?"

Jean wrinkled her forehead, then said slowly, "The voice of a young girl."

Clues were coming too fast. I tried to slow her rate of recall. "Some brat playing a trick? When I was a kid we used to ring people at random—after midnight—and when somebody answered we'd ask if they wanted to go to the john."

She laughed. "We used to tell 'em to check their garage doors."

From there we moved on to reminiscences of our child-hoods, and then to telling each other about ourselves. An exchange of truths from her and part-truths from me. A pleasant interchange we continued in the bar after dinner. Usually I do not get along well with intelligent women—I'm a frequent target for the insults women hurl when you dare to reason with them—but I got along well with Jean Grayson. It was nearly midnight when I drove her back to the block of apartments by the lake where Princeton houses its junior academics.

She did not invite me in and I did not hint she might. I had had sufficient stimuli for one evening and my mind was filled with questions I had to answer before asking more. We did, however, arrange to dine together again if she remembered anything else about her source of inspiration. Or if I wanted another interview.

As I walked with her to the elevators, I said, "Phone me if you get another dreamy call!"

"I will." She frowned as she remembered the reason for our meeting. "I sure will!"

I drove back to Annandale exhilarated by the evening, excited by what I had discovered, and alarmed by finding myself attracted to a pretty young woman in whom I had sensed no duplicity. Such uniqueness should be suspect. Especially in a woman academic. How could such delight-ful honesty flourish in the academic jungle? Were great talent and a charming personality sufficient in themselves? With Jean Grayson it seemed so. Associate Professor with tenure at twenty-six!

My next target was an exobiologist who had dreamed up a new theory of amino-acid genesis that was causing ex-citement among exobiologists. Exobiology, like theology, is a discipline based on faith without facts. I say "dreamed up" advisedly, for this exobiologist went into silent shock when I suggested a dream as the origin of his theory, and started stuttering when I hinted at a telephone awakening. After that the interview went nowhere and he excused himself before I could mention girls' voices.

The telephone pulled me out of a dream in which Justine Ladrich was chasing Ebermann, Haskard, and myself along corridors between immense filing cabinets. I grabbed the instrument and heard Jean's voice, high-pitched. "Richard—thank God! I've just had another!"

"Another what?"

"Another call from that girl."

"What girl?"

"Another call from that girl I dreamed about." The pitch of her voice dropped as irritation replaced panic. "Just now. Woke me and asked if I was Dr. Jean Grayson. When I said I was she started to sing."

"Sing?" I sat up in bed.

"Well—warble. I cut her off. Said I was busy and to ring back tomorrow night."

"Busy at three in the morning?"

"I'm alone in bed—if that's on your mind!"

"I didn't mean—" I came fully awake. "What did she say?"

"Said she would, and hung up."

I was on my feet. "Where was she calling from?"

"How should I know? Tokyo—Paris—next door? They all sound the same these days." She paused and her voice softened. "No time delay so it wasn't from overseas." Alarm returned. "Richard—what shall I do?"

"Nothing—not till I get there." I reached for my pants.

"Take it easy." She relaxed on hearing I was coming. "No need to rush."

"Don't say anything to anybody till we've talked."

"I won't. You'll get an exclusive for your article."

"Damn the article. It's you I'm worried about."

"I'm not crazy—and I'm not dreaming."

"Of course you're not." My own exasperation was showing. "It's just that something—well, something strange is happening and we'd better try to find out what before we go public."

"That's sensible. And I'm more sensible myself now. If you come this evening I'll cook you dinner."

"Are you sure—"

"Sure I'm sure. But thanks for caring. Can you make it around seven?"

"Earlier, if you like."

"Seven's the earliest for me. I have a lecture to prepare. Now go back to sleep. I should have waited till morning to call."

I was glad she hadn't. After she had hung up I subsided onto my bed, digesting two major facts. The mysterious inspirer of scientists might telephone again, and Jean had invited me to dinner in her apartment. I drove to New Jersey excited by both prospects.

Her welcome was warm and genuine. She greeted me with a bourbon and water. "I'm probably getting worked up about some kid playing tricks, as you suggested."

"Maybe. We'll find out if she phones again tonight."

"You'll stay here?" Caution and hope.

"If you'll let me. I can sleep on the couch."

"Thanks." Relief. "I'll go and start dinner." She disappeared into the kitchen while I wandered round her living room.

The room of a woman interested in more than mathematics. The usual collection of mildly left-wing literature remaindered from the previous academic generation. Good reproductions of a Constable and an early Gauguin plus an original Persian miniature. Ivory chessmen set out in some end-game problem. Neat, tidy, and yet lived-in. Piles of *Science* and *Nature*. I was skimming the latest issue of *Science* when she came from the kitchen, a sherry in her hand. "I only understand the survey papers—and not all of those. That's why I enjoy the kind of articles Syndicated puts out." She sat down on the couch, sipped her sherry, then asked suddenly, "Richard, what's going on?"

I joined her on the couch. "Some kid has your name. Some kid who talks higher math. Or who's being used by somebody who does."

"Used for what?"

"God knows. Maybe we'll find out tonight."

Jean cooked an excellent dinner, during which we avoided talking about mystery phone calls, and after dinner we turned to more personal matters. We also generated considerable warmth. It was after midnight when she disengaged herself, stood up, and announced she was going to bed. She disappeared into her room and returned with pillows and blankets. "You'll be comfortable on the couch?"

"Comfortable—but lonely." I was tempted to play upon the emotions I sensed, as I had played on the emotions of women in the past. A quick play for a quick gain with no rematch. Instant passion followed by resentment at being tricked. I wanted Jean's warmth to last so I didn't nudge Nature. Instead I patted her bottom when she bent to make up the couch and kissed her when she shot upright.

She stiffened, pressed against me for an instant, then bolted to her bedroom. I borrowed a large bath-towel to wear as a sarong and was adjusting it round my waist when she reappeared in a wrapper, heading for the kitchen. She stopped when she saw me. "Sorry! I'm just going to get some milk."

"Then pour a glass for me, and let's drink together."

She stood, studying me for a moment, before continuing into the kitchen. She returned with two glasses of milk, moist lips, and bright eyes. She hesitated, then perched on the edge of a chair, looking at my bare chest. "What's that?" she asked suddenly.

"That?" I put my finger on a small round scar. "That's where the bullet went in. It came out here." I bent to show her the larger scar on my back. "I was lucky—it missed the lung."

"A bullet?" Like most women she was both shocked and stimulated by the sight of an old wound. "What bullet?"

"A 9mm—I think. We never found it. His second's still in me."

"In you?"

"Somewhere in my right buttock. The surgeon said he'd have to probe around to find it. Do more damage. Apparently it's hell to find a bullet in a large muscle mass. Advised me to leave it unless it gave me trouble. It never has." I stood and turned. "It hit me here."

"Oh Richard! Who shot you?"

I sat down again. "A guy I was interviewing."

She gave a nervous laugh. "You investigative journalists sure meet people."

"None like you. Come over here and I'll show you why."

She hesitated, then came. She was wearing only a wrapper and nightgown. I had only a towel. With no practical problems to give us pause, we went ahead. Around two in the morning we fell asleep.

The phone rang just after three. I rolled off the couch as Jean ran naked to her bedroom. By the time I had found the extension a girl's voice was asking if that was Dr. Jean Grayson, the mathematician?

"That's me. Who are you?" I heard Jean say.

Instead of replying, the girl started to whistle a series of notes. The whistling was interrupted by the voice of an irate woman. "Alice! What are you doing? Calling long-distance again! Give me that telephone." Then the woman was speaking to us. "I apologize to whoever Alice has woken up this time."

"Wait. Please!" Jean was quicker on the uptake than I was. "Is that Alice calling?"

"Yes. Do you know the child?"

"I have a niece called Alice." Jean started to lie with instant originality. "Haven't heard from her in ages. Where is she?"

"In Richmond. Running up long-distance telephone calls. If you're her aunt—?"

"I'll gladly pay for her phone calls. Is my sister there? We've lost touch."

The woman's voice softened. "I'm afraid not, Mrs.—?"

"Grayson, Jean Grayson."

"Please speak louder, Mrs. Jenson. I'm a little hard of hearing. I'm sorry to have to tell you that Mrs. Drummond died some years ago."

Jean allowed a moment of silence. "I was afraid of something like that. We never got on well. Is Jack there?"

"Jack? You mean Dr. Drummond? I'm afraid that Alice's father died last year. She went to live with her grandmother, but was too much for the old lady. The court placed her with us. We didn't know she had any other living relative."

"The poor child. Can I speak to her?"

"I've sent her back to bed."

"Can we come and visit her?"

"I'd be grateful if you would." A moment's hesitation. "Alice is a troubled child, Mrs. Jenson."

"Poor thing. Without a father or mother at her age. How old is she now, Mrs.—? Who am I speaking to?"

"I'm Miss Lister, the Supervisor of the Manse. Alice is fourteen."

"Fourteen? How time passes! If you could tell me the

address I'll come to Richmond as soon as I can. Tomorrow, I hope."

"I'll look forward to seeing you. This is the Manse, 783 River Road, Richmond."

"Perhaps—my sister may not have mentioned—" A sigh. "These family feuds—"

"I understand." There was sympathy in the woman's voice. "I do hope Alice is your niece, Mrs. Jenson. Finding she has a relative who cares may be the saving of her." And a click as Miss Lister hung up.

Jean came bursting into the living room. "Did you hear that?"

"I heard you were married. And your husband—"

"I'm not married. Never have been. Please God, never will be! But that woman may be more willing to let me see this girl if she thinks I am. You heard what she told me?"

"You were magnificent. You are magnificent!"

Jean suddenly realized she was still naked and dived back into her bedroom. During the last hours she had shown she had a beautiful body; during the last few minutes that she could be a polished liar. I dressed thoughtfully, both relieved and disturbed. When she returned, zipping up her dress, I asked, "Who the hell was that kid?"

"A mathematical genius."

A juvenile genius in math was just possible. A genius in physics, chemistry, and metallurgy was too much. Jean didn't know the span of the kid's telephoned knowledge. And she mustn't learn. Not yet.

"No wonder she's troubled." Jean disappeared into the bathroom. "Poor child. Locked up in some orphanage. Nobody to understand her. That's why she was ringing me. Must have heard my name." She emerged from the bathroom to drag a suitcase from the hall closet.

"Where are you going?"

"To Richmond of course! To rescue the child before she's permanently scarred." She stopped packing and looked at me. "Want to come along?"

"I have to, don't I? You've got to produce a husband for the dragon's inspection."

7

JEAN MIGHT BE an instant creator of appropriate fictions but she was an unusually honest academic. Most of those I have known would have indignantly denied telephoned inspiration; Jean was intrigued. All she could talk about on our way to Richmond was her delight at discovering a child prodigy and the importance of rescuing that prodigy from some horrible orphanage. She assumed that a girl who could telephone with a fruitful hint about the nature of prime numbers must be one of those idiot savants or mathematical prodigies who occasionally appear.

I restricted myself to murmurs of agreement. I was as eager as Jean to meet this Alice Drummond and arrange her release—to learn what group of anonymous scientists were using her as a front for some bizarre plan. Genius does show itself early in pure mathematics, music, and chess. There are teenage virtuoso musicians and chess grand masters. But youthful universal geniuses—if such people ever existed—died out with the Renaissance and I could not imagine any modern genius producing breakthroughs in chemistry, physics, and mathematics at the same time. It is impossible for even the greatest natural intelligence to make a major discovery in modern science until he or she has spent years learning all that has been already discovered. Contemporary brains, however brilliant, have to spend time climbing onto the shoulders of earlier giants before they themselves can see ahead.

But Jean did not know that she was only one of several people in quite different disciplines whom this girl had been telephoning in the middle of the night. And she'd be furious when she found out. For the moment I needed her trust, and at the moment I still had it.

Also I enjoyed her company. Even driving to Richmond

as the sun was rising was enjoyable. There was a flush of excitement in her cheeks and voice. Already she was fantasizing a grand mathematical career for this unknown Alice. "Helping her to realize her talents justifies the fibs I told Miss Lister."

I agreed that, under the circumstances, some imagination on our part was excusable. Jean, like any woman, accepted ends as justifying means. "And let her go on calling you Mrs. Jenson."

"But she mis-heard me. I told her my name—Grayson."

"Miss—not Mrs. You plan to correct her on that too?"

"Probably not." She hesitated. "Why do you want her to think we're the Jensons? She'll have to know my real name later."

"Later may be okay."

"Why not now?"

"Call it the suspicious mind of an investigative journalist."

"I guess a bullet in the rear does inject suspicion." She laughed. "Okay—another white lie."

We stopped for breakfast on our way to Richmond and turned onto River Road soon after seven. A series of large and imposing mansions. After we had located the Manse I insisted we scout the surroundings before invading the house.

A paper-boy came whistling down the gravel drive and skidded his bicycle to a stop when I asked if he had a spare *Times-Dispatch* to sell. He had, and while he was extracting it from his bag, I waved toward the mansion. "Is that the Hartley residence?"

"Hartley? Nobody on my route by that name."

"Then who lives here?"

"Back there?" He jerked his thumb over his shoulder and laughed. "It's a chick pen!" And he rode off, whistling.

"A chick pen?"

"Home for delinquent girls," I translated. "It may be tougher to spring Alice than we thought."

"Then we'd better begin." She started toward the house. "Let me do the talking, Richard."

She was the naive mathematician and I was the experienced lawyer, but I was glad to let her try persuasion before I resorted to more direct methods. As I had learned, Jean could be very persuasive. And she was in top form when the large front door opened and we were confronted by an elderly lady with "Supervisor" written on her as clearly as if she were wearing a name-tag.

"Yes?"

"Miss Lister? I'm Jean Jenson. And this is my husband. I spoke to you last night. About Alice."

"Mrs. Jenson—please come in." The dragon's initial hostility was replaced by what I sensed as embarrassment. She led us across a highly polished hall to an office. From elsewhere in the house came waves of girlish chatter. "You've come to see Alice?"

"If we may."

"I'm afraid that is not possible." Miss Lister hesitated. "Alice ran away last night—again."

Jean's shock and my disappointment were both real. She sank into a chair; I checked a curse. "When—when did she leave?" asked Jean.

The dragon sat down behind her desk, adjusting a hearing aid. "Soon after I sent her back to bed—I suspect. For several days she's been more unsettled than usual. She has probably been planning this latest escapade for some time. I wish I had told her who you were and that you were coming to visit. Then she might have stayed."

"You didn't tell her?"

The dragon shook her head. "I did not think it wise at that hour of the night. She was already confused and half asleep. These long-distance telephone calls she makes are an index of her confusion. The psychiatrist says they are symptoms of her search for an identity."

"Where can she have gone?"

"I'm afraid I have no idea. According to the court records she has no living relatives except her grandmother. And she certainly will not go to her."

"Court records? Is Alice—?"

"Your niece, Mrs. Jenson, suffers from a form of kleptomania. At least, that was the opinion of the Childrens' Court. She makes long-distance telephone calls from other people's telephones without their permission. Expensive telephone calls. And that is a form of stealing. I'm afraid she's a marginal delinquent. Since her father died she has lived in several foster homes and has run away from every one—usually after an episode of unauthorized telephoning.

Six months ago she was placed in our care—we have some experience in dealing with difficult adolescent girls who have been in trouble with the law." Miss Lister paused. "Apart from her fascination with the telephone and her tendency to leave without permission, she has not shown any sign of serious delinquency. This is the second time she has left us during the past three months. The police brought her back the first time. I have notified them, of course, but they are not hopeful. They have files full of teenage runaways."

"This is most disturbing, Miss Lister. Especially as I can see you operate a very attractive home for young people." Jean wrinkled her brow. "Now that I have found where Alice is, I want to help her all I can. Do you have a recent photograph of her?"

Miss Lister opened the file already on her desk and pushed it across to us. A thin-faced youngster with long blond hair frowned up. A girl who one day might be beautiful. "That was taken when she came to us."

"I can see the likeness to my sister," murmured Jean, studying the photograph and lying with class. She stood up. "You have been a great help, Miss Lister. If I can repay you for the cost of those calls—?"

"There is no immediate need, Mrs. Jenson. Of course we are always glad of gifts to help purchase extra amenities for our girls."

"If you have any news about Alice I would appreciate your calling us." I scribbled the number of my Philadelphia answering service on a pad.

As we moved toward the door, Jean asked, "Has Alice shown any talent for mathematics?"

"Mathematics?" Miss Lister walked with us across the hall. "Alice is an intelligent child and does well at school—when she attends. But her grades in mathematics were not outstanding."

I asked, "Are there any bus stops nearby?"

"There is a city bus route at the corner. But the buses were not running at the time she must have left." Miss Lister hesitated. "I'm afraid that Alice borrowed a maid's bicycle."

"Oh dear!" said Jean. "If it's not returned, please tell

the owner I'll pay for it. I wouldn't want the poor child to get into worse trouble than she is."

Miss Lister assured us that no charges would be leveled and that she would call us as soon as Alice was found. Jean walked in disappointed silence to my car. She got in and sighed, "That's that, I suppose."

"Let's try the bus station." I started the motor. "Somebody there might have seen her."

"Do you think the fact her call to me was interrupted made her run away? If I'd listened to her last night—?"

"Jean—this was a planned take-off." I threaded through the morning rush hour of downtown Richmond. "You heard what the Lister woman said. The girl had been planning it for days."

"Thank goodness—or I would be feeling guilty."

I parked opposite the station under the disapproving eye of a policeman while Jean went to look for Alice Drummond. He was starting to move toward me when Jean returned, smiled at him, and got in beside me. "Charlottesville! The bus station there."

"Why Charlottesville?"

"Because the agent remembered a blonde child with a tote bag who bought a ticket for Charlottesville." She was studying a bus schedule as I headed for the thruway. "We've got to get there before she catches an express to New York."

"You think she's got friends in New York?"

"I doubt the poor kid's got friends anywhere after the runaround she's been getting. Now she's trying to lose herself. And, at her age, the big city's the only place to hide. We've got to catch her before she goes on the streets."

"The streets? She's only fourteen."

"That's where runaway girls usually end up," said Jean in exasperation. "When you've no place to go you go on the streets. She knows the police are probably searching for her. And they are. The ticket agent said somebody looking like a detective had been asking after a girl like Alice."

I drove a little faster, anxious to get to the girl before the police. There were enough complications already in this crazy operation without including the law governing adolescent runaways.

We arrived at the parking lot behind the Charlottesville bus station in a little over an hour. Jean disappeared into the depot. Moments later she was back outside, signaling to me. The youngster whose photograph we had seen was sitting slumped, apparently half-asleep, on the end of a bench next to the women's washroom.

8

A THIN-FACED straggle-haired girl in faded jeans and a soiled windbreaker, slumped on the bench with her eyes closed. I started toward her. Jean caught my arm. "Wait! She's not asleep. And she's ready to run."

"Run? Where?"

"Into the john, of course. We've got to gain her confidence before we say who we are. Let me talk to her. You stay here."

I glanced round. The waiting room was filled with underprivileged who have to travel by bus. None looked as if they'd interfere if we had to grab the girl and carry her off kicking and screaming. But best to let Jean try the soft sell first. "Okay. Go ahead." Then it was my turn to catch her arm. "Hold it!"

"Why?"

"That pair." Two men had walked into the waiting room; one was the bodyguard who had kept a seat for Justine Ladrich in the Grand Ballroom at Baltimore.

Jean glanced over her shoulder. "Police?"

"Perhaps." Though one certainly was not. The situation was deteriorating. Already the two men had seen the girl and were pushing their way across the room toward her.

Jean pulled free. "I'll block them."

By this time they were standing over the girl. One was flashing a wallet, showing some kind of badge. The other was reaching for her arm. The girl stood up slowly—then came to sudden life. She dodged the reaching hand and disappeared through the washroom door. Both men started after her and were confronted by a large lady emerging from it. Her glare stopped them, and they stood hesitating as they found themselves the center of the waiting travelers' attention.

''Smart kid! I'll escort her out.'' Jean shot across the room, and tapped one man on the back. ''Yours is over there.'' She pointed to the men's washroom. ''Excuse me.'' She eased him aside and disappeared into the women's.

Frustrated in their attempt at persuasion and hesitant at invading a women's washroom, the two men would grab the girl when Jean brought her out. I glanced around for allies—the sight of even a local cop would have been welcome—but there was nobody in sight who looked as though they wanted to become involved in a fracas over a runaway kid. Already this 'safe project' was threatening to turn violent. I steeled myself to face it. The very fact that Loucher Freres were after her showed the girl was too valuable for Justine Ladrich to snatch.

The pair were approaching the door again when Jean emerged—alone. ''Looking for somebody?'' she demanded. ''Or is this just sexual harassment?''

One man showed his badge. ''We want to talk to that girl who just went in. A blonde kid.''

''She's sitting on the john. Crying!''

''Tell her to come out.''

Jean glanced at his badge, then said slowly, ''You're police? Okay, I'll tell her.'' She turned and went back through the door.

For a moment I thought she had been fooled. When she reappeared I saw she had not. ''I told her. She'll be out when she's stopped throwing up. Now, excuse me—I have a bus to catch.'' She pushed past them, heading for the exit and whispering, ''Follow!'' as she went by me.

I followed. She turned down an alley beside the station. Halfway along, a pair of jean-covered legs and a slim bottom were emerging from a small window high up in the wall. As we reached it the rest of the girl emerged, hung a moment, then slid down into the alley. She picked herself up, saw Jean, and grinned. ''Thanks for that leg-up.''

''You're welcome. Let's move before they gather enough nerve to invade. This is Richard, my husband. We've got a car in the lot.''

The kid looked at me. A peculiar look, as though she

was scanning me while I was scanning her. "Your husband?"

Jean nodded and took the girl's hand. For a moment she hung back. I sensed doubt turning to trust. "Okay." She walked between us toward my car, but stopped at the door. "My bag! It's in a locker."

"Leave it. We can get it later."

"I won't leave without my bag." Her stubborn mouth emphasized what I sensed. The kid meant what she said. She fished a locker key from the pocket of her jeans.

Cursing, I took the key. "Number forty-eight? I'll fetch your bag. You two wait in the car."

The two men were still hesitating outside the washroom, doubtless debating whether to use their standard technique for persuading a reluctant woman—grip her lower lip and lead her to where they want her to go. I walked casually over to the bank of lockers, opened number forty-eight, and pulled out a battered totebag. I looked round. The thugs were still debating. One of them was speaking on a CB radio. I strode from the station onto the parking lot and started toward my car.

A woman was walking toward it ahead of me. A slim woman who was taking a penlight from her handbag. Only it wasn't a penlight. It was a gasgun. I broke into a run, but she reached the car first and was leaning through the open window, gasgun in hand, when I arrived. She half-turned. Justine Ladrich! I swung the totebag. Something solid in it caught the corner of her jaw and sent her sprawling onto the ground beside the car. I kicked her as she reached under her skirt, wrenched a muscle in my side as I jumped into the driver's seat, and roared out of the lot.

"You hit her!" Jean was horrified. "Why? She was only asking the way."

"She's with that pair inside."

"You kicked her when she was pulling down her dress." Jean sounded even more horrified.

"She was reaching for a gun."

The kid was rubbing the side of her jaw. "Those women carry guns under their skirts." Bright kid!

I weaved through the traffic on Main. "Anybody following?"

"There's a car a block back driving like you are," said the kid calmly, still rubbing her jaw. "And she's in it."

I rubbed my own jaw in sympathy and drove faster. I'm no getaway driver but I've evaded pursuit before. I lured the car astern onto a crowded shopping plaza and turned sharply toward a vacant parking space. Then I signaled the lady I had preempted. She waved her thanks for my courtesy as I drove out the far side of the space. She pulled in just ahead of our pursuers. I got a bonus. He rammed her. She emerged taut with the fury of the innocent motorist who has just been hit in the rear. He tried to back up and was blocked off by other drivers supporting a wronged fellow shopper. I drove sedately off the plaza and took the road out of town.

"That was real neat," said the kid.

"What was it all about?" Jean's face was white.

"Those thugs were trying to snatch Alice."

"Police—"

"They weren't police," said the kid. "I know cops when I see 'em." She reached down to the floor at her feet. "That woman you slugged dropped her flash."

"Give me that!" I screeched to a stop and snatched it from her. "This isn't a flashlight. It's a gasgun."

"A what?"

"A thing crooks use to knock people out. Or kill them. Depends what gas she's got in it." I stowed the gasgun in the glove compartment and spun back onto the highway. "That woman was aiming to knock you out before she carted you off."

Jean was shivering and staring at me. The kid only said, "I've read about things like that." She paused. "How come you know my name?"

"You phoned me last night." Jean recovered and took her hand. "I'm Jean Grayson. Miss Lister told me where you were and we came to Richmond to meet you."

"You're Dr. Grayson?" The girl's face crumpled. For a moment she looked as though she was going to cry. "I didn't mean to cause you trouble. I'm sorry. Drop me here and I won't be." She reached for the doorhandle.

"Wait!" Jean checked her. "Where will you go?"

"I'll be okay."

"Do you know who those people are? Why they were trying to kidnap you?"

"I think they're white slavers. They've been hanging around the Manse—asking about me. Those Arab sheiks pay a lot for young virgins. To put in their harems." She seemed more intrigued than alarmed.

"Do you want us to take you back to Miss Lister?"

"Please—no! I've had enough of that place. The Lister'll be glad to get rid of me."

"Would you like to come with us?"

"Are you trying to kidnap me too?"

"No. But we'd like to help you. Pull over, Richard." Reluctantly, I stopped and Jean opened the car door. "You can leave now if you like. Or after you've had a meal and a night's sleep."

The kid hesitated. "I'd like something to eat. I'm starving."

We stopped at a McDonalds and I sat watching her eat, intrigued by how much food a thin child of fourteen could consume. Jean questioned her gently while she ate and she chattered freely enough until long-distance telephone calls were mentioned; then she clammed up. Jean, wisely, did not press her and she came back to the car with us and got in without protest. "Where are we going?"

"My apartment near Washington," I said, before Jean could answer. "There's a spare room you can have." The reply seemed to satisfy her and by the time we reached the thruway she was curled up on the back seat, asleep.

"Poor child. She's exhausted," whispered Jean.

I gestured her to silence. The child might be asleep, but appearances were deceptive—there was something very unusual about this child.

There was something very unusual about this whole operation. I took a roundabout route back to Annandale in case Loucher Freres had spotters on the main highways, and it was evening by the time I reached my house. Alice woke when I pulled up outside and stood on the sidewalk with Jean, clutching her totebag, while I opened the front door. I do not usually return home via my front door and, as I do not trust keys, it unlocks through a tap-code. The pair watched with interest as I played the code on the three bell-pushes, but they entered without comment when I swung open the door and ushered them into the hall. "Go on upstairs while I put the car away," I said, anxious to get my car out of sight. A leased auto, registered in the name of the leasing company, but with Justine Ladrich involved it was wise to minimize risk.

By the time I got back to my apartment the two were engaged in cleaning up the kitchen. As I had been away the housekeeper from the agency had not been able to get in and the apartment was as I had left it. "Do you really live here?" Alice was asking Jean as she loaded dirty dishes into the dishwasher.

"I spend most of the week at Princeton." Jean was being hoisted by her own landmine. "This is Richard's place."

"Are you two really married?"

"Well—in a way."

"A common-law marriage? Cemented only by love." The kid poured powder into the washer. "That's the best kind."

I interrupted the threatening exchange. "Alice—you can have the spare room. Over here." The spare room had not been used for some time and was reasonably tidy.

"I'll fix us something to eat first," said Jean, inspecting my freezer. She was not excited by the contents but as all of us were showing signs of wear she selected three TV dinners and put them in the micro-oven while Alice continued to clean up the kitchen. Both these females were evidently obsessive-compulsives. Perhaps characteristic of female mathematicians; unusual in a girl of fourteen.

More typical of a fourteen-year-old, she almost fell asleep while she ate and went off to bed immediately after she had finished. After she had gone Jean asked suspiciously, "And where do I sleep? If you think that common-law stuff—!"

"I'm too exhausted for such thoughts. You take my room. I'll use the couch in my study downstairs." I yawned, anxious to postpone discussion about the events of the day until I'd thought them over alone.

One thought was clear. The kid was the crux of the whole problem. And the kid was preparing to bolt again. I had sensed that when she went off to bed. I settled down to wait.

It was three in the morning when I caught her, carrying her totebag, trying to open the front door. I grabbed her arm, took her and her totebag into my study, and sat her down. Then I demanded, "What is all this? Why are you phoning people?"

9

ALICE STARTED TO snivel. When she realized I was not impressed she shifted to sullen. "It's silly! You'll laugh if I tell you."

"I won't laugh. There's nothing funny about any of this. Yesterday I rescued you from a fate worse than death. Why was that woman trying to snatch you?"

"I don't know. I really don't!" She didn't.

I shifted my questions. "What's behind those phone calls you keep making? Who's telling you what to say?"

"Nobody! Well—no person." Her eyes filled with genuine tears. "I can't explain. You'll think I'm making it up! Or call me crazy. Like the others did. When I tried to tell them." She wiped her eyes with the back of her hand. "They sent me to a shrink."

"Told them what?"

"What I hear—from Teddy."

"Teddy who?"

"My teddy bear. It's not Teddy. It's what's inside him." She looked directly at me and her eyes went wide. "You'll understand. You can feel things—like I can!"

"What do you mean—feel things?"

"You know what I mean." She began to rummage through her totebag. "I'll show you."

This scruffy straggle-haired teenager could sense subliminal clues and had recognized I could. We could both sense lying. I was still digesting this when she produced a battered teddy bear from her bag. "It's inside him."

"What's inside him?"

"It's quite a story."

"We've got time."

"Promise you won't laugh?"

"I promise. Now get on with it!"

"And don't turn angry?"

"I won't turn angry if you'll get started."

"Okay then." She wriggled in her chair. "When Daddy and Mommy were alive we lived out on the coast, in Oregon. We were very happy. Daddy was a scientist—he worked for the Government in a research station they had out there then. After Mommy died everything changed. Daddy changed. When I found the egg and asked him what it was he didn't know and didn't really believe me when I tried to tell him what I heard in it. And when I made him listen he said he couldn't hear anything."

"What egg?"

"The one I keep in Teddy." She jumped up, took a pair of scissors from my desk, put her teddy bear face down, and cut the stitches up the back of its head. Reaching inside she pulled out a shiny metal object, the size and shape of a large egg. "This is what I found." She offered it to me.

I took it, weighed it in my hand. A hard metal I did not recognize. Heavier than it looked. This was what had turned the totebag into a club. I glanced at her.

"Listen to it!" urged Alice.

I put it to my ear.

"Hear anything?" She did not sound hopeful.

But I did. Cadences of distant chimes, running up and down some strange musical scale. Faint but clear. Notes and chords. No words.

"You're hearing it?" Alice was on her feet, hope in her voice.

"I'm hearing something. A sort of music."

The child was hugging me, kissing me. "You can hear? You can hear it too! So I'm not crazy. Or we're both crazy. Nobody else could hear. And I've made quite a few people listen."

"What is it?"

"I don't know. It doesn't open or anything."

"You were telling me you found it. Where was that?"

"In the woods near our house. Inside the station. Years ago, when I was a kid. After Mommy died."

After Mommy died (she said), I was alone a lot. I was only eleven then, just a kid, and there weren't any other kids of my age living at the station. The station was something to do with radio or radiation—I think. Daddy knew a lot about radio. I used to walk through the woods inside the fence trying to imagine that Mommy was back and that Daddy was happy. Wondering about monsters and fairies and all that stuff young kids read about. I used to sing to myself, but silently so as not to worry Dad. One day I heard something sing back. I wasn't really surprised. You know how silly kids are.

Anyway, I started searching for what was singing and found the egg. Under a pile of dead leaves. When I put it to my ear, like you listen to a seashell, I heard it singing. Not the kind of sea noises you hear in a shell, but the kind of singing you heard just now. And I saw fairyland. I really did!

I took it home and showed it to Daddy. He didn't know what it was and couldn't hear anything in it. He thought it must have fallen off some airplane and said I could keep it. Didn't want to report it because of the papers he'd have to fill in. Daddy was getting sick—even then. So I kept it and listened to it sing. And learned how to sing back. I sewed it into Teddy so I could take it to bed with me. It used to sing me to sleep—like Mommy used to do. Not so well but Teddy's touch was nice. Like—inside my head. And he helped me to dream about his fairy city. Happy dreams!

After a while—it must have been months though it seems like years, you know what time is for young kids—the singing turned into songs. Words which didn't make much sense at first. Then it began to make some kind of sense. I'd whistle that tune you heard when I wanted to talk to Teddy—the way kids talk to dolls. That's Teddy's call-sign. Daddy didn't mind but other people thought I was regressing. So I only talked to Teddy when we where in bed. And when I was dreaming. We could talk better when I was dreaming.

In dreams Teddy used to take me to his City. He lives in a beautiful dream-city. A kind of fairyland. When we're there we can talk easily. The only thing wrong was when he tried to make me listen to sermons. Religious stuff. Not Mommy's religion. I didn't like it and, anyway, I was too young to understand what the preacher was talking

about. After a while Teddy gave up trying to make me
listen. Instead he asked me to read to him.

What kind of things? Mostly fairy stories and science
things. Teddy liked me to read from Daddy's science journals. I used to read for hours, not understanding what I
was reading, of course. I went on whispering to Teddy
to keep him talking. I was real lonely. They were closing
the station and most of the other families had left.

Finally we left. Daddy went to be a Professor at Virginia Tech. I began to ask him about the science things
Teddy had told me. He thought I was getting interested in
science and started taking me with him to meetings. He
took me to a big one in Washington. That's when I first
saw Jean. I didn't speak to her or anything but I heard
somebody say she was tops in her field. I read Teddy part
of the program and her name was on it. He gave me
messages for some of the speakers—things that should
interest them. And religious things to tell them. Like
everybody should help everybody.

I did try—to please him. At that meeting I tried to pass
his messages on. I went up to the speakers after they'd
spoken. But I couldn't explain clearly and they didn't take
a young kid seriously. I even took the egg out of Teddy
and asked them to listen. Some did, but none of them
could hear anything. Several wanted to examine it in their
labs, but I wouldn't let them keep it. The egg was mine—I'd
found it—and I was afraid they wouldn't give it back.

After Daddy died I went to live with Granny. That was
when I started telephoning. Teddy kept bugging me to pass
on his messages. He didn't understand that I couldn't
because they wouldn't listen. When I told him about telephones he said that was the way. He told me to whistle his
call-sign to get their attention. I think it puts them to sleep!
Teddy knows an awful lot of science, but he doesn't know
much about people. It took him a long time to understand I
was only a kid. That I couldn't communicate like a grown-up.

It was at Granny's that I started telephoning some of the
scientists I'd seen at the meeting with Daddy. I wanted to
please Teddy a lot, especially after Daddy died and there
was nobody I really wanted to please. But Granny was
mad when I called long-distance. So I had to use call-
boxes, and that takes money. I had to borrow it and sneak

out at night to call. Of course I was caught. At twelve one isn't very sophisticated. Now that I'm fourteen I'm a lot smarter. They wouldn't have caught me this time. And now I've found you!

She was kissing me again when Jean arrived.

10

"WHAT IS GOING on?" Jean, wearing my wrapper, was standing in the doorway of my study. "Richard, what are you doing with this child?"

"Me? Nothing! What did you think?"

"She thinks you're trying to seduce me." The child giggled. "It's okay, Jean. It's just that Richard caught me trying to escape."

"Escape? But why?" Jean was across the room in quick steps, catching Alice in her arms. "Why were you trying to escape?"

Alice's voice was muffled against Jean's chest. "I'm causing you both trouble."

"Trouble? Nonsense! I'm the one who should be grateful to you. That first phone call—that hint you gave me about primes—that really helped me."

Alice pulled back and looked up. "It was right? What I said?"

"It certainly was. Didn't you know?"

"I wasn't sure."

"Listen, my dear, we'd like to help you in return. And I think you need help. If you want to leave us you can—at any time. But please don't."

"You really want me to stay with you?"

"Of course! Don't we, Richard?"

"We sure do."

"Then come back to bed. We can talk things over in the morning." Jean saw the egg on my desk. "What's this?"

"It was inside Teddy. I was showing it to Richard. It sings." Alice held the egg up to Jean. "You listen!" There was hope in her voice.

Jean put the egg to her ear, then shook her head. "I can't hear it."

"Can't hear anything?" Alice's disappointment was clear.

Jean listened again. "Still nothing. You can show me in the morning." She put the egg and the teddy bear into the totebag. "Bring your things with you and come back to bed." She slipped an arm around Alice's shoulders, urging her toward the door. "You need a good night's sleep." She looked back at me, radiating suspicion. Still horrified at my kicking a woman? Or at Alice kissing me?

Alice's story was crazy, but the kid believed she was telling the truth. That egg was the focus of the whole business. My impulse was to grab the bag, but Jean's expression warned me to stay where I was. I watched them disappear up the stairs. Tomorrow I must get hold of the thing one way or another.

"Breakfast's ready," Alice was shouting into my ear, pushing a cup of coffee into my hand. "This'll help you mobilize." She dropped her voice to a whisper. "Promise you won't tell Jean about the egg." Bringing me coffee was not entirely an altruistic gesture. She had wanted to speak to me before Jean could.

I sat up, slurped coffee, and answered loudly, "Thanks, kid." Then, softly, "Why not?"

"She couldn't hear. She wouldn't understand."

"I'll not mention it to Jean unless you say." Then, because I couldn't fool Alice any better than she could fool me, "On one condition."

"What's that?"

"You let me keep it safe for you."

She hesitated. "Okay. But only if you'll listen to Teddy and try to understand what he says. Then you'll tell people— like I was trying to do. They didn't believe me because I didn't understand what I was trying to tell them. But you will." I sensed she welcomed this chance to be rid of a task which had brought her much grief but which she had felt impelled to attempt. "You're grown up. You can phone scientists and they'll listen to you."

Our conversation was interrupted by Jean in the doorway. "What are you two whispering about?"

"Richard's promised to look after that musical egg for me."

"He has, has he? Then he must think it's valuable! Both

of you, come and eat your pancakes while they're hot."
She stared at us and went back to the kitchen. Alice
squeezed my hand and followed her. I went into the
bathroom, glad to be getting hold of the egg so easily,
wondering what other problems the child had offloaded
onto me.

Jean treated me with silent suspicion during breakfast
but only after I had eaten did she start her interrogation.
"Richard, just what do you do? You told me you were a
science writer."

"I am. I publish under a pen name—as I told you. But I
have to earn most of my living as a lawyer."

"A lawyer who specializes in defending pornographers?"
She had evidently been examining my library. "Your
tastes are certainly catholic. Or should I say Byzantine?"

"I'm a patent lawyer, and I practice copyright law as
well as patent law."

"But you are a writer, aren't you?" Alice broke in,
admiration in her voice. "You said you were an investigative journalist."

"I'm writing a series of articles for Syndicated Scientific. The first's due for publication. You know that, Jean."

"You can't judge writers by ordinary rules." Alice was
again defending me. "Writers need all kinds of references."

"Keep away from them, Alice. Writers and references.
Richard, what are you investigating?"

"Sources of inspiration—like I told you." I drank coffee and switched the subject. "Those thugs who tried to
snatch Alice yesterday—"

"Who were they?"

"I don't know. But they didn't look or behave like
ordinary crooks."

"I suppose lawyers and investigative journalists learn to
recognize the various types of criminals as part of their
training." She bit her lip. "Do you think they're still
looking for Alice?"

"Perhaps." I hesitated. "And they probably read my
license plate."

Jean jumped up. "Then we'd better go to the police—"

"Not the fuzz!" Alice protested. "They'll really lock
me up. They said they would last time."

"Not after I've told them what happened."

"Even if they believe you—they'll take me into protective custody. And you're not so well protected in protective custody." She looked at me.

Alice was righter than she realized. She and I had instant rapport. "It'll land Alice in a confused mess if we report to the police now. But we should get her out of here."

"I still think the police—"

"I'll run away if you try to give me to the cops!"

"Take her somewhere safe," I urged Jean.

"To a safe-house. Like in that movie."

"To a safe apartment," said Jean with sudden decision. "Which this one isn't. For several reasons." She frowned at me. "Alice, would you come and stay with me in Princeton?"

"Oh yes. Please!"

"That's a good idea—pro tem," I agreed. "She'll be safe with you while I'm trying to work this thing out."

"Richard, I want to know just what you're trying to work out."

"Take Alice away with you now. Then I'll explain."

Jean hesitated, but Alice was already on her feet. She had sensed what I wanted. "Let's start before those men find I'm here."

"You've a lot of explaining ahead, Richard. Kicking that woman. And how did you know that—?"

"I'll tell you when I know more. And after Alice is safe." I glanced at my watch. "And you'd better move. The vehicle registration office will be open by now and it's easy for anyone to find who owns a Virginia plate." In fact I had an agreement with the leasing agency that they would only reveal my name to a policeman with a warrant.

But the threat was enough to spur Jean into action. "Come on then, Alice. We can get a train to Princeton Junction from Union Station. Richard, please ring for a cab."

"Better if we walk to the rank. It's not far." And there'd be no cab-driver to say how he had picked up a fare at my house.

After Alice had collected her lightened totebag I led them out through my furnace room and Mister Wang's kitchen—a route which interested Alice and raised Jean's eyebrows. But I managed to dodge questions while I escorted them to a cab. I watched it disappear down Columbia Pike with a mixture of relief and regret. Jean would inevitably fit together bits of the puzzle and produce an incomplete picture. But one likely to end our relationship.

I sighed but I had something more exciting than a woman to worry about. I had promised Alice I would listen to her egg and try to understand what it said. Imagination and emotion peak in early adolesence. During the night I had reduced her imaginative story to semirational facts and produced a kind of hypothesis. Some underground group of scientists had planted a radio receiver on the kid and were using her as a safe outlet for knowledge larded with their political creed. It was not a very convincing hypothesis, but better than none.

11

THE EGG SAT on the desk in my study. A metal ovoid the size of a large pear. Smooth, hard, and shining. The thing that had been inside Alice's teddy bear, that had added weight to her totebag. A radio link with some science underground? An engineer with a warped sense of humor? In itself it could hardly be dangerous. The kid had slept with it beside her.

I picked it up and listened. Warbling notes running up and down a strange scale. Teddy's call-sign? Why hadn't Jean heard it? The notes were clear enough—!

I dropped the thing. Jean hadn't heard because the warbling was inside my head! I backed away from the desk. The sounds faded and died. I stopped, then edged in again. The egg remained silent.

It had sung in my mind. The singing that Alice claimed to have heard when she first found it. A singing that had later become words. Words about primes, and superpure silicon, and quarks. What was it? And how did it do what it did?

Whatever it was, it wasn't magic. The product of some research lab? Alice's father had been a scientist. She had found it among trees within the perimeter of a federal research station. I left the egg on my desk and went to my computer terminal. Was there a dead Dr. Drummond in any of its files?

A flashing moment, and dead Dr. Drummonds came sinking down the screen. Among the last, a professor of physics at Virginia Tech. A professor who had previously been a scientist in the Federal Civil Service.

Alice had talked about a research station in Oregon where her father had been a radiation specialist. I accessed more files and found there had indeed been such a station, closed three years before. A station dedicated to investigating unusual methods of communication. The jargon for research into ESP.

During my time as a consultant to the DIA there had been a burst of ESP research funded by the Defense Department, research stimulated by the discovery that the Russians had several large establishments investigating wild fields. The Soviets may not believe in God, the Devil, or the supernatural but, perhaps because they don't, they're suckers for pseudoscience. Several Russian crackpots had converted clever fakery into comfortable careers.

As certain plausible psychics had fooled some of our own credulous Generals. ESP, paranormal perception, psionics, parapsychology, and other forms of fortune-telling had become fashionable—as they had been fashionable back in the fifties. The Defense Department, under pressure from scientists who should have known better and a President who routinely consulted clairvoyants, had succumbed and spent a great deal of the taxpayers' money investigating nonexistent phenomena. All under top secrecy. Not because there were any secrets to protect. Top secrecy to prevent the public from learning that Defense was again making a fool of itself.

Nothing demonstrable had ever emerged from those labs—the lab in Oregon must have been one of them—nor from their Soviet counterparts. After it had become obvious that Defense was spending millions chasing myths the labs had been phased out, although the Reds, so I had heard, were still showing their usual bearish persistence. Because my ability to sense deceit had led to suggestions of clairvoyance—while I believed it only sensitivity to subliminal clues—I had always ridiculed the paranormal as nonsense.

Now I was staring at a thing which had injected sounds into my head. And messages into Alice's head? I sat down, picked up the egg, and listened again.

Warbling as before. Then scanning. Mutual scanning. Before I could react to the light touch sweeping across my mind my own touch was sweeping across another mind. An utterly alien mind. Yet direct contact. Scanning each other by mutual consent; both of us equally confused. We pulled back together.

Contact with what, by what, through what? A kaleido-

scope of images and a complex of sounds. Mutual scanning by mutual agreement. A not unpleasant sensation.
Mutual mind-stroking! No trace of fear or hint of threat. I
went upstairs and poured myself a bourbon. Below, on my
desk, was the enigma of enigmas. A microrecorder packed
with information? More than a recorder. I had stroked a
mind—not a brain or a mechanism.

And felt the same fascination, the same hunger to listen,
that Alice had implied. I fixed myself a second drink and
took it downstairs. I examined the smooth surface of the
egg more carefully, searching for any sign of an antenna.

Nothing! I again put it to my ear.

No warbling. Only a sense that a channel was open, that
another mind was waiting for a call. A call-sign? Teddy's
call-sign? I remembered the cadence, ran through it in my
mind, and we were again in contact. A moment of shifting
colored shapes. Then the flashes locked on to a mental
image as clear as any video.

The familiar image of Earth seen from space. Then a
long hull glowing as it entered atmosphere. An impression
that the hull contained the other mind. The picture of Earth
zoomed in as the hull dropped toward the Pacific.

High above the ocean a small silver ovoid, like the one
on my desk, shot out from the hull. The hull continued its
downward course and splashed into the sea. The ovoid
curved toward a distant shore. Rushing in toward a rocky,
wooded coast. Crashing through trees, landing on a pile of
dead leaves.

The picture blanked. I pulled out. The other had shown
me what it was and how it had arrived. Metzler had
mentioned something from space splashing down into the
Pacific. Alice had found the egg under a clump of trees in
Oregon. Unless this was some complex scam the thing on
my desk was an extension of the mind I had stroked. A
mind in that hull, now somewhere under the Pacific Ocean.

Paranoia exploded. An alien spaceship or a human trap?
What the hell should I do? Obvious solution—give it to
Metzler.

What would he do? Turn it over to Defense Research
Labs and us to the interrogators. With open-ended orders
to plug a top-secret leak. If they didn't hear anything in the
egg they wouldn't give much credence to my claim of

seeing a spaceship arrive. None at all to Alice's fairy story. I didn't relish the prospect of the kid and myself sitting under the lamps, trying to convince skeptics of the unbelievable.

I believed what I had seen, but only because of my sensitivity to deceit. Nobody except Alice shared that sensitivity. It wouldn't be safe to give Metzler the egg until I had demonstrable facts to go with it. Sufficient to stop the Unit from trying to squeeze more facts out of Alice and me. About telepathy, for example.

Telepathy? Telepathy was not an explanation. It was only a word to cover something unknown. A word which I had previously equated with bullshit. Telepathy had never been demonstrated in repeatable experiments, despite the best efforts of scientists, wishful thinkers, and university charlatans. With the egg on my desk and its images in my mind I had to accept that something real was happening. As an earlier generation had been forced to accept radio as real.

But radio had been explicable in terms of hard science. There was no hard science—nor soft science—to explain mental telepathy. Until now nothing convinced me that telepathy existed or could exist. Only a collection of dubious anecdotes and still more dubious experiments in reading hidden cards, with results just outside the range of probability. I had always written them off as flaws in statistical theory rather than proof of exotic happenings.

I picked up the egg again. Alice had said that it talked to her, but only after some months. Would it talk to me on this first day? I renewed the contact, felt the mental scan, and tried a silent question. "What are you?"

The answer was barely intelligible. "Bringer of Word."

"What word?"

"Word of Truth and Knowledge."

"Where are you from?"

A brief interval, then the answer. "Far away."

"Where is that?"

The words in my mind were becoming clearer, almost as if we were starting to understand each other's accents. "World not your named."

"How far away?"

"Four hundred and sixty-five your light-years." The figures were given clearly.

"This thing I have here, is it a remote terminal?"

"Yes."

"Are you in that spaceship you showed me landing in the sea?"

"I am the spaceship."

"A machine!" Surprise forced it from me.

"A machine kind."

"And what am I?"

"A mature sapient." Clearly, without hesitation.

"You spoke to another human. How do you classify her?"

"An immature specimen."

"You know our language?"

"Not well. Deduced from readings of the immature."

"I heard you sing."

"Attract notice. Ensure attention. You do not use?"

My paranoia awoke. I might be talking to an alien machine. Or I might be revealing my credulity to a Defense Department gadget. The thing interpreted my silence. "So even matures do not sing for attention. So immature difficult to spread words."

We were going faster and deeper than I dared. "Can we talk together again?"

"Sing when near. I answer."

"How near?"

"Within one point three five meter." It handled figures better than words.

"Then I will call you later."

"At pleasure." The kind of closing remark my computer makes when it signs off after a session.

Whatever the range of this remote I could not let myself think freely with it still on my desk. I took it up to my bedroom and stowed it in a drawer under my shirts. I couldn't evade the problem by saying that what I had found didn't make sense. I had to make sense of what I had found.

12

FOR THE REST of the day and most of the night I vacillated between panic, euphoria, and caution. Panic at being jumped by some alien goat-foot. Euphoric at the prospect of gifts like superpure silicon. Hesitant at the possibility that I was being sucked into Alice's structured delusion. I fell asleep fearing it was all a crazy dream. Waking the next morning I went straight to my bureau.

The egg was still nesting among my shirts. I slammed the drawer shut and retreated to the kitchen. Saturday—no housekeeper or secretary to intrude. I breakfasted on coffee and a cigarette, stared at the wall, stared out of the window, went into my bedroom and sat on the bed. Finally retrieved the egg and took it down to my study. Put it on my desk and stood inspecting it, trying to rationalize what it was.

The thing claimed to be a remote extension of an alien machine. To believe that, I had to suspend disbelief and accept the doubtful evidence of my senses. The implications were too vast to consider until I was certain I was neither a madman nor a dupe. That the egg was neither an alien trap nor a human fake.

Trap or fake, it had told Alice things no one human could possibly have known. That was my anchor to reality. I sat down, gripped the edge of the desk, throttled my imagination, and stiffened my mind. Then I whistled the call-sign cadence.

Again the sense of touching and being touched. Word-pictures forming. Doubts surfacing. As though answering those doubts, an invitation. "Enter and see my world."

"Your world—here?"

"Image. Enter safely. Return safely."

An invitation which should have raised my paranoia to

80

new heights. It did not. I believed Bringer. I looked away from the egg, out of the window, across a waste of back yards, sheds, rubbish, piles of garbage. My belief that the machine was telling the truth could be a false confidence inserted into my mind by the machine itself. I hesitated. Then curiosity, and perhaps greed, tipped me into giving a mental nod.

The dreary view from my study window shivered, began to fade into background. A miniature brightness in the foreground enlarged into the image of a white city under a bright sky. A well-ordered city of block buildings and straight streets beside a blue bay. A busy city, automata scurrying among buildings. A city filled with people going briskly about their business. A calm and prosperous city, shining in the sunlight, bounded by plantations and pastures. A human city?

"No—my City." The picture expanded, spreading out across green woods toward distant hills. "My world."

"Your world? Here?"

"A recorded image of my world. My City is real, though far from us in time and space."

"But—?" I stared as the city zoomed in to fill my visual field. "But that's a human city. Those people— they're human beings."

"Human in the highest sense. Physically very different, but sapient entities much like yourself. Similar intellectually to all sapient entities throughout the known cosmos."

"They look damned human to me."

"What things look like is a function of the viewer's perceptual system. The most powerful and important forces in the universe cannot be seen or sensed by most sapients. True reality can never be perceived through the senses. What you are seeing now are the outputs of your own decoders. Coded signals from the recording are entering your central nervous system via inductive taps into your sensory input channels. They are decoded into familiar percepts by your brain, the image produced being the closest match in your imagination or memory to the input signal. You see a familiar translation of the true reality. The recording is a reality, so you can see my City as you would were you indeed looking down upon it."

The import of Bringer's words hit me. "You're in my mind!"

"Superficially—as you are in mine. Be assured I can never invade your mental privacy. The search for matching concepts is a purely machine process. Similar to your computer's search for matching words, which it does effectively but without any understanding of what the words mean."

"Like I hear you speaking English?"

"Exactly. You hear the words you yourself would use to describe the percepts I am transmitting."

That was not quite accurate. Bringer was using my words but not in my way. For the moment I accepted its explanation, one which would have satisfied Bishop Berkeley, and enjoyed the pleasant scene spread out before me. Only a fringe of back yards and garbage cans remained to remind me I was still sitting at the desk in my study, staring out the window. The image of the City was satisfying. The kind of city I would have built were I in the business of building cities.

A vision like a vivid dream. The kind of vision described by the seers. The scene was moving below me as if I were floating across the city in dream-flight. "It's a kind of three-D videotape?"

"It is a stochastic recording. A recording which includes all possible outcomes. You are observing one of many potential realities. The individuals are image, but each has alternative actions. In brief, the recording is of a non-deterministic system governed by heuristic constraints."

In searching my brain for matching words Bringer had evidently acquired the fashionable jargon of systems engineering and information theory. "You're saying that you don't know what I'm going to see?"

"I know only in terms of conditional probabilities. The individuals below will act in individual ways but the group action is predictable at a high level of confidence."

The City faded and I was back in my study, staring through the window at piled garbage, recovering from the beauty of the vision. Still in mind-touch with Bringer. "Why have you come to Earth?"

Bringer seemed ready for my question. "To bring you

truth and knowledge. That is the purpose for which I was
created."

"The kinds of things you told Alice—that immature
sapient?"

"The kinds of things I tried to tell her, but which she
could not understand."

"Will you tell them to me?"

"After we have communicated more." Our minds touched
and we parted.

Before the arrival of Bringer I had judged the probability of intelligent aliens making contact with Earth to be
about as likely as life after death. Hopes created by us
humans as cushions against the evidence that we were
alone in an indifferent or malignant universe. By now
Earth's modulated radio albedo must be the loudest signal
in many alien skies. For decades our most sensitive
radioscopes had been searching for extraterrestrial signals
and hearing nothing but noise. For millennia human prayers
had been floating upward toward heaven. As both our
radio signals and our prayers were being ignored, any
deities or aliens who did exist must be too remote to notice
or too wise to answer.

Yet the popular beliefs in God and aliens had seeped
into my thinking. I was not as astounded as I should have
been at Bringer's arrival. Nor did I doubt that it had
traveled so far for so long to get here. Even our own
solidstate high-tech machines could probably survive such
a voyage in near vacuum. The manufacturers of probes
heading out into the universe were advertising that their
products would outlast the solar system. The alien ship
was manned by a machine. Which spoke well for the
aliens' good sense. Only entities with the life-span of
machines would set out on space voyaging.

Why had these intelligent aliens dispatched Bringer on a
voyage across the galaxy? Conquest or material gain was
impossible. Perhaps the ship was packed with embryos or
germ-dust—or something unimaginable. Stuff for a horror
story, not for a machine with a mind like Bringer's.

The machine claimed that its mission was purely altruistic. Its makers had built it to spread their knowledge
among fellow sapients on other worlds. Despite my in-

stinctive suspicion of altruism I had to accept that, for the moment, as a working hypothesis. My more immediate concern was what had made me the fortunate sapient chosen to receive these handouts? Why had Bringer, with four billions on Earth to choose from, only spoken to Alice and me? Reason forced me to face the obvious answer.

We were both sensitive to whatever the egg radiated. Alice's father had been on a team investigating wild methods of communication. Maybe they'd succeeded better than he'd thought? The station might have radiated something that had attracted the egg. The egg had attracted Alice. And, indirectly, my sensitivity to deceit had led me to her.

The mind I'd touched was the mind of a machine. I was relieved rather than shocked. If telepathy existed—and I was being forced to believe it did—then it was a physical phenomenon and could not be restricted to biological minds. Nothing occult about it. Rational thought was a property of all higher intellects whether the shifting patterns moved across a substrate of neurones or across a matrix made from something more robust. Terran Artificial Intelligence, the big thing in fifth-generation computerdom, was only a few human generations away—if we gave ourselves a few generations. But alien AI was already on the floor of the Pacific.

During the next few days Bringer and I talked frequently and misunderstood each other constantly. Partly because Alice had not understood most of what she had fed into its memory. She must have spent many evenings reading to her Teddy, reading from her children's books as well as from her father's scientific journals. Bringer's colloquial English, juvenile at first, became superficially adult from its conversations with me. Its scientific vocabulary was excellent. Emotionally loaded words such as "love" had a different loading and seemed to refer to an emotion encompassing all true sapients.

Between conversations with Bringer I worked on the series for Syndicated Scientific. The publication of my lead article on Slipe and his superpure silicon had been delayed not, Jackson assured me, because of editorial policy but because of corporate directive. "There's some patent problem involved, Richard,'' he told me over the telephone. ''But that's being cleared and I want to get the series started. The Slipe story's first rate. You've sure got the touch—and the insight. We'll have more assignments for you when this lot's out.''

Jackson was as honest as any editor can be, so I continued to write up my interviews, chiefly for my own satisfaction. The real goal of the operation was already achieved. Sooner or later I would have to tell Ebermann and Haskard what I had found, but what I had found was so bizarre that I needed something concrete to soften them up first. I reminded Bringer of its mission to dispense knowledge and suggested it start by telling me something useful.

It considered my request. ''First, you must visit my City again.''

''Gladly. But Alice said you looked like her teddy bear. Can you show yourself some way? So I don't feel I'm talking to myself.''

''You wish total immersion?''

''Total immersion? Yes—if that's what it takes.''

Therefore one Sunday morning in early August I locked myself in my study with the egg on the desk and prepared to experience whatever it meant by ''total immersion.''

13

TOTAL IMMERSION INVOLVED instant transfer. My study flicked into faint background. The City was spread out before me in hard detail. Still the same well-ordered city, gleaming white in the sunshine. But now only a few hundred meters from the grassy hill on which I was standing. And standing beside me was Colonel Metzler.

"Colonel, what the hell—?"

"I'm Bringer." Spoken with Metzler's sharp voice and brusque manner. "You asked to see me, Ryan. Searched your stored images for one that matched your concept of me. This was the best fit. Not good, but the closest."

"You searched my memories?"

"Superficial only. No prying around. Couldn't if I wanted to. Any more than you can pry into mine." The figure gave a tight Metzler smile. "Like the word-search I told you about before. You made the match—not me. Prefer someone else?"

"No. You'll do." If Bringer matched its appearance to some other images floating in my superficial memory, God knows what I'd see.

"Trust me?"

"Yes," I said slowly. "I guess I do."

"Break off any time you want." Another tight smile. "Take a look around first. Any changes?"

I stared at the sea, the sky, the City. At the green forests fading away into the distant mountains. The same overall image as before but with much greater detail and a far firmer reality. "It's more—well—convincing."

"Because now you're in it. We're in it. Both of us together." Bringer gave a typical Metzler shoulder-jerk. "Let's move!"

"Move where?"

"Into the City, of course. Let you see how things are run here. That's why you came, isn't it?" He started down the hill with his usual purposeful stride. Hard for me to think of that upright figure as anyone but the Colonel. I went after him.

The grass was springy under my feet. The tang of the sea came on the breeze from the bay. Reality increasing as belief increased. You can only see what you believe, and you often see only what you think should be there. This was indeed total sensory immersion. My study was a faint shadow in the margins of my mind.

He was waiting for me on the road at the foot of the hill, waiting with typical Metzler impatience. "Move it, Ryan, we've a way to go. Can't loaf along like these civilians."

I swung out beside him, nodding with him at the men and women we overtook. They smiled silent greetings in return. A bunch of 3-D puppets, yet they mimicked life well. As we reached the first buildings I asked, "Colonel, when you were Alice's Teddy—did you bring her here?"

He looked at me sharply. "Several times."

"And she saw what I see?"

A barked laugh. "I doubt it. She's a child. Too young to spread knowledge. But through her I found you."

"Have you made other contacts?"

"Not on Earth. Can't waste probes. Lot of worlds still to convert. One probe per world should be enough. But before you turned up I was thinking about trying a second. Shouldn't need to now."

I licked my lips. "How long are you planning to stay?"

"Only long enough to deliver knowledge to Terran sapients. That's *your* job, Ryan."

"My job?"

"Of course. That's why I'll be giving you knowledge. You're telepathic. Needs an adult telepath to start spreading knowledge. Sapient able to talk mind-to-mind. You're the first I've recruited here. So that makes you the local CO." A tight Metzler smile. "Richard Ryan, Commander of the Knowledge Militant on Earth. How does that sound?"

"Impressive." It sounded terrible. Why the hell had Bringer thought I'd want it to model itself on Metzler? And why was Bringer talking more and more like I imagined Metzler himself would talk in this situation?

"Get yourself some troops, Ryan. Contact more telepaths. Snowball effect. Know what I mean?"

"Sure." I hesitated. "But that may take time."

"Takes a lifetime. Your lifetime. My lifetime. We've both got assignments for life." He laughed. "Spreading knowledge among sapients. My job's to take knowledge to all the worlds I can reach for as long as I last. That's why I was made. That's my duty." Duty—genuine Metzler. "Maybe that's why you were made, Ryan."

I hadn't been made—I'd been born. I'd had no "duty" pinned on me. "I may have problems finding telepaths to recruit."

"If you're a truly sapient race there must be enough around. Otherwise—?" He shrugged. Otherwise we wouldn't be worth wasting knowledge on?

So Bringer believed all sapient races contained numerous telepaths. I had almost betrayed myself—and humanity—by telling him that telepaths were, at most, a tiny minority. If any existed. Alice and I, the only two people who, so far, had been able to communicate with Bringer, could not communicate with each other mind-to-mind. At best we could only sense emotions.

If Bringer thought that telepaths were too thin on the ground to spread knowledge, then it might decide we were not a truly sapient race worthy of knowledge. It might move on without unloading our quota of gifts. For the moment I was reassured that Bringer did not seem to be aware of what I was thinking as we walked together up the boulevard toward the agora, the square at the center of the City.

"Did Alice tell you much about Earth?" I asked, glancing at the solid white buildings on each side of us. The architecture was mostly "brutal modern." Utilitarian rather than beautiful, now that I was seeing it close up.

"Soon as I realized she was a child I knew her perceptions might be inaccurate. But she told me enough to show things here are much the same as on any ignorant sapient world. Saps having to defend themselves against subsaps with magic. Like that story of Jack killing subsapient giants."

"Magic?"

"Another word for science, isn't it?"

"Some people think they're the same."

"Alice is too young to make fine distinctions. But she told me a hell of a lot of details about your science. Mostly didn't understand what she was saying." He shook his head. "Your people seem to educate your young in reverse. Fill 'em with detail before you give 'em the structure."

"I'm afraid we do. Perhaps you've suggestions for improvement?"

"Education is species-specific. What suits one species may not suit another. Most species transfer knowledge to their young in a pattern of increasing complexity, pausing for understanding at each step. From my interactions with Alice it seems you transfer large amounts of specialized information early in the learning process. Alice was crammed with stuff she won't be able to use yet." Bringer again shook his head. "Illogical—but it must suit your species."

"It's one way." I did not try to imagine the educational processes on Bringer's home world. A truly telepathic race might not need books and journals. Bringer had not, apparently, considered that Alice could have been reading to her Teddy. "Perhaps you learned more about us from television?"

"I took station underwater immediately after entry. Minimize deterioration from EM radiation. Also improves probe range. But blocks radio. However, while passing through the atmosphere, I recorded snatches of programs. Allowing for her age, they support what Alice said about your society. Same general pattern I've found in other sap societies. As expected. All saps have the same goal: to discover Truth. My makers were close to reaching Truth when I sailed. By now they must be there."

"How long since you left?"

"Hell of a long time. Too long to mean much to you. And time-flow's not a constant." The hint of a sigh. "My makers sent me to spread the knowledge they had found. Knowledge to aid saps threatened by subsaps. Threats you must know about?"

"I do." I pressed the point. "Your aid may be vital to our survival."

Bringer said nothing and we continued to walk together through the crowds toward the agora. They appeared more human than ever. A certain sameness and lack of expression perhaps; nothing I could put my finger on. I had to remind myself that these were only three-dimensional images, projections from some recording made aeons ago. Remarkably lifelike all the same. Talking together as Bringer and myself were talking together.

"Like you to see this, Ryan." Metzler paused at the edge of the agora, pointing to a statue at its center. "What do you think of it?"

"It" was a gigantic piece of sculpture, a monument in the best Victorian tradition, of a half-clothed man embracing a half-clothed woman. I moved closer and stared up. Bringer expected me to be impressed. "It's—it's striking."

"Know what it represents?"

I had no idea what it represented. I hesitated. "I'm not sure."

Metzler showed his disappointment at my lack of vision. "Knowledge Embracing Truth. That's what it shows. In some form familiar to you, of course."

"Of course. I see it now. Impressive symbolism."

"You're damned right it's impressive. Those are the twin foundations of this City." Bringer-as-Metzler looked up at the statues with much the same expression as I'd seen on the face of the real Metzler when saluting the flag. "Knowledge and Truth. Those are what I'm here to deliver. What you've got to spread."

"Spread?"

"Spread the Word. That's your job now, Ryan. May take guts—warn you of that. Lot of saps—sensitive and insensitive—serve the Lie. Same here as other worlds, I expect, eh?"

"There are some who reject knowledge and truth." So these aliens used Truth as their God and Falsehood as their Devil. Depressing to realize the high-tech civilization which had made Bringer had made the same mistake as had we primitives. "Preaching truth and spreading knowledge can be tough here."

Metzler-Bringer studied me. "Think you're the man to do it, Ryan." He paused. "If you can't hack it, bring me somebody who can."

"Give me the knowledge and tell me the truth, and I'll

hack it." The kind of unwilling committal Metzler as Colonel had maneuvered me into before.

"That's the spirit, Ryan. Now head back to base. When I've sorted things out here I'll contact you with a catalog."

The City faded and I was back in my study with the Metzler-Bringer's voice ringing in my mind's ear. I sat there for some ten minutes, wondering what the machine was "sorting out" and trying to make sense of all I had learned. Then, suddenly, a series of images started to flow through my mind, almost as though I really was flipping through the pages of a catalog. One image caught my attention. "Stop."

The image froze, then faded. A query. "Molecular memory?"

"Yes."

"You wish to have?"

"Yes." I sure did. Molecular computers could be here within the lifetime of a patent.

Again the flurry of images. "Coded self-organizing long-chain. Your formula." A string of carbon codons floated clearly. I seized pencil and paper and copied them down. "Suspend in gel. Modulate electromagnetic three dimensions. Organize. Learn. Reorganize. Tetrabits per cc."

I stared at the paper, starting to understand. "What modulation?"

"Appropriate wave-forms." It droned on, using terms it must have learned from Alice's readings. By the time it finished I had the outline for the basis of a molecular computer.

"This is better than anything I know."

"Better always replaces less good. That is the Word. You have knowledge. Now you spread that knowledge."

That was what Bringer expected me to do. Recruit other telepaths and establish a knowledge network to distribute the snippets of information it was proposing to give me. During my immersion in the City the image of Bringer-as-Metzler had been overwhelming. Talking through the egg in my study Bringer proved to be a mixture of erudition and naiveté. It believed everything it said. It believed most things I said. It seemed incapable of lying and acted as if I, a sapient, always told the truth as I saw it. I might be mistaken, but I couldn't lie.

It had probably been programmed not to doubt the veracity of anything told it by a mature sapient, although it could and did question the accuracy of details. It had shown me an image of its home port but it would not, or could not, tell me much about its makers. That was probably classified information and not part of its programing.

For the past three years Bringer had been learning about human society as presented to it in fairy stories, comics, and scientific papers read by a child who was herself living a kind of fantasy. It had made allowances for her youth and inexperience but had accepted the overall pattern she had presented because it agreed with its preconceptions of sapient societies.

Bringer's mission was to spread the knowledge of its creators through the galaxy. To preach the brand of truth it started to call "The Word." To give converted sapients information which they could use to protect themselves against subsapients and unbelieving sapients. And it gradually became clear to me that I wouldn't get any more handouts until I had produced some sensitive sapients to show I was doing my share of the spreading.

I didn't know any telepathic sapients, apart from Alice, and as I was busy making the molecular memory patent watertight, I didn't press Bringer for more knowledge gifts. I did listen to its quaint sociology. For much the same reason that Alice had continued to read to her Teddy. Mind-stroking was mutually pleasant and Bringer encouraged it. The thing might have only a machine mind, but any sort of mind isolated for eons cruising across vast empty spaces must grow weary of its own company. That might be anthropomorphic thinking but Bringer did seem to enjoy conversation. And I enjoyed learning about Bringer.

It was in societics that it most clearly showed machine zeal and machine rigidity. It was a natural master of Aristotelian logic—the way that Aristotle thought men should think. Men don't but machines do. And Bringer did. Its picture of intelligent life on Earth had been formed by imposing the social behavior of its builders upon the mixture of childish myth and scientific beliefs which Alice had fed it. Its premises were therefore bizarre but its logic was perfect so that its conclusions about us were grotesque.

Bringer assumed as an absolute that the nature, the motivations, the goals of all sapient life—biological and machine—must be basically the same throughout the universe. No alternative was conceivable. Any lifeform that did not match that pattern could not be truly sapient and therefore did not warrant being treated as sapient. Somehow or other it had acquired the idea of "soul"—probably from hearing Alice's bedtime prayers—and had assumed that was how we humans differentiated between sapients and nonsapients. Sapients had a soul; others did not.

The machine was still waiting for me to produce sensitive sapients for its inspection. No more total immersions and no more knowledge-gifts until I did. Perhaps it would accept Alice as a mature telepath if I explained to her why I needed her aid and coached her in her role?

With this in mind, and because I wanted to see Jean again, I phoned to tell her I'd be coming through Princeton at the end of August and might I drop by? I could not read her true emotions over the telephone and she did not show any obvious joy at the news—I wondered what Alice had been telling her—but she did say she'd meet me at the station.

14

JEAN WAS THERE when I got off the two-coach train which shuttles between Princeton Junction and Princeton, but her greeting was not warm. She pulled back physically and pushed me away mentally when I tried to kiss her. Repulsed, I looked around. "Where's Alice?"

"In summer school. She'll be home for lunch. But I want to talk to you before you talk to her."

"How is the kid?"

"She was doing fine—until she heard you were coming. Now she's upset again."

"Upset? About what?"

"That egg thing she gave you." Jean started across the station yard. "The news you were coming has revived her fantasy."

"What fantasy?" I caught Jean's arm and held her to a halt. "What's she been telling you?"

She jerked her arm free and faced me. "The same that she told you. And she says that you encouraged her in it."

"I'm not sure it's all fantasy."

"Of course it is! She was an unhappy child and she's still trying to hide a talent she's afraid of."

"Talent? What talent?"

"Her mathematical talent, of course. Pretending that it was her teddy bear who told her about infinite prime numbers."

"Not her teddy. The thing she sewed inside it."

Jean gestured impatiently. "Children of her age imagine all kinds of fantastic things. Fairies at the bottom of the garden stuff."

"Children of fourteen?"

"She told me she was eleven and her mother had just died when she found that egg." Jean continued toward her car. "She developed a structured delusion to avoid having to deal with the problem of her mathematical talent. And she's maintaining that delusion to protect her ego."

"Jean—you're not talking like a mathematician. You're talking like a psychologist."

"I'm repeating what the psychologist told me. The only explanation that makes any kind of sense." She got into her car.

"You've taken the kid to some psychologist?" I walked round the car and got in beside her.

"Not some psychologist!" she snapped, starting the motor. "I took her to see Professor Gershin. He's a clinical psychologist with an international reputation who specializes in the problems of adolescents. Alice wouldn't cooperate. He arranged for her to be examined by a noted psychiatrist and she said she'd run away before she'd let another shrink fondle her. And Gershin didn't touch her. I was with them all the time."

The fondling must have been mental and unconscious. "He was the one who diagnosed her as repressing her math talent to hide it?"

"Suppressing—not repressing. She doesn't know she's doing it. Gershin advised me to leave her alone, let her talent flourish at its own rate, now she's safe among friends. And Richard—" She swung her car out of the station yard—"she's developing into a normal happy youngster ever since I stopped asking her about mathematics. Miss Crossey, her teacher in summer school, reports she is a bright child and is starting to come out. I don't want you to distort that."

"Neither do I. But how could I?"

"She's got a crush on you. Ever since she saw you kick that woman, you've been a hero to her. Not to me! I dislike unnecessary brutality. Children of Alice's age are infected with it. Every television show—"

I exploded. "That woman was out to gas her and you!"

"You're very sure of that, Richard. You claimed that flash of hers was a gasgun, but I never examined it. Where is it?"

"Around the garage, I guess." The thing must have rolled away under the seats when I opened the glove compartment or fallen out of the door. Anyway, I hadn't been able to find it. "But I can recognize a gasgun when I see one. And I, at least, had the sense to recognize a kidnap attempt."

Jean turned onto Main. "Oh, I don't question the kidnap attempt. I'm only questioning your overreacting." She glanced sideways at me. "Has that woman or her helpers shown up?"

"Not yet. She couldn't have read the number of my car."

"I suspect they were people from the Childrens' Aid."

"You think we rescued Alice from the Childrens' Aid?"

"Perhaps. I don't know. Anyway, the child's much better off with me than with them or with that grandmother of hers. I want to keep her with me. I want her to be able to live a normal healthy life and get a good education. And I don't want you upsetting her with a lot of investigative reporting—or whatever it is you do."

"I won't upset her," I promised. "And I'll try to crush any crush."

"Don't be brutal!" Jean parked in front of the lakeside apartments. "Be kind, but be firm. Adolescent girls, even growing up under normal circumstances, pass through emotional storms. They interpret everything in terms of sex."

"You have an excellent memory, Jean."

She glared at me as she got out of the car. "I was like any other young teenager. I fell in love with the most horrible creatures. Thank goodness I had a family to protect me. Alice has had nobody—until now. And I'm going to protect her."

"Against horrible creatures like me?"

"You're not a horrible creature. You're just a devious liar." She suddenly smiled her old smile and put a hand on my arm. "A damned attractive liar—the last kind of person for Alice to get a crush on."

I sighed and followed her to the elevator. "I'll keep the kid at arms's length."

Physically that proved impossible. The moment I entered the apartment she threw herself into my arms, her thin body pressed against mine, her emotions flooding my mind. I managed an avuncular response to her hot kisses, put her back on her feet, and asked the question guaranteed to shoot down any teenager. "How are you getting along at school, Alice?"

She heard my words and sensed my rejection. From then on throughout the visit she was either sullen and silent or noisy and sarcastic. When Jean drove me back to the station that evening she thanked me for having behaved so well and rewarded me with a gentle kiss. I got onto the train feeling like a true sonofabitch for hurting the only other sensitive I had ever met.

During the journey back to Washington I rationalized my part in the situation and tried to feel relieved that Jean had accepted the superficial psychological explanation for Alice's lack of demonstrable mathematical talent. Amazing how brilliant mathematicians and physical scientists accept psychological explanations whose equivalent they would jeer at in their own disciplines. As my only encouragement, in the few moments I had managed to be alone wtih Alice, I had whispered for her to go on playing the same game and that I was starting to find out something about the egg. Using Alice to con Bringer was obviously some way in the future.

By the time I reached Annandale I was exhausted, cursing all females, adult and adolescent alike. I repressed my hurt over Jean and Alice by concentrating on the preparation of a molecular memory patent. A task that challenged my art and my skill. An application that must show sufficient present value to attract licenses and yet conceal aspects which could promote it to a master-patent when the time came.

My article on Slipe, delivered to Syndicated in June, was still unpublished in September when Jackson phoned to say that Slipe wanted to meet me in Washington. Syndicated, sensitive to possible legal complications, would like me to humor him. A request that Jackson had to pass on although it offended his editorial ethic. A victim should only see what's been said after it's in print. I reassured Jackson that I'd be happy to humor Slipe. Somebody was leaning on the little chemist. It would help to know who.

We met in Slipe's suite at the Mayflower. Interesting in itself. Professors do not rent suites with their own money. He offered me a drink and then sat fidgeting, trying to be ingratiating but obviously worried. After a few fulsome remarks about my skill as a science writer, he came to the real reason for his visit. "That remark you made—about a dream and a telephone call. What prompted you to make it?"

I shrugged. "As I explained, Dr. Slipe, I'm interested in the origins of original ideas. Of what triggers insights such as yours. Kekule's own account of his sudden vision of the six-carbon ring—of his half-dream while sitting in front of the fire—made me ask if you had experienced anything like that. You said you had not."

"At the time I rather resented your suggestion. Thinking about it later I was reminded that I was, in fact, awakened by a telephone call during the night previous to the morning when I suddenly saw the key to superpurifying silicon. And that I did have a kind of a dream."

"Really?" I leaned forward, looking fascinated. "Do you remember anything about the call?"

"Not much." He hesitated. "The caller seemed to be a young woman. And her voice was vaguely familiar."

"A lady-friend, perhaps?"

He stiffened. "None of the ladies I know would call me at three in the morning!"

"I didn't mean—"

He waved my apology aside. "And this sounded like a young girl. I don't know any young girls. Also—" He hesitated—"she sang!"

"Sang?"

"Well—chanted. Meaningless notes. I must have gone back to sleep. A silly dream. Forgot all about it. But it was the next morning that I got my key idea on superpurification. Your remark during our interview helped me remember that telephone call. Also where I had heard that girl's voice."

"Where was that?"

"Two years ago I chaired a session at the AAAS meeting in Washington. The New Year's meeting. After the session a young girl—a child—came to me and tried to tell me something about silane gas. I didn't pay much attention. She had some kind of a toy with her—a silver egg-shaped thing. Asked me to listen to it."

"And did you?"

"She was very insistent, so I did. Couldn't hear anything, of course. She seemed disappointed and went away."

"Did you know who she was?"

"Not at the time. Later I found out that her father was a Dr. Drummond, a physicist who used to take his daughter to meetings with him."

"Where is she now?"

"I don't know. I was hoping you might have some idea. Because you mentioned a dream and a telephone call. Perhaps some other scientist—?" He spread his hands.

"This is all news to me. Exciting news! Have you spoken to Dr. Drummond?"

"He died last year. Her mother was already dead. She went to live with her grandmother. A year later she ran away. She has since run away from several foster homes."

"Why do you want to get in touch with her?"

"Well—" He paused. "If her telephoning stimulated that dream—triggered my insight—then I owe the child something and I'd like to help her. She seems in need of help."

"The thought does you much credit, Doctor. I wish I could suggest something. Especially as this adds human interest to your story. Perhaps I can mention it in future articles. Some reader might recognize the girl."

"No! Please! The whole thing sounds too laughable. I'd appreciate it greatly if you could treat this conversation as confidential. But tell me if you do hear anything to corroborate it."

"You can rely on my discretion, Doctor. As a reputable journalist I always respect confidences."

"It's not only my desire for personal privacy. There are certain legal aspects. I have a patent application pending. An application for a very valuable patent. And you know how those lawyers would leap at any excuse to question the originality of my discovery."

"I can appreciate your concern. As I appreciate your being so frank with me. If I hear anything about this girl I'll tell you. Otherwise, I'll say nothing about her." I paused. "Have you told anybody else?"

"No!" He had. "Why?"

"Because Ladrich was listening to you give your paper at Baltimore."

"Ladrich?" Slipe shook his head. "Who is he?"

"Works for some financial analyst." Slipe had never even heard of Justine. "I recognized some of the others monitoring your presentation. Greig from Dupont. Metzler and Culbertson and Simpson, for example."

His startled reaction to the name "Metzler" was so obvious that I didn't need my sensitivity to pick it up. "Greig I've met, but not the others. Who are they?"

"Talent hunters—I think." I shrugged. "Seen them hanging around scientific meetings, and they're not journalists. Better not talk to them if you do run into them."

"I won't! I won't!" He thanked me and showed me out, looking more worried than when I had arrived. I was relieved that it was Colonel Metzler and not Justine Ladrich who was squeezing me. But how had she learned about Alice? One of the other regenerated academics must have talked under trickery or pressure. Which suggested Justine knew that Slipe was not the only example of revived originality.

My interview with Slipe, the first in an important series of articles on recent scientific advances (according to Syndicated's blurbs), came out at the end of September under my pen name. It was well received and reprinted coast-to-coast. I glowed anonymously.

15

"RYAN?" IT WAS Metzler on the phone. "You've some explaining to do. Be at the House. Fifteen hundred. Today!"

My article on Slipe had come out the week before and I'd been expecting Metzler to yell for me. With Bringer-as-Metzler still so strong in my mind, I did not relish facing him in the flesh. "Colonel, I'd like to see you, but—"

"Ryan, I don't want to see you! I want an explanation. Not that Grayson business. Something more recent. Be here at fifteen hundred or I'll send a patrol to bring you in." And he hung up.

I doubted whether even a colonel in the DIA would infringe civil liberties to the extent of having a patrol bring in a civilian lawyer. And the Grayson caper was a flawed lever; it would fracture if he tried to hoist me with it. Nevertheless caution took me into Washington that afternoon. This was no time to offend Metzler.

The House on K Street was still the headquarters of the Association of Military Photographers and Artists, and the colonel still looked more of a soldier in civilian clothes than most soldiers do in uniform. He had a copy of my Slipe article open on the desk in front of him and he challenged me as I came through the door. "I see you're reverting to journalism, Ryan."

"Why do you assume I wrote that?"

"The style—like your old consultation reports. Nobody around here can put things the way you could. We miss 'em." He had never shown any signs of appreciating my style when I had been a consultant, but his present praise was genuine and I felt flattered, despite myself. "Also the subject. Sit down and tell me about the new journalism."

I took a chair. Then I took another which didn't wobble. Metzler mined his office with items that tended to keep his visitors off-balance. "Are you planning to wreck my writing career a second time?"

"Still clutched up about that negative radar business? How was I to know you're blessed with second sight? Sorry just the same." He frowned at the memory of one of his few errors. "Anyway, you've made more from pirating patents than you'd have from raking muck. Though this job you've done on Slipe's good." He leaned forward across my article. "What did you find?"

"Find? How do you mean?"

"This interview was just a front so you could scan Slipe close up, wasn't it?"

"My client suggested that writing an article about Dr. Slipe might give me new insights into his inspiration."

"And you scared him spastic. Did you know that?"

"I sensed that he was alarmed by some of the questions I asked."

"Slipe started to jagger as soon as I pulled him in. Said you'd reminded him of incidents he'd forgotten."

"What incidents? What did I say that shook him?"

"You don't know?"

"I sensed—" I broke off. "If you don't tell me, why should I tell you?"

He stared at me, then said slowly, "I wish to hell I could read your mind, Ryan. I know I'd dislike what I'd read. But at least I'd learn the other half of the truth you tell. Slipe's been after you, hasn't he?"

I nodded. "I couldn't help him. He kept asking me about some young girl." I hesitated. "There's not much more that I can say, Colonel."

"Can say or will say?"

"Can say." Without involving my client, I added to myself.

"You don't know any young girls?"

"I prefer mature women."

"I'm aware of your commercial preferences, Ryan. I mean this girl Slipe talks about. Do you know who she is?"

"I do now. Slipe told me. He said her name's Alice Drummond. That she's the daughter of a physicist. A dead physicist."

"Slipe told you that? The blabbermouthed fool. Did he tell you why he's looking for her?"

"To help her—he said. Now, I guess, it's because he's helping you?"

"Slipe's only interested in helping himself. I put the fear of Mammon into him. Threatened to block his patent. He thought those questions were plants and you were working for us." Metzler paused. "Wish to hell you were."

Thank God I wasn't. "Colonel, who is this Alice Drummond?"

"A child somebody's using as a courier." He cracked his knuckles. "We think she's been kidnapped. When I catch whoever has—!" His fingers clenched and my throat tightened. "We're searching for her."

"Justine Ladrich was at Slipe's lecture. Think she's involved?"

He stared at me. "Do you?"

"Seems likely. Though Loucher Freres would hardly be the source of Slipe's silicon. They trade information— they don't give it away through young girls." I paused. "That Ladrich woman could be after this Alice Drummond for the same reason you are."

"And you, Ryan?"

I shrugged. "Haven't said anything about her to my clients since Slipe gave me her name. A kid—they'd think I was kidding."

Metzler did not smile. "This girl's the daughter of a Federal scientist. Apart from anything else, she deserves Federal protection. From the bastards who are using her and any bitch who's trying to grab her. Or has grabbed her." He paused. "Are there others besides Slipe who've risen from the academic dead?"

"Unless Slipe's unique—there must be."

"Ryan—you're a fast man with an empty phrase. Do you know of any?"

"Colonel—I'm only interested in patentable discoveries. And superpure silicon's the only discovery made by a has-been I've heard about. I've interviewed several other scientists for that Syndicated series, but none of 'em have produced anything worth a dime. Commercially, I mean."

"And the commercial angle is the only angle for you!" Disgust at my avarice diverted the thrust of his interrogation. "You've a talent for spotting deceit—and you love hunting for it. You're not in that fool patent game just for the money—though God knows, you love that too. You enjoy hidden intrigue. Why not come back to us—as a consultant. The real action's here."

"I dislike violence."

"Good intelligence avoids violence. Violence is a last resort. An admission of failure."

"That's what you always said. I believed you—until Chicago. I've still got a nonviolent slug in me."

"Wasn't I right? An admission of defeat—by the reds." He sighed. "If you pick up anything about that girl—tell me."

I could make an honest promise. "If I hear anything that doesn't affect the rights of my client I'll pass it on."

The colonel studied me the way a cat does; the look that wishes you were small enough to eat. "I suppose I'll have to be satisfied with that. For the time being. Keep in touch, Ryan. And we'll keep an eye on you." He waved me from his office.

When I reached the safe phone I tried to call Jean, to warn her that the DIA were after Alice. I failed to reach her. Since my visit to Princeton she had moved and now had an unlisted number. Neither the phone company nor the departmental secretary at Princeton would reveal what it was. I left a message for her to ring my answering service. She did not.

By mid-October I had polished the molecular memory patent bright enough to shine while still sufficiently tarnished to hide its full value. Overworking is a temptation in any art form, and one to which my competitors are subject. I took the final draft to the penthouse and showed it to the partners.

Adam Haskard made no pretense at understanding the application. Harold Ebermann leafed through it with interest but without noticeable enthusiasm, reassurance that I had hidden its true value well. "Might be able to peddle this, Ryan. But what's so great about it?"

I stripped back the verbal overlay and showed him the mother lode hidden beneath.

He looked through it again with a skepticism that turned to admiration, then at me with frank suspicion. "Why are you letting us in on this?"

"Because I got the idea through the Slipe operation. Our agreement gives you a cut in any product."

"Who'd you steal it from?"

"Dammit—I don't steal!"

"Then how'd you get it?"

"Well—I did graduate from MIT with honors."

"And I won the Divinity Prize at Episcopal High," said Adam, standing behind his partner. "Richard—is this really yours?"

"It's my discovery. To all intents and purposes it's mine. There's not a soul, living or dead, with any claim. It's completely new. There's nobody to contest me. Molecular computers have a hot future. Even a minor patent like this will bring that future closer. A lot of firms will snap up licenses. A quick profit. For all three of us."

"So you say."

"Start filing. Then show it to Conray. Hear what they offer—as is. They could run lab tests in a week to show the idea'll work."

"You're very sure of yourself."

"I've good reason to be."

"We don't want to tangle with Security or Defense."

"Nor do I. You know that. I give you my word that nobody'll be able to accuse us of anything. After you two are convinced that it's what I claim—then perhaps I'll tell you how I got it."

"Why not tell us now?"

"Because you wouldn't believe me."

"Something to do with your clairvoyance, Richard?" asked Adam.

"Maybe." I stood up. "After you're satisfied that patent's going to be good, let me know. Because there may be more where it came from."

"You've found what's leaking?" Ebermann was dangerously accusing.

"No. I can tell you this much now. There's no leak. Not from any lab. And this isn't Beltway Bandit stuff."

"Then where the hell?"

"First get that nailed down. So the cash inflow will convince you I'm not crazy."

16

THE CALL WAS a fake but I can't sense deceit on the telephone and its subject diverted my suspicion. It purported to come from Julian Haladner, the Executive Vice-President of the Law Society, and the caller identified herself as Mr. Haladner's private secretary. Mr. Haladner would like an unofficial chat with me about a matter raised by Bruton, Barton, and Wiggin, one of Washington's more prestigious firms specializing in corporation law. They had tangled with me the previous year and shown themselves incompetent in patent challenges. I had extracted myself with my professional conscience clear, leaving them caught in their own convolutions.

I jumped to the conclusion that BB&W were now trying to square accounts through a complaint to the Ethics Committee of the Law Society. Haladner, who had dealt with similar complaints about me before, would know that I never moved without adequate cover and the secretary hinted that her boss would like to avoid another time-wasting episode. So could I come to his office in the Warren Tower at eleven the next morning. Mr. Halader was tied up at the Attorney-General's or he would have invited me himself.

I asked her to thank Julian Haladner for his courtesy, agreed to be there at eleven unless something urgent came up, and spent the evening checking through the BB&W files. The next morning I drove into Washington through the November murk prepared to refute whatever charges of unprofessional conduct they were raising. I was so occupied in wondering which one they'd pick that I didn't pay particular attention to the three men waiting by the elevators in the foyer of the Tower, and hardly noticed them crowding into the elevator after me. When I did sense what they were the doors were closing. I jumped to escape and the three threw me back. Then the gas hit me in the face.

Not cyanide, thank God, I thought and then stopped caring as the gas took effect while the elevator dropped to the parking level. One of the new supertranks, I decided. I could still think but I didn't care. And I didn't object to walking between parked automobiles until we reached one with a driver. I got in as asked and heard the driver say something in a language I didn't recognize. Soon after that I stopped thinking.

Started thinking again lying on a couch, bright spotlight, black room. Under the light! Whose light? Hands free. Sit up. Stand up. Fall back. Feet tied. Sitting, face in hands. Starting to reason. Where, who, what?

"Don't pretend, Mister Ryan. I know you are conscious." A woman's voice from behind the spotlight. Accent? European, educated in England. I hunched, my face in my hands.

"Sit up!" Voice like a whip.

"Light—hurting my eyes." Mumbling, sitting up, hands down, blinking against the glare, trying to see past the light into the darkness. Interrogation situation. Sudden anger—right response. "What the hell? Where am I?"

"You don't know. And you won't know."

"You can't get away with this—whoever you are."

"It is easy to get away with murder, Mister Ryan, when there is nothing to connect the victim to the killer. You are a lawyer. You know there are many unsolved murders."

I did. I stared into the darkness. The woman was sitting just behind the spotlight. And she was alone in the room. Except for me.

"However," the voice went on, "I hope that nothing so drastic as murder is needed. I hope no drastic action of any kind is needed. In short, I am hoping you will cooperate."

"Cooperate? In what?"

"Where is Alice Drummond?"

Suspicion approaching certainty. I felt the flavor of her thoughts as I heard her words, looking at where I sensed her to be. "Alice Drummond?"

"Your client, Mister Ryan. I presume she's your client.

Ah—so she is.'' The bitch was reading me. ''Where is Alice?''

Metzler had been right. The woman behind the lamp was a sensitive. And I could feel her emotions. Prepared to hurt to get what she wanted. ''Where is she?'' I mumbled. ''Somewhere in North America—I think.''

''Exactly where?''

''I don't know.'' I gave her time to appreciate the truth of my words. This woman was ruthless. I was forced to gamble. ''Why do you want to know, Justine Ladrich?''

The shock-wave reached me. And her quick recovery. ''Justine who?''

''Ladrich. Justine Ladrich. You work for Loucher Freres. Is this how they usually open a deal?''

An instant of silence from behind the light. Then calm imposed on rage. ''Who I am will not help you if you don't cooperate with what I am.''

''But it does.'' I could see her silhouette. ''It helps me to know that you'll be in jail soon after you do anything more foolish than you've done already. Under the lamp yourself.'' I produced a laugh. ''You were seen at Slipe's lecture. I was there. So were the DIA. They know we were both there. And I've visited DIA HQ. If I don't visit them again they'll send a patrol out after me—and find you.''

The spot went out. I smelled her perfume near me in the darkness. And felt her mind. Her recoil of surprise as she touched mine and knew I was speaking the truth. The perfume faded as she moved away.

''For God's sake, Madame Ladrich. Why this absurd scenario? Put on the lights and untie my legs. Before you wreck any chance of a deal.''

''Are you with DIA?'' A trace of uncertainty.

''No.'' Emphatic. ''I'm an occasional consultant. That's all. But Colonel Metzler looks after even the part-time help.'' Full truth in that. He did.

And she knew it. The silhouette moved, standing up. The spot went off. The room lights came on. An apartment. And the woman facing me was the woman from Baltimore. But not an unremarkable woman in glasses with untidy hair. The beautiful woman in the photograph. Wearing an elegant pantsuit. A woman with black groomed hair, a firm mouth, dark eyes. And an expression of frustrated fury. Beautiful and deadly dangerous. But alone. No sign of her muscular support.

"Madame Ladrich—we've met once before. Briefly."

"When you hit me." She sat down slowly, facing me. "You also kicked me. While I was on the ground." She smiled thinly. "It is considered unsporting to kick a woman when she's down."

"It's unsporting to try to snatch a young girl."

She shrugged. "At the time I did not know my attacker was talented. Nor that he was an occasional consultant to the Defense Intelligence Agency."

"You know now."

"I had heard there was a talented operator in Washington. I have been hoping to meet whoever it was for some time—though not under these circumstances."

"What talent?"

"A talent for sensing deceit. You know it because you have it." She stood up and walked toward me, stopping just beyond my reach. Her dark eyes were on my face. "And you know I have it." She returned to her chair. "What a relief! No need to lie. No need to suspect lying."

"Then you'll know I'm not lying when I say I won't attack you if you untie my feet."

She hesitated, then picked up my challenge. "I have to believe you, don't I?" She came to the couch, knelt down, her head bent as she started to pull away the adhesive tape binding my ankles. I concentrated on admiring her smooth black hair, the graceful curve of her white neck. She looked up and smiled. "Thank you, Mr. Ryan." She ripped away the last of the tape. I stood up, swayed, and felt her hand on my arm, steadying me. "That gas has only minor aftereffects. But muscle weakness and vertigo are among them."

So I couldn't have attacked her had I wished. I subsided onto the couch. She returned to her chair. "Perhaps we share other abilities—and ambitions, Mr. Ryan. Might we also share certain interests?"

"Such as?"

"That girl—Alice Drummond. I accept that you do not know where she is. But can you discover where she is?"

"Why do you want to know?"

Her eyes narrowed. "That girl has a toy. A valuable toy. I want to purchase it from her—or from her attorney."

"Purchase? With a gas-gun?"

"She is an evasive child. I was only intending to take her to a place where we could bargain in peace, Mr. Ryan."

"As we know each other so well, why don't you call me Richard? I'll call you Justine."

That threw her slightly off balance. "Very well, Richard. You may not know where the girl is but you can communicate with her, can't you? I sense you can. If you're her lawyer, will you pass on my offer?"

"What's the offer?" I let avarice surface. Greed is an affect easy to detect and tends to swamp all other emotions.

She shrugged. "My offer to you? Or my offer to the girl?"

"Justine, I'm an ethical attorney. I would only expect my fees—plus a modest commission."

"Your fees and your commission will be excellent. And your client will gain both a fair monetary reward and personal safety. Do you have a figure in mind?"

"Do you know what that toy is?" My question shot out through my surface greed like a missile from a submarine.

She didn't. Her anger flared as she sensed I had read her. "I know it's potential value. I suspect you know more." She paused. "So you do! That is one reason why I am suggesting we join forces to ensure we both benefit."

"One reason. Are there others?"

"Several. Your own well-being, for example. Loucher Freres will go far to get what they want."

"I knew that before you tried to grab Alice. Before you snatched me." I paused. "Colonel Metzler also knows."

"Colonel Metzler." She spat the name. This woman had more emotion than she allowed to show. A hot-blooded woman with surface ice. "I had no idea that I was facing such strong competition." She came and sat beside me on the couch, touched my hand. A gesture implying trust. "As colleagues we could achieve great things. With the toy—even greater."

The wrong movement by me and her reaction would be instant. I reached slowly into my pocket, felt her readiness, and took out a cigarette. I lit it and laughed as she relaxed. "You see, Justine? We can't really fool each other. Why should I try to fool you? In that cliché—you have me in your power. Whatever happens to you after you've killed me can only give postmortem satisfaction. Violence by either of us will bring disaster down on both of us." I turned to face her. "Won't it?"

She stared back, nodded.

"I can't negotiate under duress and keep my integrity. I must think first of Alice. In my business, as in yours, success depends on trust. Con even one client—and you're kaput."

She nodded again. Her eyes were luminous. Her perfume enticing. A faint smile of pleasure as she sensed my enticement. "Of course. She'll benefit. The way you protected her in Charlottesville was admirable. You hit me with her bag. The toy was in that bag, wasn't it?"

I nodded. "Gave the bag some weight."

She touched her jaw. "I found that out. And I do not hold it against you. You acted in an honorable and decisive way. Rescuing a young girl from kidnappers. But Richard, you are not noted for aiding ladies in distress. So I suspect your reasons were somewhat more cogent than her safety."

"Justine, you don't seem to know much about what you're after. That toy may be too valuable to sell. And why should I team with you on an equal basis—if I know more than you do?"

"For your health, of course. And for her health." Her mind was ugly. "Ryan, I keep my threats."

"Ladrich, your firm has that reputation." I held my fear deep. With opponents like Justine, to show fear is to lose the play. "I bargain hard, and I won't bargain under threat." I put on a show of exasperation. "For God's sake, woman—if you want us to work together, don't start by threatening me."

"I was impetuous. Forgive me. To talk with someone like oneself is novel." Again she touched my hand. "One slips into habits acquired when dealing with the untalented. To harm you would destroy my hope for cooperation, would it not?"

"It would. But forget it. I know what you mean. I've hardly ever met another sensitive either. But—about this deal—I don't want to be trapped into treason. And there are rumors—who's your client in this operation?''

"In this project Loucher Freres has only one client—themselves. And they have no intention of involving any others—from the private or public sector.'' She watched my face. "You can sense I am speaking the truth.''

"I do.'' And I did. I stood up. "I want time to think this over. Show me the way out.''

"I'll have you shown out. Blindfolded. I don't want you adding details to whatever you say to Colonel Metzler.''

I showed I felt insulted. "Say anything to a third party while a deal is under discussion? I hope your firm has more integrity than that.''

She laughed. "In this particular instance—we have. And Richard, we must meet again under better circumstances.''

"Justine—it won't be easy to forget you had me helpless.''

"I'll try and make up for it. And I'll get in touch with you after you've had time to consider your terms.'' She went toward the door. "My people will give you a lift to wherever you parked your car. Where is it?''

"In the lot under Warren Towers. Was that how you traced me? From the number of my car?''

"Finally. I should have suspected there was more to you than a small-time lawyer when I had so much trouble tracing you through that car-hire agency. By the way, don't blame them for giving me a lead.'' She opened the door and called something in the language I did not recognize.

When her men arrived I allowed myself to be blindfolded and taken down to the basement of an apartment block. They only took off the blindfold after we were back under Warren Towers. They left me standing beside my car.

17

"I DON'T WANT to know where Alice is," I said slowly and distinctly into the telephone (Jean had at last responded to my attempts to reach her via the math department). "I only want her to call me."

"You're the last person in the world she wants to call!" Jean paused and her voice went from sharp to sympathetic. "You were hard on her last August, and you know what teenage girls are like."

"I'm learning." I was doing my best to pass on Loucher Freres' offer so I could honestly report I had tried. "Just ask her to call me back."

"As she'd say—don't hold your breath! You really hurt her. But I'm sure she'll come around, given time—and explanations!" Jean hung up.

I slammed the instrument down. I'd hurt Alice at Jean's request. By protecting both of them I'd made myself Justine Ladrich's target. And now they'd cut me off without a hearing. I wanted to shake the pair of them—physically and emotionally. That being impossible I phoned Selected Escorts.

Alice didn't call. To maintain my honesty I tried again the week before Christmas. The departmental secretary would only say that Dr. Grayson was out of town until after the New Year. She had not left a number or forwarding address. Dr. Grayson wished to be free from interruptions while working on a new theory. The secretary spoke as if mathematicians were anchorites who withdrew to solitude in search of inspiration. As that was not Jean's style I assumed she and Alice were on vacation and could only trust it was somewhere safe.

In early January what I had been hoping and fearing happened. Justine called. My heart raced at her voice.

"Richard, I've been waiting to hear your client's response to our offer."

I crammed sincerity into my answer. "I don't know where my client is, right now."

"But you've presented our offer?"

"I haven't been able to get in touch with Alice Drummond since we met. I advised her to stay under cover and she's doing better than planned. She hasn't called me, although I said—"

"She's with that woman, I suppose?"

"What woman?"

"The one in the car with you. The day you kicked me."

"Oh her? I guess so. But I don't know where she is either."

"Are you trying to tell me that you don't know where Alice is and you can't get a message to her, Richard Ryan?"

"Justine Ladrich, would I lie to you?"

"On the phone my talent doesn't work."

"I'm telling you the truth." And being doubted when I was. In desperation I added, "I'd tell you to your face. Then you'd have to. If you really are sensitive?"

A quick intake of breath, as though to an insult. "You'd meet me?"

"Well—yes—if you insist."

"I do insist. The bar at the Hay-Adams. Seven this evening."

I recovered and refused to be stampeded. "Too secluded and too dark. Better we meet in the open. Lots of light and plenty of people."

"If you're afraid I'm going to jump you again—I'm not."

"Justine, my talent doesn't work over the phone either. The lounge at the Hilton. Eight p.m. Okay?"

"The Hilton? Among those people? All right. If that's what you want."

I didn't want, and yet I did. After I had put down the phone I left my office for fear that Alice would call and leave me helpless when I faced Justine. I wasted the afternoon watching an SF movie with incredible aliens doing unbelievable things. Not half as incredible as the reality in which Alice and I were involved. But weird realities are rejected in realistic fiction. I forget who said that first.

When I arrived in the lounge bar at the Hilton a little before eight it was crammed with the usual collection of salesmen, visitors, and assorted women. But no signs of Justine's bodyguard. I paid a waiter to get me a wall table and reminded myself I was only here to protect Alice, Jean, and the interests of E&H Inc. Later, after I had learned more from Bringer, we might be able to reach an understanding with Loucher Freres. But it was the prospect of again meeting the only woman who shared my talent which had my pulse racing. A woman who was both beautiful and breathlessly effective. Under other circumstances I'd have been tempted to take up her partnership offer. I was even tempted now.

She arrived at exactly eight and came directly to my table. I jumped to my feet. She dropped into a chair. A waiter appeared with the speed waiters show when mink coats and diamonds arrive in their section. She snapped, "Dry Martini!" then stared at me with eyes that matched the hardness of her diamonds. "Say that again, Richard."

"Say what?" I sat down.

"Tell me again that you haven't been able to get in touch with your client since we last met."

"I haven't been able to contact Alice Drummond since I saw you last. In that darkened apartment of yours. And I have left messages for her to call me which haven't been answered." I spoke slowly, allowing her to sense the truth of every word.

She muttered something in her unfamiliar tongue, something that sounded obscene. "I have to believe you, don't I? I was wrong about you. You are a small-time attorney. Losing such a valuable client."

My pride smarted. "I emphasized to Alice the importance of keeping out of sight. You gave me damned good reason."

Her Martini arrived. She rewarded the waiter with a sweet smile, then turned a hard face on me. "What are you going to do?"

I spread my hands. "What can I? I'm one guy on my own. I haven't got the back-up facilities of Loucher Freres." She sipped her Martini in silence. "I know Colonel Metzler's looking for Alice Drummond too. And I think he suspects you've got her.''

Justine didn't do anything as dramatic as choking over her Martini, but she did put it down on the table with controlled care. ''That's not true. About my having her, I mean.''

''I know—because you say so. But Metzler hasn't our nose for lies.''

''Did you—?''

''No—I didn't tell him that you'd tried to snatch her. After we entered negotiations, that would have been unethical.''

''Richard—I admire your commercial ethics. I hope they match your good sense. Does Metzler know about your client's toy?''

''He knows less than you do.''

''I know—'' She checked herself. ''All I know is that egg-shaped thing of hers contains a valuable data store.''

''Good guess, Justine.''

''But it's more than that—isn't it?''

I shut down and stood up. ''Convinced I've lost contact with Alice?''

''Don't panic, Richard!'' She laughed, reached out, and caught my hand. ''Is it just me—or do all women frighten you?''

''Of course not.'' Her laugh was a challenge. ''But this is a business discussion. And it's over.''

''The evening's just started. I'm all dressed up with nowhere to go. And you're wearing a clean shirt. Let's relax and talk about ourselves. No more business.''

''No more probing?''

''No business probing. But I can't help being interested in you, Richard. As a man.''

I sat down slowly, fascination competing with good sense. Was she really as attractive as she seemed to me? Or was she playing the game I had so often played— matching her actions to my reactions? Showing me those aspects of herself which she sensed pleased me? Subjectively, she was a very beautiful woman. From the way half the men in the lounge were admiring her, that was objectively true.

She saw me glance around and looked around herself—

with distaste. "Let's go somewhere quiet for dinner. Still suspicious? Then you pick the place."

"You're inviting me to dinner?"

"Only because you haven't invited me. And I can't wait any longer. I'm hungry. My treat!"

"In that case—the Jockey Club."

"The Jockey Club? Aren't you a little behind the times?" She stood up.

"Probably." I moved to help her with her mink. "Haven't taken a lady out to dinner in Washington for years." And never a lady as beautiful as this one.

She caught the emotion and I sensed her pleasure in my pleasure. I overtipped the waiter. The doorman got us a taxi in seconds. Her perfume scented the cab and she leaned against me as the driver screeched in an illegal U-turn. The pressure of her shoulder and thigh against mine sent a wave of emotion through both of us. The lights of Washington streamed past. For the moment it was as magical a city as the City of the Word. And the maître d' at the Jockey Club showed unusual enthusiasm when we appeared—or rather when Justine appeared. Even the waiters were unusually attentive.

Justine approved of the food and ate with an appetite which showed she was indeed hungry. I tried to enjoy the haute cuisine, but most of my pleasure was in watching her eat. There is something fascinating about watching a beautiful woman enjoy a meal—I suppose it confirms she's human. And with her—another sensitive—there was also a shared enjoyment.

The wine and the food brought a softness to her face and a sparkle to her eyes. Afterward I welcomed her suggestion that we move to a more intimate place to dance. A place she knew. "Trust me?" She squeezed my fingers.

"For this evening only—yes."

The music was slow and dancing close in the old fashion was a unique pleasure—because she was an excellent dancer and because of the instant sympathy which flowed between us. As we went back to our table after the first dance I said, "As dancers—we're a prize-winning pair."

"I haven't enjoyed dancing so much in years." And her pleasure was genuine.

We danced, we drank, we talked. Both of us enjoyed the

game of matching each other's emotions and avoided questions which might arouse suspicion. Justine was the epitome of all I desire and fear in women. We ignored the dead past and the doubtful future. We delighted in the precious present. Dancing with her, sitting beside her, evoked an absurd contradiction. The touch of her mind brought as much pleasure as the pressure of her body.

Only at the very end of the evening, as we sat close in the cab, did I push the magic away. "Justine—forget about Alice and her toy. It's not worth it. While you're hunting her, there's no hope for us."

She was tempted. That was a triumph. "There's always hope. Why can't you—?" She laughed with a touch of her old hardness. "There's no discharge in the war."

"What war? This is commercial competition—not war."

"A quotation, my dear. It means that neither of us can retire—not yet." She patted my knee. "You're a delightful opponent, Richard. Would you like to visit my apartment again? The lighting adjusted to your taste?"

An offer I had enough residual good sense to refuse and which she regretted as soon as it was made. I kissed her, watched the guard welcome her home, and returned to Annandale and my empty rooms with the craziest plans running through my mind.

But not so crazy that I failed to check whether she had planted a bug on me. And the plans fell apart when the phone rang while I was checking.

18

IT WAS JEAN on the phone and her first question was a typical female assault. "Richard—I've been ringing you for hours. Where have you been?"

"Where—?" That was none of Jean's business. "Dining with a lady."

"I doubt she's a lady." A pause. "Have you heard from Alice?"

"No—but I'm glad to hear from you. They're after her again."

"Who? That Colonel?"

"Him too. Also those thugs—" I stopped. "What Colonel? Why a Colonel?"

"Because some Colonel's looking for her."

"How—where is she?"

"I don't know."

"Good girl. But this line's safe. You can tell me."

"I wouldn't—even if I could." Jean hesitated. "Alice has run away. Last week."

"Bolted? Where to?"

"I don't know." Jean sounded angry and exasperated. "She phoned some friends at the Manse. They said the army was asking about her."

"What?"

"Some Colonel's been to see Miss Lister. Claimed he wanted to talk to Alice about work her father was doing at that research place in Oregon. The excuse was that the child might remember something he'd like to know."

"Christ! Did the kid tell you this?"

"Not directly." Jean hesitated. "I was listening on the extension. In case she started calling long-distance again."

"Did she tell you anything?"

"Not a word. Not a hint. We were staying at the

119

YWCA in New York. She went to bed early. The next morning I found she'd run away during the night. She left a note thanking us for everything and telling me to forget her. Didn't want to drag me into more trouble. Not to tell anybody I'd known her. And to burn the note.''

"You better had. Burn the note, I mean. Where do you think she's gone?''

"Probably—the streets.'' Jean sighed. "Poor child!''

"Maybe she'll phone you—or me?''

"She hasn't called me yet. I was hoping she'd have called you. But if she hasn't by now—then I doubt she will. She doesn't trust you.''

"Alice said that?'' The hurt stung.

"Several times. I can't blame her. I don't trust you myself.''

"Trust me when I tell you the kid's in danger. It's the DIA who are after her.''

"DIA?''

"Defense Intelligence Agency. Probably because of the egg thing she kept in her teddy bear. Must be some secret gadget they lost when they dismantled that research station of her father's.''

"You've still got it?''

"Yes. Maybe I'd better turn it in. But you stay out of this. Like Alice asked.''

"I don't even know what I'm supposed to stay out of.''

"The less you know, the better off you are. There's no reason for the DIA or anybody else to backtrack to you. So don't start anything. It'll only make more risks for Alice. Now give me that unlisted number of yours. So I can call you if I hear from her.''

She gave it reluctantly. I repeated my warning to stay away from army and police, and to keep Alice well hidden if she did return. We hung up without exchanging endearments.

This promised to be worse for me than for Alice. While fourteen-year-old runaway girls are the prey of pimps and pushers, she was not a classic victim. Her sensitivity to deceit should keep her out of the hands of those vermin. Alice could look after herself. But I needed her.

Bringer was becoming increasingly insistent that I produce sensitive converts. No converts, no handouts. If I couldn't persuade Alice to act the convert, no more presents from Bringer. I'd be forced to team up with Justine, and though that might be delightful for the moment it would be ultimate disaster. For now I could only stall them both and hope that Alice would finally come to me for her Teddy.

What was I doing? Sitting on a secret far more important than patents. What was holding me from confessing all to Metzler? Fear? Fear of claiming something I'd always jeered at? Fear of ridicule? Or fear of being regarded with distaste as a mind-reader?

With the information I could give the colonel, and with the DIA behind him, he should be able to take her within weeks. But with Alice in Metzler's hands I'd be out of the action and under the lamps. So would she. And while she might be an ungrateful brat I didn't want that for her.

Three evenings later she walked into my study, looking as though she had been living in doorways and laughing at my expression.

I jumped to my feet. "How the hell did you get in?" I had thought my house secure against intruders.

"Through Mister Wang's kitchen and what he runs on the second floor. Do you know what goes on?"

"No." And I preferred not to.

"I told him I was looking for a job and he sent me upstairs. I dodged down to the cellar and came through your furnace room. Well, aren't you glad to see me?" She ran across the room and kissed me.

I pushed her off my knee and rubbed my cheek. "Of course."

"You don't sound ike you are. Maybe I should go back and work for Mr. Wang?"

"I forbid—"

She was laughing. "Relax, Richard. It's only some card game. Fan-tan, I think. Mr. Wang remembered me leaving with you. He's very nice."

He was also one of the few people I trusted. "What have you come for?"

"To seduce you, of course. Oh Richard—you look so funny! It's a good thing we have instant understanding and I know you're not really alarmed." She plumped down into a chair. "I came because the DIA are after me, and I didn't want Jean to get mixed up with them.'' She pulled up her legs. ''This is the safest house I know. And you're the only person besides Jean I trust.''

''That's not what Jean told me.''

''Silly! I said I hated you so she wouldn't think I'd come here when I took off.''

The deviousness of women—even at fourteen. ''On the phone she said something about you calling a friend at the Manse.''

''How did she know? Listened, I guess. Jean's smarter than you'd think for such a nice person. I called a friend who said that a Colonel Metzler of the DIA had been looking for me. He didn't learn much. The Lister told him about people who'd been asking after me—you and Jean among them. But she called you Mr. and Mrs. Jenson— and her description was grotesque. The Lister's eyesight's poor and she won't wear contacts or glasses. Vanity in a hag of her age—I ask you? She told the colonel the number you gave her. But I guess that won't help him much. Not when you cover every avenue—like this house.''

''Not much.'' Eventually perhaps—if Metzler put the full team to work on my Philadelphia answering agency. Anyway, I'd had that number trapdoored against inquirers. ''How did your friend know all this? Is Miss Lister telling the girls you're wanted by the DIA?''

''Tell us inmates anything? No way! Lister's the ulti-mate clam.''

''Then how did your friend find out?''

''We've got the Lister lair bugged.'' Alice gave a squeal of laughter. Poor Miss Lister, having to deal with a gaggle of teenage delinquents like Alice. ''We hear lots! When I heard I was a fugitive from the DIA I dodged out on Jean while we were in New York—at the YWCA!'' She made a face. ''Cruised around long enough for her to check I wasn't with you. Then headed here.'' She leaned forward, suddenly intense. ''And you mustn't tell her I am.''

''I certainly won't. But you must write her you're safe— for the moment.''

''I'll mail her a card. You've got an out-of-town drop, I'll bet. I left to get out of Jean's hair—and into yours.'' She giggled, sensing my reaction.

For she roused a reaction. In six months Alice had

developed from a skinny youngster into a nubile adolescent. And the way she was sitting would have been immodest had she been wearing a skirt. Even in tight jeans the effect on me was obvious to her. "Stop it, Alice!" I snapped.

I didn't have to tell her what to stop. She sat up and put her legs down. "I really came to find out what my egg's been saying. Have you told anybody about it?"

"Not yet."

"Richard, I'm glad. I don't like the look of the people who're trying to find out."

"Any idea of why they're onto you?"

"I guess one of the guys I showed it to at that meeting must have talked to someone who knows what it is. What is it?"

"I'll tell you after you've eaten. Take a bath while I fix supper."

"Okay." She jumped up. "I'm ravenous."

"You always are. You also need a bath."

"I've had to sleep in my clothes this last week."

"So I smell."

Alice sat at the kitchen table, finishing steak and starting on apple pie. She still had a healthy appetite but otherwise, glowing from her bath, wrapped in my robe, she was a much improved version of the straggle-haired child who had left for Princeton with Jean six months before.

Then she had seemed a street-smart brat, impertinent and unwashed. Now she was comparatively polite and very clean. She'd locked herself in the bathroom for so long that I'd had to hammer on the door and bawl that her food was getting cold before she'd come out. When she did emerge she showed that Jean had taught her more than mathematics.

Her yellow hair was brushed golden to her shoulders. Her lips and eyes were made up to better effect and with more restraint than is usual in girls of her age. And she smelt like fresh flowers. She had not, however, put on her clothes. As she ate she explained, "All my stuff's filthy. May I wear this robe while I put my things through your washer?"

"You're welcome. As long as you keep the front pulled

together." Every time she leaned forward to take a mouthful she was showing me her young breasts.

She giggled. "Richard, you liked what you saw!"

During my career I had read the emotions of many
aroused women but never until I met Justine and Alice any
who could read mine. Discomforting. The backwash from
the emotional maelstrom of a teenage girl was a warning to
stay out of range. These days to show any interest in a
young girl is to be suspected of voyeuristic prurience. The
few who have interested me have been intelligently confused and usually unhappy.

Alice was neither confused nor unhappy. She continued
to enjoy the taste of my apple pie and the savor of my
reactions. At last I snapped, "Alice, if you go on display-
ing yourself I'll—I'll— "

"You'll do what?" Her smile was impish.

"Send you to bed."

"That might be fun."

"Oh God! Finish your supper."

"I've finished." She made a face and pushed away her
plate, but pulled my wrapper tight across her front. "Richard, you're a real good cook."

"Thanks. Go and make yourself decent. Then we'll try
to get the dirt out of your clothes."

"I want to hear what you've found from Teddy."

"You'll hear. After your things are in the drier."

She made a face but ran off to return in one of my
shirts. "Is this decent, sir?" She rotated for my benefit.
The tails of the shirt came below her knees.

"If you keep your feet down—it'll serve." I finished
my coffee and stood up. "You load the clothes-washer. I'll
do the dishes." Sucked into domestication already. I usually leave such chores to my daily housekeeper. But memory of Jean's reaction to her first view of my kitchen
goaded me into cleaning it up myself.

By the time I had scoured the pans I had used with the
abandon of a cook who's forgotten he'll have to clean up
his own mess, the clothes-drier was spinning and Alice
was bugging me to show her Teddy. We went down to my
office and I put the egg on the desk between us. Then I
told her what Bringer claimed to be.

"Teddy's from an alien spaceship?" She was only mildly

astonished. Growing up in an environment of real spaceships and video aliens, that was not as fantastic for her as
it had been for me. "I'd guessed he must be something
like that."

"Calls itself 'Bringer.' I'm not yet sure what it's
bringing."

"Nothing bad. Teddy may be dumb, but he's not bad."

"We've only got the machine's word for that. But—
yes—I don't think it intends any harm." I paused. "It
showed me the City."

"He did? How wonderful. Let's visit together! Teddy
stopped taking me. Said I was immature. I'm mature now.
Well—almost!"

That was what I wanted, but a sudden spasm of conscience blocked my immediate acceptance of her offer.
Involve this child in something that might not be as safe as
it seemed? "I'm not sure—"

"The egg's really mine!"

It was hers. And it was Alice who had involved me. She
was in this up to her young neck already. She'd shown she
could look after herself better than most adults. And if
Bringer did accept her as a convert, then both of us could
profit. "Okay—it probably won't work, but I'll try. If you
promise to do as I tell you." I hesitated. "I don't think
there's any danger. But this is all so wild—"

"I'm sure Teddy wouldn't hurt me—us."

"Promise you'll do as you're told?"

"Why? Teddy's mine!"

"No promise—no trip."

She scowled but promised. I fetched the egg and put it
on the kitchen table. "Remember—let me handle everything. Okay?"

Alice nodded. I whistled the call-sign, felt the touch,
and said I was bringing a sensitive visitor. Could a guide
meet us please?

19

WE WERE STANDING together under a rose arbor in a sunlit courtyard, Alice decently dressed in a clean T-shirt and jeans. The air smelt sweet. And a smiling young woman in a neat brown dress with white cuffs and collar was walking toward us.

"Richard, welcome to the Gates of Perception. Is this the sensitive convert who wishes to visit the City?"

"Who are you?" Alice burst out.

"My name is Edwina Bringer.'" A bright smile. "I am your guide." She indicated a button on her blouse. "Edwina Bringer—Official City Guide."

Something new from Bringer's repertoire. An illusion typical of the young women who serve as guides at conventions, expositions, trade fairs, and so forth. The same easy superficial charm. "You're what?"

"I am the image of what both of you perceive as a 'guide.' When you accepted intimate contact and requested a guide I scanned your mental reactions to the term 'guide' and this image best matched both your percepts." She smiled a professional smile. "Come and sit down so I can explain to your guest what is happening, before I take you both on a tour of the City." She walked toward a table and chairs in the corner of the courtyard.

I pushed Alice after her and we sat round the table. Edwina Bringer gave another smile. "First, be assured that however real this appears, you still exist in your own reality and may return to it whenever you wish." She spoke with the brisk confidence of one who has made the same set speech many times. The tone of an experienced tour guide addressing her flock. The equivalent of telling us we could return to our hotel if we became hot, tired, thirsty, bored, or needed to visit the washroom. "Do you understand?"

I nodded and hushed Alice.

"What you experience here is what your senses are telling you. My signals are entering your brains via taps into your sensory channels. Not physical taps of course." Another reassuring smile. "Inductive taps in your terms. The signals I am feeding in are being decoded by your own perceptual decoding mechanisms. So that, for example, if I give my coded signal for the concept 'one' you decode that into your percept of 'one.' " She held up one finger to demonstrate. "You hear the word 'one' or see the alphanumeric for 'one.' In brief, the concept 'one' has been transferred from my mind to your minds, transmitted by me in a form familiar to me and decoded by you into forms familiar to you. If you spoke French, for example, you would hear me say 'un.' Is that clear?"

"Clear as mud," murmured Alice.

"Basic information theory—slightly skewed," I muttered. "I'll explain when we get home. What she's trying to say is that we'll see and hear everything as something we know—however weird the thing itself actually is."

Edwina Bringer waited for me to finish. "Perhaps you would like to convince yourselves that you are indeed able to leave here at will?"

"I don't think that's necessary—" I began.

"I do," said Alice. "Richard, let's call time out. So we can talk this over. By ourselves."

"Be assured I can never invade your mental privacy. As I told Richard before." She smiled at me. "Richard, you are better at explanations than I am. Perhaps I should leave the task to you, when you bring future visitors." She stood up. "If you do take a break now, I hope you will return so I can escort you round the City of the Word."

"We'll be back. Couple of minutes—that's all." A mental jerk, and we were again sitting in the kitchen with the egg between us.

"City of the Word!" said Alice. "She's sure full of 'em. And why does she call it that?"

I shrugged. "Bringer's drawing on both our vocabularies. And getting confused. But it's made itself look human."

"Human? That female phoney?"

"She's your Teddy in another shape."

"I wish she was Teddy. And why do I have to pretend to be a first-time visitor?"

"Because Bringer said the kid it knew was too young to visit. And I'm supposed to bring only mature sensitives to the City. So act impressed. And don't ask awkward questions."

"Okay." Alice shrugged. "I'll play along. Let's go back to the game."

I whistled and we were again in the arbor. Three glasses of orange juice were waiting for us on the table.

Edwina waved toward them. "You may not be thirsty, but this juice can serve as an example of induced sensory input. If you care to taste you should find it suits your palates."

I took a mouthful. Alice sipped hers cautiously. "Seems okay," she admitted. "But I didn't come here to drink fake orange juice."

"Of course not. I only had these brought to serve as a sensory introduction." Like any professional guide, Edwina was impervious to insults from rude clients. She rose gracefully. "If you care to come this way."

We followed her across the courtyard to a pair of ornate white doors, the panels rimmed with gold. She turned to us. "We call these the 'Doors of Perception.' "

"That's what Huxley called 'em," muttered Alice.

For a moment Edwina was confused by the interruption, "I use familiar terms whenever appropriate." She pushed open the doors. "The City of the Word!"

We stood and stared. My austere city had become a city to dwarf all cities. In outline and order it resembled the city I had seen before, but glorified by Alice's dream. Spires and towers rising toward a blue sky, white buildings with golden roofs gleaming in the sun. A walled city now, with battlements and gateways, surrounded by green pastures and flowering orchards. The same blue sea but with sailboats gliding across the bay. People were strolling along the seafront and the roads leading into the city.

People of various races and colors, dressed in a variety of earthly costumes.

"It's beautiful!" Alice laughed with delight. "Like the New Jerusalem we used to sing about in Sunday school."

That, of course, was it. This was a composite image formed from both our ideas about how an eternal city should look. An illusion which might be extravagent but which, to us, was lovely. No nonsense like gates of amythest and streets of gold. Just a storybook city of walls and towers, shining in the sun.

Alice was staring at the crowds moving leisurely along its boulevards. "Those—they look human."

"They are all sensitive biological sapients of various races," said Edwina Bringer. "You see them in familiar form, in varieties equivalent to the varieties on Earth. Physically, of course, they are quite different. But intellectually they are very similar to sensitive sapients such as yourselves. So there is no trickery in what you see. You see what they are. If you follow me."

"Not very well. But skip it for now."

"What about nonbiological sapients like yourself?" I asked. "Any in that crowd?"

"We gather elsewhere." A reproving frown for a rude question. "Shall we proceed?" She started down the hill.

"Hold it!" I was responsible for the safety of the kid. "What's going to happen?"

"Anything that can happen. But nothing physical can happen to you. And few unpleasant events occur in the City of the Word. As I mentioned on your earlier visit, this is a nondeterministic system governed by heuristic constraints. We three are watchers with only minimal effects on system dynamics."

"What the hell's she talking about?" muttered Alice.

"She's saying this place is as large as life and twice as natural. Treat this as real, kid. We may even see some action."

"It's feeling realer and realer. I just stubbed my toe!"

The sense of reality was growing. Alice and I must be reinforcing each other's illusions. We followed Edwina into the crowd streaming through the City gates, walking among them as I had walked with Bringer-as-Metzler. By the time we reached the main boulevard leading toward the agora Alice had evidently accepted Edwina as the equivalent of Teddy and was chattering away.

I dropped a little behind the pair, looking around me. What lay beyond the buildings on each side of the boulevard? Were they just a façade, like the plywood fronts of some movie set? What would I see if I slipped up one of the side streets? Would the whole illusion fade out? Would I be snapped back to Edwina's side? The exploratory itch was overwhelming. Alice and Edwina were deep in some discussion. On an impulse I dropped farther behind and turned along the next street we passed.

Nothing much did happen. There were fewer people about, but they still ignored me. The buildings were higher so the street was darker but the sky was still blue and the sun still shone. Tall houses with shuttered windows, the external anonymity of old apartment buildings in a French provincial town, houses looking inward to a central courtyard, presenting blank faces to the outside world.

I rounded a corner and came on a small square. Then jumped into a doorway at the sound of many feet, stood staring as a squad of soldiers came marching across the square. Not toy soldiers. Not ceremonial guards. A squad of effective-looking fighters, men and women, all dressed and armed alike.

Dressed in black Roman-style armor with Roman-type swords on their hips, each carrying a short spear. Not quite Roman. They wore knee-boots rather than sandals. And they all looked much the same; a squad of brothers and sisters with faintly familiar features.

I stood watching them. No sign of a leader or commander, yet they turned in unison, a well-disciplined squad. The faces went past. Not the faces of automata. The set expressions of crack troops on parade. The similarity between them was striking but not absolute. And teased my memory. Then I remembered where I had seen such a face.

A picture in my bedroom as a boy. A picture that had hung in my father's bedroom when he was a boy. A Roman soldier standing at a gateway, holding his spear, staring at something outside the picture. The sentry at the gates of Pompei, staying to die at his post because he had not been relieved. The Victorian image of an unlikely myth. A picture to impress on a young boy the devotion to duty expected of a man in my father's boyhood. As a child I had admired it. As a teenager I had ridiculed it as an example of military idiocy. But, buried in my subconscious, that picture must still be my idealized image of a soldier. Whatever these creatures were, they were some kind of soldiers. Stamped with the image of my childhood ideal.

The squad disappeared up another street. I walked slowly back toward the boulevard, vaguely discomforted by what I had seen. I found Alice and Edwina standing in the agora, admiring the heroic statue of Truth Embracing Knowledge. They did not seem to have noticed my absence.

I touched Alice's hand. "Time to go home, kid."

Edwina frowned. "Are you leaving before the commentary?" Her expression told me I'd better not if I wanted any more handouts.

"Commentary?"

"The recorded words of Truth and Wisdom. That is what you came to hear, did you not?"

"I guess so," said Alice as I nudged her.

"Then hear the Word," said Edwina as a voice rolled out across the agora, rolled down from the top of a tower at one corner of the square.

The crowd fell silent, faces turning upward toward the tower. "Hear the words of Knowledge and know the Truth!" Edwina, Alice, and I looked upward with the rest. "The greatest good is the good of all. The whole remains; the many change and pass!"

I had been bracing myself against a torrent of unwanted cosmic wisdom. I found myself listening to a string of banal aphorisms. The crowd stood in awed silence. Edwina was gazing toward the tower with an expression which in a human would have been called devotion. A machine listening to its own preaching? Alice had started to listen with an equal awe but flickers of amusement were showing in the corners of her mouth as the voice plunged on into a series of redundant non sequiturs, sentimental statements just this side of nonsense. The kid was not easy to fool.

The last empty phrase floated down and the voice finished with an impressive injunction. "You have heard the word of Truth. Go and spread it among the peoples!"

The crowd relaxed. Alice turned to Edwina. "I'm converted. Can I go home now?"

We were back in my kitchen, Alice staring at me across the table. "What's happened? Everything's changed. That's a different city!"

"Different for me too, kid." I fumbled for a cigarette. "Edwina wasn't the guide I had last time. Or rather—Bringer had another shape last time." I lit the cigarette. My hands were shaking. "And the city's changed. I guess it's like Bringer said."

"Said what?"

"That we see what we imagine. The city we're both seeing—it's a compromise. Between us—well—we created it."

She bit her lip, pulled at a strand of her hair. "You mean—we did it together? A kind of joint vision?"

"Something like that." I remembered the towers gleaming in the sun. "More beautiful than mine was."

"More practical than Teddy's fairyland. But I miss Teddy."

"You seemed to be getting along with Edwina."

"Oh—she's okay." Alice paused. "Everything seemed more real. Is it true? That place only exists in our heads?"

"In our heads—and outside 'em!" I shook mine. "It's a recording. A variable recording. Real high-tech. But still only tech."

"And we think it's magic? Like a couple of savages facing TV?"

"Not savages. We're sure faced with something we can't understand. But we know it's a recording."

"A recording? I get it! An open-ended recording. Like one of those TV shows where people phone in to vote what happens next."

"Kid—you've got insight. A play written by a transrealist writer."

"A what?"

"The new wave in literature." I laughed. "The writer dreams up characters, puts 'em in place, and lets 'em go. To do as they like."

"Sounds weird to me!" Alice frowned. "But that place is weird. Weird but beautiful." She sighed. "I wish Teddy had recognized me."

"You've changed, kid. For the bigger."

"You too—for the better! You were real mean to me before." She came round the table and slipped her arm round my neck. "Dick—you and me—we're special."

"Bringer called us 'sensitive.' Kind of telepathic. We can sense each other's emotions." I disengaged her arm. "As you can sense I don't like being called Dick."

"But you do! Underneath! I'll only call you Dick when it's important. Dick, what's with us?"

I stood up. "Whatever we are—we've got what it takes to contact Bringer. It thinks there's a lot more humans like us. And it wants to teach us things."

"That knowledge and truth stuff? That sermon in the City?"

"Maybe. But useful things too." I paused. "It's told me one useful thing already. It knows lots more. It wants us to spread the knowledge it gives us. What you were trying to do on the phone. But when it finds out that there aren't many telepaths or whatever on Earth it's liable to take off."

She sensed the hunger behind my words. "You want to get as much as you can out of Teddy before he goes, don't you, Dick?"

"That seems sensible." For me it was. "Let's try and collect what we can, while we can."

"You want to visit the City again?"

"Only if you're willing."

"And you want me to pretend I'm somebody different when we do?"

It was no use my trying to fool Alice. "We could try it."

"Con Teddy into thinking you're collecting converts while you collect payoffs?"

"That's a crude way of putting it." Six months of intensive education by Jean had fed her natural intelligence so that at one moment I was talking to a sensible and informed person and the next to a smart-assed teen.

"But it's what you'd like me to do?"

"Only if we can't think of anything else. You're the only sensitive I know. Besides Justine Ladrich. The woman who tried to snatch you. And I sure don't want to recruit her—unless I must.''

Alice regarded me with a mix of emotions. I winced. ''Richard—Jean warned me about you. Fool Teddy into giving? Okay—I'll think about it.''

20

SHE THOUGHT ABOUT it for several days and, while I could think of little else, her thoughts were diverted from exploiting Bringer to ideas of exciting me.

Alice was no nymphet—only a healthy young girl entering that tumultous period when natural intelligence is highest, imposed morals are lowest, enthusiasm greatest, and glands firing at blast-off. Consciously or unconsciously she was seeking a consenting male. As I was the only male around, she concentrated on me.

That may sound amusing or exciting; I found it alarming. Alice could sense my emotional reactions to her attitudes, expressions, and particular parts of her body. That led her to evoke the kind of responses she sought. Her main asset was the compact behind of a well-formed young female. She knew it and she exploited it by wearing tight slacks and bending over frequently when I was around. Something she did more often when I wouldn't let her leave the house.

On the third morning after our visit to the City she came into my study to borrow a book from the lowest shelf of the bookcase, presenting me with an excellent view of her ass. Still bending, she asked, "Why didn't Teddy recognize me? Edwina recognized you."

"I'm the local Word-rep, supposed to be out collecting converts. And you—like I said—you've changed a lot in the last six months. Mentally and physically."

She stood up and turned toward me. "Do you think I'm pretty?"

"For a skinny brat, you're not bad."

"I'm not so skinny anymore. And I am fifteen. That's the age of consent in Virginia. I looked it up."

"Alice, for God's sake stop trying to seduce me. I go for women over forty."

"That girl who was coming from Selected Escorts was twenty-six. I asked her."

"What girl? When?"

"The one you'd ordered for Friday night. She rang to confirm and I deconfirmed for you." She giggled. "I told her I was the mistress-in-residence."

"Alice—oh hell!" I'd forgotten my standing order with Selected Escorts. "We were going out to dinner."

"Now you can't. Not unless you take me."

"We've been over this a dozen times. The DIA, Justine Ladrich's gang, and God knows who else is after you. For the moment the safest place is here."

"I'm bored with being stuck in here. With you like you are." She came across the room and plumped herself on my lap.

I pushed her off. "Alice—stop it!"

"Stop what?"

"Stop acting like a bitch-puppy in heat."

She jumped away, her mouth open, her face shocked. Her hurt rolled over me. Trying to give me pleasure—and I had responded with verbal brutality! Tears filled her eyes. "Richard!"

"That was cruel. But I'm trying to ram something into your young head that you've taught me. Something I wish to hell I'd known when I was fifteen."

"What?" Curiosity outweighed hurt. She wiped her eyes. "What did you do at fifteen?"

"Hunted girls. Hunting—that's the word. I'm using it now, but I didn't realize it then."

"But boys chase girls. Thank God! If they don't they're either wimps or gays."

"Chase—not hunt. Alice, I was a sensitive, like you. And I didn't realize I was—like you didn't. But I knew I could get inside most girls' pants if I took the trouble to try out different passes. If I altered my pass to match a girl's reaction I'd set up a positive feedback that would often end—you can guess."

"Copulation is one of the few examples of positive feedback in nature," said Alice in a burst of erudition.

"Copulation? Sure, but that wasn't what I was after

most of the time. When you can manipulate people you do it to get what you want. Sex, money, admiration—you name it. I went after it. And Alice—by the time I left high school I didn't have a friend in the world. And I haven't had a real friend since—not until I met you and Jean.''

She stared at me. "But I wasn't trying to get anything out of you. I only want to be—well—loved. Does being like we are mean we can't be loved?''

"The only other sensitive I know about—Justine Ladrich— isn't exactly lovable. But you're lovable. And you'll stay lovable if you don't do what I did. It was only after I'd felt you sensing me that I realized how the girls I seduced—the guys I fooled— must have felt afterward. They didn't know they were being manipulated—but they knew something was wrong with me. That I was a selfish sonofabitch— which I am. Alice, I'm too fond of you to let you wreck things like I did without warning you. That's why I said stop acting like a bitch in heat.''

She flushed and muttered, "You've been touching me too!''

"Then you know what I mean." I hadn't realized that I had. Not consciously.

She scowled. "I'll try to keep my feelings under control. And you sure are a sonofabitch!'' Then she ran to put her arms round my neck. "Oh Dick, we must never fight. Not when we're the only two like we are. Or are we?'' She straightened, brightening. "We need more sensitives to con Bringer. Perhaps we should look for cold-hearted sonsofbitches who are exploiting everybody? Maybe some of them are sensitives?''

"That's an idea. I hope it's not true.''

"You still want to present me to Edwina as a new convert?''

"Only if you want to go.''

"I do. And if you take me I'll pretend to be someone different. Like you suggested.'' She fetched the egg. "Let's try now.''

Whatever her motives, this was what I needed. "Okay—if you'll stick with it.''

Total immersion took longer than before, and when we did arrive in the courtyard Edwina's professional greeting was perfunctory. "Welcome to the City of the Word. Richard, I'm busy at present. Do you think you could escort your visitor into the City without me?"

"Be glad to." I led Alice through the Doors of Perception, murmuring reassurance. On the hillside beyond I started pointing out the glories of the City. It hadn't changed noticeably since our previous visits.

"What's with her?" muttered Alice.

"Who knows? But she has to keep this whole outfit operating. Something important must have come up."

"Well, she's gone now. You can stop faking."

I glanced behind me. The Doors of Perception were closed. That didn't mean Bringer wasn't monitoring. "Alice—no risks!"

"We're safe here. Bringer said so. And now's our chance to explore." She looked down the hill. "Let's start with the beach. Leave the City for later. Lots of people along the sea-front. I want a close-up on 'em." And she was away running.

I cursed and started after her. Down the hill, across the road, over green lawns to the sandy beach beside the bay. In the short run an untrained thirty-five is no match for a healthy fifteen. She raced ahead along the sands, then bounded up steps onto the esplanade. The City wall, ornamental rather than functional, ended at the open sea-front.

Alice was gazing at the lawns and flower beds, the small cafes with their bright-colored umbrellas along the City side of the esplanade. People were swimming in the surf, sunbathing on the sands, sitting in the cafes, strolling along the sea-front. The picture of an idealized seaside resort. She turned and laughed when I arrived.

"What's so funny?" I gasped.

"Cigarettes there wreck your wind here. This is sure some illusion."

I leaned on the rail, recovering my breath. "No more snap decisions. Bringer may be watching us. I'm supposed to be showing you round the City."

"And if Bringer thinks we're not behaving like devout converts, then you won't collect the payoff? Is that what's worrying you, Richard?"

"Something like that." I wiped sweat from my forehead. "Remember this is an illusion. We're really back in my study. You can still see bits of it if you try."

"Ugh! I'd rather not. It's nicer here." She started to walk along the esplanade. "Among live people. Not shut up in a house with one elderly drip."

"They're not live people. They're three-D puppets. Images projected by Bringer."

"I know! But they seem like people. And you're not a drip. You just act like one. A silent drip!" She studied the passing images. "They're talking to each other. I wonder if they'll talk to me? Let's test!" And she started across the esplanade toward what appeared to be a good-looking young man. She caught his arm. "Can you talk?"

"Can I talk?" He stopped and looked down at her. "If you call this talking—yes, I can. So, apparently, can you." He smiled. "What's your name, young lady?"

"Alice." She let go of his arm and moved back.

"I don't know how this sounds in your language, but mine's Jerry."

"Jerry?" she repeated faintly.

"You're really Bringer, aren't you?" I demanded, joining them.

"Bringer?" He looked at me and laughed. "Good God no! Bringer's a machine. It doesn't go around incognito. If it turns up, it'll look like it did when you saw it last." He glanced along the esplanade. "Can't see it at the moment. Why did you think I was Bringer?"

"Well, I assumed—"

"Richard thinks only Bringer can talk."

"Only Bringer talk?" The young man stared at us in sudden realization. "You're not citizens. You're visitors!"

"Does that matter?" Alice was again uneasy.

"Not a bit. Except I'm delighted to meet you. What the hell's going on? Visitors wandering around without a guide?" He pointed to a table outside one of the open-air cafes. "Come and sit down. Let me explain."

"You're sure that's okay?"

"Okay? Of course it is. We imagons like to meet visitors." He ushered her toward the table.

I held her back. "We don't know what we're into."

She jerked free. "Jerry's a nice guy—or I'm no judge of guys."

"He may be anything. You know this is all distorted perceptions."

"Jerry's as real as you—or me. Whatever he really looks like—he's nice. And he's offered to tell us things." She went to join the nice guy at the table. I followed. Was this some trick of Bringer's?

Alice evidently didn't think so. She perched on a chair and stared admiringly at the young man. "Jerry—what are you?"

"An imagon."

"An imagon?"

"Stored projection pattern. Stored in Bringer's data banks. Energized to full perception." He smiled. "Like you are."

"I'm not a projected pattern. I'm real!"

"Of course you're real. Real as I am. Only you're not physical here. Like I'm not physical. The physical you is back on whatever world Bringer's trying to convert right now. Hardly able to bring a physical body into this recording. It's the imagon you that's sitting here." Jerry laughed. "And looking very pretty."

Alice blushed. I'd never seen her blush before. "You're a recording?"

"We're all recordings." He waved his hand toward the sea and the City, at the people strolling along the esplanade, at others sitting at the tables around us. "But, for the moment, this is reality." He smiled at both of us. "Relax and enjoy it. I am."

"Where—where are you? The physical you?" faltered Alice.

A faint shadow on Jerry's face. "Far away. And long ago. I'm one of the locals from the City. I—this I—left my physical behind me when we sailed. By now—?" He shrugged. "What's left of my physical must be part of a lot of other physicals. Back to distributed amino acids or whatever you call 'em. So this is the only me now. You feel real, don't you Alice?"

"Sure."

"So do I. Only difference between us is that you'll go back to your physical when your visit's over. Me?" He shrugged. "I'll go back to electronics."

I cut in. "Why didn't Bringer tell us about imagons."

"Bringer's a machine. Doesn't really like visitors and

locals mixing. Visitors sometimes introduce ideas which upset our quiet lives. Bringer's ideal life is quiet. No unscheduled disturbances.''

"Will she get mad if she finds us talking to you?"

"Mad? Bringer?" Jerry laughed. He had a pleasant laugh. "No way! A bit anxious maybe. Bringer takes its job seriously. Typical machine.''

"Intelligent machine?'' I said.

"Intelligent all right. Superintelligent. Needs to be to keep all this operating. Sure, this is a recording and we're imagons. But the ship itself is no recording. The ship's as solid as any reality. And cruising the galaxy's no job for anything not superintelligent. Ever thought of the navigational problems of galactic space?''

"I don't get it." Alice thrust aside questions of cosmic navigation. "You live here? In the City?''

"I've got an apartment in the City. Everybody does. But mostly I live in a village in the woods. A lot of us do.''

"For how long?"

"Me? Subjectively—about a quarter life. Objectively, in external time—since Bringer sailed. Millions of your years, I guess." He saw our expressions. "I'm only as old as I look. All of us are only as old as we look. We imagons, we only live in short spasms." He gestured toward the City. "This place only energizes when Bringer's docked on some world it's converting. Like it's docked on your world now, I suppose. And not all the time it's docked. Generally, we only come to life when visitors like yourselves are aboard." He grinned. "When you leave— I'll go electronic soon after.''

"How awful!" Alice had her hand to her mouth.

"Why? I'll hardly notice. Pattern freezes as is when Bringer switches off. Switch on again, and I'll be back. Doing whatever I was doing. Off like this." He stopped with his hand lifting an imaginary glass. "On again." He raised it to his mouth. "A day—a thousand years—between drinks. Never notice the difference." He looked at us. "When I was physical I did something like that regularly. Called it sleep. Good translation? You have it?''

I nodded. "We sleep."

"Most sapients do. Something fundamental, I guess. Also—" He paused.

"Yes?" I leaned forward.

"Well, as you may know, time isn't continuous. Everything exists by fits and starts. Even when you're back to physical, you'll be doing it. And not noticing it."

"There are theories of temporal discontinuity. But nobody's ever done much more than theorize."

Jerry was about to explain something important about the nature of time when Alice again interrupted. "Whatever you are—you're the tops!"

"Thanks." He reached out and squeezed her hand. "I'll remember that for a long time."

"For a million years after I'm dead, maybe. Break the memory record for any girl on Earth."

"And most other places." Jerry paused. "Alice, can I ask you a personal question?"

"Of course."

"Then—" He hesitated. "How many legs have you got?"

"Two. Why?"

"Because I've got six. I see you with six." He caught her fingers, calming her shock. "And all six of yours are beautiful!"

He was still reassuring her when somebody on the seafront called "Jerry!" A group of young men and women were waving and coming toward us.

Jerry jumped to his feet. "Visitors!" he shouted back. "Come and meet Richard and Alice." He looked at us. "All good friends. And three of 'em have two legs—I think."

Alice gave a faint smile. I stood to meet the approaching group. They appeared to be young, healthy, handsome human beings. One, who seemed female and was attractive, took the chair next to me. "Are you really visitors?"

"What else could we be?"

"Citizens pretending to be visitors. We've some weird types aboard this ship. I've been fooled that way before." She studied me. "You're a visitor, all right. What world are you from?"

"We call it Earth."

"Earth?" She wrinkled her forehead. "But that's what

we called my world. Oh, of course! The translator. Everybody calls their own world 'Earth.' In their own language.''

I glanced at the others crowding round our table. ''Are you all from different worlds?''

''Most citizens are from the original. Jerry there, for example. But some of us came aboard as visitors when Bringer was called in to spread the Word. And a few of us stayed. I'm one who stayed.''

This was getting more and more bizarre. I asked a bizarre question. ''Are you all telepaths?''

''Of course. Or rather we were. Why do you ask?''

''Well, for telepaths you talk a lot.''

''Richard, you certainly are a visitor. We're all imagons now. You too. Difficult job to make a telepathic imagon. You tried any mind-to-mind while you've been visiting?''

''Only with Bringer.''

''Bringer's an immense machine. Has power to spare. And even Bringer talks when it mixes with us. Which isn't often—thank God.''

''Why? Is Bringer dangerous?''

''Dangerous? Not so you'd notice. Worse than dangerous—boring! Bringer's a machine intellect—and you know what they're like. Dedicated. Duty-fixated. Et cetera. Good thing it is, of course. Otherwise we'd all have finished up inside some sun long ago.''

''Ada,'' broke in a young man who had arrived at the tailend of her remark. ''Bringer's lucky. It's got a job to do. It's got a reason for existence.'' He sat down, his fists clenched. ''We imagons haven't got jobs. We just exist. We're the ultimate degenerates. We create nothing. We do nothing.''

''Except talk!'' said Ada impatiently. ''And you do enough of that, Guy.''

The young man appealed to me. ''What kind of a life is this? Is this what we bargained for when we volunteered?''

''I didn't volunteer.''

''What?'' The young man stared. ''Has Bringer started using press-gangs to collect crew?''

''They're visitors,'' explained Ada. ''Richard and Alice—meet Guy. Our resident complainer.''

''I'm not a complainer,'' protested Guy. ''It's just that,

well—all this seems pretty pointless.'' He gestured at the cafe and the City.

"And what were you doing on homeworld that was so important?''

"Nothing! That's why I volunteered to come voyaging. I thought that I—as an individual—would be doing something that mattered.''

"And you are. You're an essential part of the Mission. We all are.'' Ada gestured in her turn. "Without us the City'd be an extended machine. Lifeless buildings plus a PA system. And who'd want to visit a lifeless City? Who'd be converted by a recorded voice?''

The others had started to listen and the discussion became general. Jerry leaned toward me. "This argument started when we sailed. It'll still be flourishing when we finally crash.''

"We also serve who only stand and wait,'' said Ada.

I glanced at her. "That's a quote from one of our poets.''

"One of ours said it too—in our language.'' Ada laughed. "All poets—everywhere—say the same things.''

Someone objected to that as a universal affirmative. All univeral affirmatives were invalid. The conversation rose and fell. Ada whispered, "They'll keep that going for the rest of this embodiment. Anything especially interest you, Richard? Now's your chance to ask.''

I asked the first question that came into my head. "I saw a squad of soldiers up one of the side streets. How do they fit in?''

"Them? They're the City Guard. The whole Guard volunteered to serve with the City's image. Complete anachronisms.'' She was thoughtful a moment. "Though there are occasional incidents— times when they're useful.''

"Incidents? What kind?''

She took my hand and led me to an empty table nearby, away from the group around Alice—now the star turn. "Bringer reacts the City to suit the tastes of visitors. So, to some extent, do we. Occasionally the taste of a visitor is—well—distressing. The Guard can help to sort things out.''

"Imagons can be forced to do things they don't like?"

"No way! If some visitor likes things I don't—I stay home. So do most people. But there are atavistic drives in all of us—even as imagons. In you, too, Richard, if you look. Know what I mean?"

I did. "You avoid that by staying home?"

"Or out of the way. Once we've found what's happening. The next switch-off returns things to normal. Trouble is—Bringer doesn't like to switch off while we've got visitors. For obvious reasons."

"You'd be stuck with detestable imagons?"

"At times—we are. We've collected a few en route." She glanced round the cafe. "None here I recognize. But there's over a million of us aboard. Still lots I've never met. Probably never will."

Over a million! "It's Bringer who decides when to switch on and switch off?"

"Yes."

"So Bringer rules the City?"

"Operates—not rules. Bringer's a dedicated machine. An absolute Believer in the Cosmic Word. As I guess we are all—at heart. But it can't control probabilities." She glanced out to sea. "For example, there's a storm coming in. Still a long way off. Bringer can shift the odds around but there'll be a storm sometime. In the end the probabilities work out. Bringer'll try to divert it. That's what it's likely to be doing now. If it can't—then it'll want to switch off before it breaks."

"And I'm supposed to be showing Alice the City. Taking a convert to hear the Word." I jumped up. "Better be moving."

Ada caught my hand. Her touch was warm. "Relax, Richard. Sit down. You'll hear the sermon as well here as you would in the agora."

"Any place in the City—you'll still get preached at." Jerry grinned.

The laughter which met his remark made me fear for a moment that we'd become involved with a gang of heretics or an imagon underground. But moments later the voice did boom from loudspeakers in the cafe. The talk suddenly stopped. Along the sea front and on the sands people stood in silent reverence as the same flood of platitudes as before rolled across the City. Even Guy and Jerry were listening with bent heads. I glanced at Alice. She was watching Jerry with frank surprise.

The sermon finished with the final invocation and the chatter started again. As if I was back in the Student Union at MIT. The same kind of intellectualized arguments about ultimate goals and vague concepts. It faded away when Ada, looking out to sea, called, "Bringer's lost out. Storm's coming in."

Dark clouds were roiling up along the horizon. Clouds that held wind and rain. The group with us were on their feet. The people on the beach were collecting their belongings like any scatter of vacationers. The strollers along the sea-front were hurrying for shelter. And Edwina Bringer was hurrying along the sea-front toward us.

"Here comes trouble," said Jerry. "Time to go home. Nice to have met you, Alice."

She caught his hand. "Will I see you again?"

He smiled down at her. "Maybe. If you come back while we're docked. I'll look out for you." Then Edwina reached us.

"Richard—you and your guest really must leave now. There's a storm approaching. I've been busy trying to reroute it, but the probabilities are too great to avoid." She turned to the others. "And the rest of you should have the sense to be getting home before the rain."

"We're leaving right now, ma'am." Jerry waved to Alice, Ada smiled at me, and then they were all running with the rest of the homeward-bound vacationers.

I caught Alice's arm. "That's it for now, kid."

A moment later and we were back in my study.

21

"SIX LEGS!" Alice was staring at me across the desk. "Jerry said I had six legs."

"All beautiful," I reminded her.

"He said he had six legs. Yet he's so human. They were all so human."

"They looked and talked human. They could be fakes. Fakes produced by Bringer to fool us."

Alice shook her head. "Jerry told me things. So did that woman who moved in on you—Ada. She said they're from other worlds. If she's only Bringer's mouthpiece, then she was lying. And Teddy—Bringer—doesn't lie. So Jerry, Ada, all the others are—were—real people."

I pointed to the flaw in Alice's logic. "If they're real people, then they can certainly lie."

"Not if they're the imagons of true telepaths. True telepaths couldn't lie."

"Not to each other," I agreed.

"Anyway, Bringer couldn't be all those imagons, and run the City, and operate the spaceship, all at the same time."

"You do hundreds of things at the same time, kid. Like breathing, and screwing up your face, and chattering. Shut up and let me think." For the moment I was more interested in the commercial possibilities revealed by the City than by the philosophical problems it posed.

"It's depressing," Alice persisted.

"What's depressing?"

"All those imagons from different worlds talking and thinking so much like humans."

"Why does that depress you?"

"All the saps in the universe being no better than us."

"Not all the saps. Just a random sample." But I appreciated her point. I had always ridiculed the tendency of imaginative writers to imagine intelligent extraterrestrials as sharing our own messy set of emotions. As I had ridiculed utopian writers who had pictured them as wise, kind, et cetera. My own image of any ETs that might exist had made them as unhuman and malignant as the rest of the physical universe. To find Bringer's collection appeared more or less human in their behavior might depress a teenage idealist—it cheered a thirty-five year old pessimist. None of them had seemed much smarter than us but neither had any of them seemed as malignant as I had feared. "That damned ship's packed with imagons. Over a million of 'em. We've only met a few. Maybe only the few Bringer wanted us to meet. Alice, we're out of our depth. What do we do?"

"Thanks for asking me—but I haven't a clue!" She rubbed her eyes with the back of her hand. "All I've got at present are emotions."

"For God's sake, control 'em kid. Or go somewhere else. At this range you're blasting me. And I'm listening for Bringer's message."

"The payoff?" She sat twisting her thin gold necklace with its jade teardrop pendant. The chain snapped and the pendant fell to the floor. "It's broken!" she wailed as she picked it up. The jade pendant had snapped in half. "Jean bought it me for Christmas!" Alice started to cry in earnest.

Blubbering over a broken pendant when we had just returned from the wildest trip any humans had ever taken. "Pipe down! I'm listening out."

"Jean told me—" She stopped crying. "Oh wow! It's there! The catalog like you said. I'm seeing it."

I wasn't. I sat silent, annoyed that Bringer was presenting its offerings to this child. More annoyed when she called, "Richard, write this down!"

I grabbed paper and pencil and begin to scribble to her dictation. When she'd finished, I looked up. "What the hell's this?"

"What I asked for. Something to fix my busted pendant. Something I can make myself to stick the bits together."

"You've wasted our payoff on stuff to fix that thing?"

"Bringer asked me what I wanted, and that's what I

wanted." She came round the table to look over my shoulder. "Will it work?"

"Bringer's gifts usually work," I snapped, staring at what I had written, glaring at her, then staring at the paper again.

"Will I be able to make it?"

"You make it?" I reread the directions. "Nothing very complicated. Most of the materials you'd need are easy to get. Of course, the temperatures and proportions seem critical. But, with care, you might be able to cook the stuff up."

"Then let's try!" Her grief was swamped in excitement. "Might be fun to make something."

Maybe not such a bad choice, after all. She'd asked for an effective, easy-to-make, general-purpose adhesive. I reread the specifications. "If this works—it could be good."

"Must be good. Remember the Word? Best replaces better."

"I know where we could get the chemicals we'd need. Plus a good thermometer. And the microwave oven—?" I was becoming infected with her enthusiasm. "Now we've got it—might as well fool around."

"Then I'll be able to fix Jean's present."

I stood up. "You stay here while I get the materials."

She was still excited when I got back with the packaged chemicals. We spent the rest of that day and evening too absorbed in amateur chemistry to worry about the City and the imagons and all the other problems Bringer had brought. After a number of failures we finally began to produce compounds that stuck. By midnight we had a sample of stuff that stuck as nothing else did. Alice happily repaired her pendant while I started to draft a possible patent.

An energetic young girl needs a target for her energy when house-bound with a man old enough to be her father. Alice rejected my suggestion that we take another trip to the City with the reasonable argument that it was too soon. "Not worth risking my being spotted by Edwina if we crowd her."

I was forced to agree. Also I was busy testing the samples of adhesive which Alice continued to cook up and preparing a patent for an adhesive which should have considerable commercial value. And which would not attract Justine's or Metzler's attention.

After a couple of days Alice got tired of making adhesives and became interested in the various aphorisms which she had heard from her Teddy and during our visits to the City. I was too busy to take any interest in it myself, but when she brought the collection to me I was impressed. Not by the contents, which were still puerile, but by the skill with which she had interwoven the various Words of Truth into an ascending order so that, given the absurd premises, they mimicked a logical argument. A kind of refined banality.

She read them aloud to me in her young girl's voice, imitating that of the invisible preacher from the tower in the corner of the agora. She had an actress's skills, and I showed my admiration. "Alice—you've got it! The right religious touch. You've almost converted me."

"Silly—it's supposed to be funny! Do you know what I'm going to call it?"

I shook my head.

She burst out laughing. "The Cosmic Creed!"

22

ALICE'S ADHESIVE WAS a winner. "Strongstik," now on the shelves of your local hardware store. Nontoxic, inactivated by saliva or digestive juices before use, once used to stick it remains stuck. To every kind of surface, molecules merging across interfaces in ways which still infuriate experts in the physical chemistry of surface phenomena.

When I took it to the penthouse office of Ebermann and Haskard there was already champagne on the credenza. Conray had made an excellent offer for a license on the molecular memory. Their people thought that the patent had some of the potential I claimed. My partners were ripe for more wonders.

I had a mundane but commercial wonder in my briefcase— one of Alice's samples. Ebermann ignored my warning and tested a drop of the stuff on his desk and touched it with his pipe. Adam and I watched while he tried to jerk his pipe free. I left them with the sample for further testing and promised to return in three days if they were interested.

They were. When I arrived three days later with a draft patent application, Ebermann's pipe was still stuck and he was being forced to choose between pipe and desk. He tugged at his pipe while I outlined my proposal. When I finished he grunted, "Is this stuff as easy to manufacture as you suggest?"

"That sample holding your pipe was made up in my kitchen with chemicals anyone can buy. There are several subtleties in making the stuff, of course. Times, temperatures, proportions, and so forth. Some of them flat against accepted chemical wisdom."

"Just how did you acquire your chemical wisdom, Ryan? I thought you majored in electronics?"

"As a patent attorney, nothing patentable is foreign to

me. With this stuff, ignorance helps. A good chemist wouldn't do the things I did. The stuff's easy to make, but not easy to imitate."

Adam, a scientific innocent, was already intrigued by something he could understand and whose commercial value he could appreciate. "But if we patent, everybody will know how to make it."

"Not through my patent," I said proudly, laying my draft on Ebermann's desk. "This only describes the process up to the gel stage. An essential step but not the whole story. It's actually during packaging that things get really tricky. For any right-minded chemist this patent will be more hinderance than help." I sensed the partners' envy and admiration. "Spent a lot of time writing this up."

Ebermann looked at Adam. "If it's as good as Ryan claims—as it seems—maybe we should go into manufacturing?"

"That dummy company down on Saint Hilda's?" Adam lit a cheroot. "We're incorporated to do anything from running ships to making guns."

A new hunger was growing in both of them. They were lusting to deal in something more material than advice and information. "Hold it!" I broke in. "Product manufacture—that's the road to bankruptcy."

"Not with an unmatched product and an open market. Like you say it is." Ebermann frowned at me, then tried once again to jerk his pipe from his desk. "And this damned stuff sure sticks."

Adam chimed in. "We market enough of it under our own trademark to convince everybody that it's the adhesive of the future. Then we sell out to a multinational—retaining residual rights. Partnership with a multinational like Sanan—and we'll have a corner on the world."

"A multinational?" I queried. "What about the Technology Export Act."

"One advantage of teaming with a multinational," Ebermann grunted. "End-run the politicos. Multinationals can save civilization. With a true multinational you know where you stand. No nonsense about social responsibility or patriotic bull. If a government interferes—move to where the government doesn't. Make an unbiased deal with the unions. Produce the goods, share the profits, and tell the bureaucrats to butt out or you will." For a Harvard Master of Business Administration, Ebermann had a simplistic approach. "We revive E&H Trading, Ltd." He rubbed his hands together. "Ryan, you'll have one third of the stock. How does that suit you?"

"Okay—I guess." That stock would form a good start for Alice's trust fund. "Maybe we won't have to sell out?" Ebermann's enthusiasm was catching. "Maybe we can build up to our own multinational. Some of the biggest started off pretty small. And with some of the other things I've got cooking—"

"Just what have you got cooking? And where?"

"When the profits from molecular start to arrive, and after Strongstik is launched, then I'll tell you."

"Strongstik?"

"Strongstik! That's my name. That's what we'll call it."

"Sounds sexy," said Adam.

"Maybe an advertising agency should give an opinion. Names are important in the retail trade." Ebermann tugged at his stuck pipe.

"To hell with the hucksters. Strongstik it's going to be. The ad people can use your pipe-desk combination for their commercials. But they'll keep my name."

Adam was laughing. "Richard's a creative writer. Can't discard his creation."

I drove back to Annandale wondering whether I should tell Alice about her future wealth. I was jerked back to present danger by Mr. Wang. He came through the door in the wall from his storeroom as I went upstairs from my garage. "Mr. Ryan, you are being watched."

"Watched? By the cops?"

"My customers think they are police. I have seen them and I do not think they are. They look like criminals."

Justine Ladrich's thugs? "Where?"

"Two automobiles on the street out front. Each end of street. Since this morning. Also in back."

So they'd have seen me garage the car. They'd know I was in the house. They probably knew Alice was here too.

"Your customers spotted 'em?"

He nodded. "They keep my customers away."

"Sorry for that. I'll cover your losses."

"No losses. My customers return later. But you and Alice—that nice young girl—will you stay till those men go? Or force their way in?" He saw me hesitate. "I leave on delivery half-an-hour. You can travel in back of my van."

"Thanks." I paused. "Will you take just the girl?"

"If you wish. But why her only?"

"If those thugs are who I think they are, they'll check everything coming out of the lane." If Justine snatched Alice I'd crumple. "Let me go out first. Draw them away."

"They will see you are alone. Perhaps if my wife went with you?"

Involve Mrs. Wang in a possible shoot-out? "That's generous of you, but your wife's got black hair."

He thought, then smiled. "I fix. You fetch the girl. She travel with me. I have blonde to travel with you." He pushed me toward the stairs. "Go and tell Alice to get ready. Bring her back down."

I hesitated, then went racing up the stairs, shouting, "Alice! Are you okay?" Foolish if she wasn't. I was not thinking clearly.

"Sure. What's wrong?" she called from the kitchen.

I raced up the second flight. "Those thugs from Charlottesville are onto us. You've got to get out of here."

"Why? They can't get in."

"Maybe not. But you'd be trapped if they do. Pack your things. Mister Wang's going to give us a lift in his panel truck."

"Among the used chop suey he takes to the pig farm? Ugh!" She started toward her room, then stopped. "Where will you take me?"

"Out of town first. From there—we'll decide later."

"Dick—I don't want to leave you."

"Brat—I don't want you to go. But you must. That gang outside are tougher than the cops. For God's sake—go get packed. Don't keep Mr. Wang waiting."

She went unwillingly, but she went. She came down into the office with her totebag in her hand. "You'll keep Teddy safe, won't you?"

"Sure will." I gathered up all the cash I had and pushed the bundle into her bag. "Hang onto this. Everything locked?"

She nodded. "All systems go. All alarms set. If they can bust into this place they're real pros."

"They are." I grabbed her arm and pulled her down the stairs to my garage, then urged her toward the door into Wang's. "You go with Mr. Wang. I'm taking my car."

She hung back. "I want to go with you." She glanced at my car. "Who's that woman in it?"

There was a blonde hunched in the front seat. Mr. Wang was arranging her. He smiled as Alice arrived. "A decoy." He looked proud. "Inflatable woman."

Alice stared at the inflatable, now more or less upright, an old windbreaker around its shoulders. "What is it?"

"Inflatable woman. I borrow from my cook. His wife still in Schezwan." Mr. Wang stood back, admiring his handiwork. "Fool you, eh, Miss?"

"It sure did!" Alice swung on me. "Richard, what'll they do if they grab you with—with that?"

"Nothing." I hoped. "Why should they?"

"She deflate fast. Valve here." Mr. Wang indicated the valve on the inflatable's left hand. "You safer with me, Miss. Mr. Ryan—he safer with dummy."

Alice scowled, but followed him through to his garage. The last bucket of part-used chop suey was going aboard the panel truck. "Real neat." She stared. "Do I get to feed the pigs too?"

Mister Wang looked at me. "Where shall I take her?"

"Washington airport. At the auto-rental desks. Alice, if I don't get there within an hour take a shuttle to New York. Then ring Jean. Okay?"

It wasn't okay but Mr. Wang loaded his reluctant passenger. I sensed he had played games like this before. At that moment I did not mind for whom—I was glad to have an experienced operator as an ally. I pressed a receipt for three months' advance rent into his hand, adjusted the pneumatic woman beside me, and drove out into the lane.

It was almost dusk. The blond hair rested on my shoulder. Apparently Chinese gentlemen also preferred blondes. When I turned out of the lane onto the side road a Buick pulled out from the curb. As I passed the street to my house a Ford and a Pontiac got under way. I turned onto the Pike with all three astern. Minutes later the Buick roared past me and took station just ahead. I was bracketed. Far back I glimpsed Mister Wang's panel truck turning off the Pike.

They were setting me up for a crunch on the next empty stretch of highway. Three cars rear-ending and the drivers trading punches. Only the police stop to get involved in that kind of fracas. Nobody questions one of the lady passengers being carried off to hospital.

I had no lady passenger, but I didn't want my car crunched. Nor did I want to get physical with this gang. Best to finish it on ground of my own choosing. Mister Wang and Alice were well clear. I started to deflate my companion, then turned sharply into a McDonald's as she collapsed. I had her stuffed under the front seat by the time the Ford and the Pontiac came alongside. The drivers grabbed me as I jumped out.

Ford bounced me up against the front fender while Pontiac flung open the door. "The dame—where's the dame?"

"What dame? What the hell?"

"That dame with you? Where is she?"

"You're out of your mind! I'm alone. If this is a stick-up—?"

"Quiet, Mack. Open the trunk!"

A gun poked my ribs. I opened the trunk. The two stared at the spare tire. The Buick swung into the lot and its driver joined his colleagues in inspecting first my car, then me.

"What are you after?" I demonstrated fear and anger. "Is this a bust?"

"He had her with him when he left," insisted Pontiac.

"You guys have the wrong car. Now beat it before I call the cops."

"Bring him along," said Buick, turning away.

I had already sensed that Pontiac was reaching for the gas. I hit him in the stomach before he got the flash free, jumped over him as he doubled up, kicked Ford, and dodged Buick. Spectators stopped chewing hamburgers. I reached the restaurant and joined a line. Looking back through the glass I saw the thugs sorting themselves out.

By the time I had forced down a hamburger they were gone. Three cab drivers were drinking coffee. I hired all three, asked them to interweave, and one finally dropped me at the airport.

Alice was waiting by the rental counter, disappointed that there had been no excitement involving her. From my expression and emotions she knew I had had enough for the time being. She watched the concourse while I rented an auto then went quietly with me to pick it up. And she stayed silent until we reached the Washington Beltway. Then she asked, "Where are we going now?"

"Jean has a safe house somewhere. I'll phone her."

"Jean? Do we have to get her mixed up in this again?"

" 'Fraid we do. There's nobody else I could trust you with. Anyway, nobody knows about Jean except you and me."

Alice didn't like it but she had to accept it, not having any practical alternative. Presently she asked, "What did those pals of yours say when you showed them the glue?"

"They were enthusiastic. Getting set to start making it." I paused. "You'll be a part-owner of the company that does."

"They sound like crooks."

"Alice—they're the two most trustworthy people I know. In their business honesty pays. And this is one of the times our talent comes in useful. I know they're playing it straight."

That satisfied her. When I stopped so she could phone Jean at Princeton she sounded genuinely penitent in asking if she could come back.

"Of course, Alice! Where are you?"

"With Richard."

"Alone? Is he there? Put him on the line. Richard, you've had that child living with you alone?"

"Just living with me. You want a medical certificate to show she's still intact? If she is! She's only leaving now because that gang from Charlottesville are hanging round my house. They're after her and I want her somewhere safe. You said you had a house."

"Some friends—I'll come and fetch her. Let me speak to Alice again. Alice—where can I pick you up?"

Alice giggled. "At the Whore's Bed."

I seized the phone back. "Teenage humor! We'll be at the Boar's Head Inn, outside Princeton. You know the place. Should get there around ten. We're driving."

"Then keep driving. I'll be there." And Jean hung up.

"She thinks you've been taking advantage of me," remarked Alice when we were on the road again.

"Maybe. For God's sake—for my sake—disabuse her of that."

"I won't be able to hide my disappointment at not being taken advantage of. Can I tell her you felt me?"

"Of course not! Dammit, I didn't."

"It was all in your mind. And in mine. Okay, that's our secret." We drove in silence for several miles. "Richard— I'll miss you."

"I'll miss you, brat." And I would.

We had agreed that Alice would explain the egg to Jean as being some kind of remote terminal, without saying what it was remote from. When Jean did meet us she accepted that explanation without pressing me further. In fact she said very little to me. Her chief concern was Alice's physical and mental state.

After she was convinced that all was still well, she took the girl to the car. Her last words were to the effect that Alice would doubtless be able to explain most things, but that I still had a lot of explaining to do. And that I was not to annoy either of them until I was prepared to give a full and truthful account of what I was up to.

I watched the tail-lights of her car disappear with a mixture of relief and regret. Then I started back toward Washington.

23

REJECTED BY JEAN, parted from Alice, fearful of Justine, I needed sympathetic company. I needed sympathetic company badly. I rang Selected Escorts and ordered a sympathetic young lady, preferably blonde. The dispatcher promised to send one round that evening.

At eight the front door chimed. The voice on the intercom was pleasant and vaguely familiar. "Selected Escorts, Mr. Ryan." A girl who'd been here before? She was standing on the front step so that the video only showed her figure and her hair. Her hair was black but her figure was promising. I went down to let her in and opened the door with a welcoming smile. I lost it when I saw who she was.

"Good evening, Richard." Justine Ladrich returned my smile and put her foot in the door. "You wouldn't come to my apartment so I've had to come to yours—alone and unarmed! May I come in?"

I would have slammed the door in her face but I couldn't slam it on her foot. I opened it wide enough for her to slip into the hall, pushed it shut and swung round on her. "My office is closed. And after your last try at snatching Alice—!"

"Richard, you're a difficult man to reach during normal business hours. Anyway, I'm not here on business. At least, not on our usual business. I'm here on Selected Escorts' business." She laughed at my expression. "You asked for a sympathetic hostess—preferably blonde. I'm a brunette, but I'm prepared to be sympathetic."

Standing close to her in the narrow hall I scented her perfume and sensed her emotions. She was not about to jump me. "What do you want?"

"Only your usual fee." She laughed again. "May I go

upstairs?'' She had started along the hall before I could answer.

I went up the stairs after her, apprehension mixed with admiration. She sensed the admiration and looked back. ''Thanks, Richard. It's nice to be appreciated.''

If this was a trap, it was Justine who was trapped. I followed her into the living room. She slid her coat from her white shoulders, dropped it on a chair, and turned to face me, holding out her hands. ''Will I do, Richard? Please don't send me back—or tell the agency I'm no good. You're among the most valued of their regular clients.''

Her black dress must have cost more than an expensive call-girl could earn in a week, and was one which no call-girl would wear on duty. Pearl necklace and diamond earrings. Her own beauty outshone both. I gaped at her. ''Have Loucher Freres bought the agency?''

''Bought Selected Escorts? My employers don't deal in prostitution or drugs. At least, not directly. But I do have friends with contacts. Friends who can get a girl a job.''

''A job. What job? Why are you here?''

''To do a job, of course. An honest job for honest pay.'' She laughed. ''What's a nice girl like you—? Please, not that cliché.'' She sank onto the couch. ''Don't you usually offer your companions a drink before you put them to work?''

Paranoia and common sense urged me to throw her out while I could. Curiosity, excitement, and a fascination with this beautiful woman blocked decisive action. Why should someone with her wealth and power risk coming unarmed to my apartment? Play the hooker to get me alone? How much did she know? What was she after? ''What do you want?''

''Cognac—on the rocks, please.''

''I meant—''

''If you have any cognac.'' Her glance around my living room suggested doubt that I'd have a decent brandy.

''Will Courvoisier Napoleon do?'' My childish reaction to her implied taunt. ''Though I don't like wasting it over ice.''

''Quite right. Then straight.'' She took a small jeweled cigarette case from her handbag and lit a Turkish cigarette.

"So you do enjoy other luxuries in addition to expensive young ladies."

"I have a modest private practice." I poured cognac into a snifter and fixed myself a bourbon and water. "I don't own a wealthy corporation." I handed her the cognac and sensed her shock.

"What makes you think I own one?"

Startling this self-confident woman restored some of my own confidence. "Both Loucher brothers are dead. And you don't operate like a hired hand." I sipped my bourbon. "In brief—I know the tigress by her paw."

"You're sensitive, all right." She did not deny my inspired guess, only looked at me across the rim of her snifter. "I came here tonight to make sure."

"You mean a sensitivity to subliminal clues? Like yourself?"

"Sensitivity to subliminal clues? Are you pretending you're only a human Clever Hans? Clever Hans—you must have heard of that German horse who could sense its trainer's breathing well enough to do arithmetic? You have?" She lowered her cognac and laughed. "More than that, my dear Richard. As I know you know." She leaned forward, her eyes bright. "You're the first talented person I've ever met."

"There are others?"

"I have heard of them. I've never met one. And I had to meet you again to make sure. On the phone you could be lying. Here—I'll know if you are. And you'll know if I lie. Which I won't." She leaned forward. "Richard—it's urgent we reach an understanding. There are others after the Drummond girl—and her toy."

"Metzler?"

"People rougher than Metzler. Rougher than Loucher Freres."

"Your goons were rough enough with me."

"The fools! They were not supposed to take direct action. I gather they collected more than they gave." She laughed. "For a man who abhors violence, you're rather good at it. The locals I have to employ lack panache."

"And your own musclemen lack English. Justine—you've tried force twice—and failed. Now you're trying to get at me by pretending to come from Selected Escorts." I sipped my bourbon. "That's a mean trick to play on a man expecting sympathetic female company."

"A trick? Oh—the idiom confuses me. But this is not a trick. I mean this is a trick—in the street sense. I am as ready to perform professionally as any dedicated whore. If I seek some extra recompense for services rendered—well, that's the way we weak women have to operate in a male-dominated world."

I stared at her. She was not lying. Give her what she wanted and she'd sell herself. "Is your gang preparing to jump me? Is there some catch I haven't seen yet?"

Her eyes did not waver and she answered with truth. "No. At present I'm an honest trader. I'll perform as you wish and the only gratuity I ask is a few minutes' conversation."

"I pay above scheduled rates but I never tip the girls. The agency knows that."

"Then I will get no gratuity." She shrugged. "It's a tough business—this whoring."

I took a mouthful of bourbon, lit a cigarette, and studied her. She was reading my emotions as I was reading hers and we were both becoming excited by what we sensed. Justine Ladrich was enjoying her role of hooker. And she was willing to play it to the full. She must have other deeper reasons which she was holding hidden. But there was one emotion we shared: curiosity about how it would feel to have sex with another sensitive. "Okay," I said after a moment. "I'll make an exception in your case. What do you want to talk about?"

"Don't clients usually tip afterward?" She stubbed out her cigarette. "About that girl, of course. Where is she?"

"I don't know." I let her appreciate the fact that I didn't. "Did you think I was keeping her here?"

"You were." A hint of anger. "On the phone she called herself mistress-in-residence."

"Well—she wasn't. Dammit, Justine, the kid's only fifteen."

"Men found me most attractive at fifteen." She shrugged. "No matter. Did you pass on my offer?"

"We're still considering."

"You realize that it cannot remain open for much longer?"

"I do."

Her face went hard. "You must not take my warning
lightly."

"Believe me, Justine, the more I learn about your methods the more weight I give to your words. Especially now
that I know you're the employee who directs the Directors."

"Then perhaps—?"

"Conversation's over. You've had your tip."

"I have to start work? So soon?"

"You can go if you want to. I won't complain to
Selected Escorts."

"Go? But you will be billed and I will be paid, whatever
happens. If nothing happens—then I would be dishonest."
She smiled and stood up. "What is your preference,
Monsieur?"

"The usual. Take off your clothes."

A spasm of anger. She might enjoy playing the hooker.
She didn't like being spoken to as if she were a hooker.
"You do not usually talk to your *belle de nuit* so roughly,
do you, Richard?"

It was her turn to sting me, to be angered at being so
obvious. I had an impulse to shake her. Her hand hesitated
at the zipper of her dress. "Please—no violence."

"The agency doesn't allow violence with its girls. Except under special contracts. And they know I'm never
violent."

"But I have other sources of knowledge. Richard, you
can be very violent upon occasion."

"You've had your tip. Now, take off your dress or get
out."

"Verbal violence. Shame, Richard!" But she unzipped
her dress and slipped it off gracefully, making none of
those movements which amateurs attempt and which tend
to be ludicrous rather than lascivious. She folded it neatly
on a chair, looked at me and, when I nodded, she un-
hooked her brassiere and let it drop. Then she stood facing
me, smiling her satisfaction as she sensed my response.
She had beautiful breasts.

"Sit down. While I fix our drinks."

She relaxed on the couch in panties, garter belt, and
stockings. Coached to dress according to custom and cus-

tomer preference. I gave her a fresh cognac and sat down opposite her. "You know what astounds me?"

"Many things, Richard. But I can't identify what in particular?"

"The fact that the effective owner of a corporation as rich and powerful as yours, should take the kind of risk you're taking."

"Am I taking a risk?"

"Any woman who's naked and alone with a stranger is taking a risk. Whoring is more dangerous than mining or testing aircraft."

"But we're not strangers. Already we know more about each other than most people know after living together for years. About each other's emotions, I mean." She leaned toward me so her breasts hung free. "Richard, have you any close friends? Have you any friends at all?" I did not have to speak. "Neither have I. We two live in a morass of deception and deceit, don't we? Who can blame us if we shear the ignorant sheep?"

"I don't loot the innocent, Justine. I only divert funds which greedy corporations are trying to divert to themselves."

She laughed. "With me—it's greedy financiers. Oh, we can justify our actions very well. But when everybody one meets is greedy and dishonest—it's hard to take them as friends. Or as real lovers. Is that why you employ call-girls? You are a handsome enough man to obtain what you want without paying."

"That's dishonest." I shrugged. "I mean—I do it. As you do. Play on their hungers—their emotions. As we are playing on each other's now. But it doesn't feel good. And—in the end—they always hate you." I looked up at her. "You've found that, haven't you?"

"It's refreshing not to have to speak." She put down her glass and stretched her arms above her head. "Richard, we might be able to make love—well—normally. Because we know it's no use trying to hide what we feel. Or pretend a pleasure we don't have." She picked up her glass again. "We could even be friends." She gave a wry smile at my unspoken rejection. "At least we ought to do some research into this weird talent of ours. That toy thing is mixed up in this some way, isn't it? I guess that girl has it?"

"Maybe." Alice had her Teddy. I studied her, at an impasse. This woman was deadly dangerous. The fact that she was sitting quietly, alone and half-naked, seemed to make her even more dangerous. She was not going to harm me physically—at least for now. I could trust her word on that. But she might be planning to manipulate me in other ways. I sat sipping bourbon. She was the loveliest woman I had ever seen in panties.

After several minutes of silence and growing tension she shifted uncomfortably. "The agency didn't warn me their client was a voyeur."

"Most professionals are happy to snag a voyeur. Same money for less work." I laughed as her lips thinned. "So take off the rest and show me the scene."

To give Justine her due she acted the hooker well. She removed her panties and stockings, stood facing me naked, then turned when I gestured. After standing with her back toward me for a full minute her anger seethed over. "What have I done for you to play this game with me? You're no voyeur, Richard."

Her emotions were too hot for her to do anything very sophisticated now. I stood up and walked toward my bedroom. "Come along, Justine. Let's go to bed like the disreputable pair we are."

She followed me into the bedroom, and stood waiting. The surface Justine regarded me calmly; the subsurface Justine radiated a mixture of anger, anticipation, and apprehension. It is very hard for anyone, man or woman, to retain self-control when naked and facing someone who is clothed. A fact well known to professional interrogators.

I closed the door to emphasize that she had put herself in a dangerous position. If she had misjudged my character she could be in for a very bad time indeed. Naked, she was without weapons or means of calling to her bodyguards for help. Her breasts started to rise and fall a little faster as her breathing quickened.

I let my eyes wander over her body and my imagination linger over the various things I could make her do—or that I could do to her. My sudden disgust came reflected back at me as her calm broke. "No, Richard. Not that!"

"Not what?"

"Whatever you were thinking about doing."

"You knew what I was thinking?"

"Not exactly. I just felt your reaction. Disgust."

So I had been disgusted. "And that made you disgusted? Maybe we don't have the same tastes in sex? Maybe what disgusts me would delight you? What we share is an outdated ability to be disgusted."

She relaxed at my laughter. "I've sensed some disgusting minds under some very smooth talk. Men who think of women as animals."

"Really? I find it's usually women who fantasize animals. Usually horses. So you do?" We both smiled and both realized how rare it was to be amused during the preliminaries to sex. "Justine, will you credit me with the decency not to ask for anything you consider disgusting."

"Of course, Richard."

"Then I have a credit?"

She nodded. I hoped I would never have to cash that credit. "Okay—it's a deal. Just normal sex. If there is such a thing. Paranormal at worst. Get into bed while I take a shower."

She was looking at me over the sheets when I got back, dripping. "Richard—your watch."

I glanced at my wrist. "I never take it off. Not even in the shower."

"Well, please, take it off before you come to bed."

"Sure. But why?"

She giggled, a sound I would never have imagined she could make. "Last time—I got my bottom scratched by a wristwatch."

We spent an enjoyable night, sleeping and making love. Better than most, but not as good as Jean. Justine, however, seemed more than satisfied. In fact, she was so satisfied that the next morning I became suspicious. She had got what she came for. A night of sex with another sensitive as she had said? That was one reason for her satisfaction. But there was another, a more important reason. And I couldn't sense what it was.

I checked her purse, her clothes, and Justine herself in careful detail the next morning and found nothing. I extracted one promise from her. She wouldn't turn her thugs loose on me again if I stayed in Washington and if I promised not to squeal on her to Metzler.

A promise I could make. After we had drunk coffee together she left with a kiss, still satisfied that the risk she had taken had paid off. Leaving me afraid it had.

Leaving me also with a hunger to communicate, for while the shared sex had been enjoyable enough, the direct contact with her emotions had been a higher pleasure. For many years I had not felt any great need for friendship. Loneliness had been my comfortable way of life. My talent for detecting deceit had let me detect it so often in others that I had learned to avoid intimacies. Deceit, I had learned through experience, was the normal human condition. Justine had said that neither of us had any friends. Distrustful of friendship, I had had no friends— until the last six months. Now I had lost the two I had—Jean and Alice. And acquired an enemy. The woman with whom I had learned the pleasures and dangers of sex between sensitives.

24

"RICHARD, WHAT'S HAPPENING?" It was Adam Haskard on the phone. "Haven't heard from you since I got back to Washington." He and Ebermann had been down in Saint Hilda's, getting Strongstik started.

"I've been busy." Busy doing nothing. I had spent most of the weeks since Justine's visit worrying about Alice, wandering around my apartment, wondering what to do next. I had lost my reusable convert and would be giftless for some time. I needed companionship; I needed allies. Adam and Ebermann were my only possibilities. Should I tell them part of what was happening? Adam's call helped me decide. "I'd like to discuss something with you and Harold."

"Harold's still down south. But I'm at your service."

"I'd rather not come into Washington. Can we meet out of town?"

"Sure. Why don't you be my guest at Talloaks this weekend. My place in Maryland. I can promise you pleasant company—besides myself."

Adam's pleasant company would be female and I could use some female company now that Alice was gone, Jean lost, and Justine dangerous. I stared out of my office window. I'd scouted the local area daily and had neither seen nor sensed any signs of surveillance. Justine and Metzler must be keeping an eye on me, but I was sure I wasn't being closely watched. "Your country place? It's secure?"

"The Talloaks estate's better guarded than Fort Knox. Some of my neighbors are worth almost as much. All of them fear intruders—for various reasons. I'm beginning to worry, myself. The rate the cash is rolling in will soon turn all three of us into prime kidnap material."

A break from Annandale was enticing. "Okay. I'll be there Sunday." Then I fished out the egg and called Bringer. "Can I bring insensitive saps to see the City?"

Bringer paused, as though considering. "What have you learned from your visits to the City so far?"

I had learned about molecular memories and about a good adhesive, but I sensed those were not what Bringer was after. "I've learned that you come from a beautiful City, from a beautiful world."

"Beauty is the product of Truth and Knowledge. That you must have known already."

"One of our poets said beauty is truth, truth, beauty."

"Most poets, everywhere, are sensitives. Have you not learned anything else?"

"I have seen how your makers live in a happy and well-ordered society."

"A society of sapient sensitives, secure from assault by insensitive saps, can hardly be other than happy and well-ordered. Does the Word I bring carry no more for you than such mundane teachings?"

My answers were not satisfying Bringer and I was starting to feel the desperation of those oral examinations when I had sensed the examiner was not satisfied with my answers but was trying to help me with hints. I glanced around my study for inspiration and my eye fell on a copy of Alice's Cosmic Creed. "You mean, have I appreciated the spiritual aspects of the Word?"

"I am beginning to fear you have not."

"Well, I have. Part at least. For example, the Word has taught me that the best must always replace the less good. That the individual serves best in the task for which it is best suited."

"Then you have received part of my signal." Bringer sounded pleased at my answer. "Have you learned more?"

I began to read the Cosmic Creed verbatim. When I had finished reciting Alice's ordered collection of platitudes Bringer spoke in a voice that verged on the emotional. "At last you have extracted the Sacred Signal from the Profane Noise. You are fit to spread the Word among your fellows. To that end you may bring a few selected insensitive converts to view the City and hear the Word. But insensitives cannot be immersed."

I thanked Bringer for its permission, relieved that I had fed the machine what it wanted. I started to drive out of Annandale on a fine Sunday morning in April, still uncertain as to whether I could risk treating Adam as one of the insensitive few. Several blocks from my house I got the impression that I was being followed. I made several detours, laid several of the standard traps, and caught nothing. But I still had the feeling that I was carrying a tail. A feeling so strong that I swung into the parking lot at the Seven Corners shopping center. A Sunday morning, the lot was almost empty and most of the stores were closed. Nothing suspicious pulled into the lot after me.

Being jumped once by Justine's goons had probably made my paranoia overactive, but it could not be ignored. I left my car and walked into the shopping center itself, wandering through a maze of glass-fronted boutiques, all closed. Still nobody I could spot trailing me; still the feeling somebody was.

The revolving doors to the lobby of an office building were unlocked. I paused, uncertain, put my hand into my pocket for a cigarette and felt a squeeze-tube sample of Strongstik. On an impulse I pulled it out, checked to see nobody was watching, and squeezed a few drops of the stuff into the bearing of the doors. Then I walked across the lobby to the far exit, pausing beyond it to look back through the glass.

After about a minute a woman tried to come through the doors, assumed they were locked, and went off. I was about to move off myself when a large man came walking quickly from the maze between the boutiques, pushed at the doors, then pushed harder when they failed to rotate. A glimpse of him was enough. One of Justine's thugs. I left him pushing in frustrated fury. I was being trailed, but how? Outside I had the luck to catch a cab on the far lot. I was being lucky with cabs. It took me to the nearest Hertz. Fifteen minutes later I was driving into Maryland, no longer feeling I was being followed and with increased respect for the shadowing skills of Justine's team.

Talloaks was both secluded and secure. A guard admitted me to a fenced estate of what the agents called distinguished executive homes, scattered across miles of landscaped countryside. I found Adam sitting beside his indoor pool, flanked by three lovely girls. He jumped up to greet me, "Richard—it's good to see you. Ginny, Judy, Karen—meet Richard Ryan—my brilliant partner."

The girls surveyed me with half-closed eyes. Their smiles were friendly and they shared one readable emotion—greed. I smiled at each in turn as I was introduced. Adam's introduction was an invitation to take my pick.

That could wait. "Is there somewhere we can talk—privately?"

"Come into the library. Excuse us, girls. But don't go away." Adam led me through the house. "Conray's have started to pay on the molecular. And Strongstik's going well. Got something else in that case of yours?"

"Maybe. Is the library clean?"

"It's been swept. The whole house is swept regularly. It's all clean." He led me into the library. "Why so cautious?"

"Natural paranoia. And because of this." I took the egg from my briefcase and placed it on the table between us. "That's it."

"That's what?"

"I got the molecular and Strongstik out of that."

"What is it? Some new kind of recorder?"

"It's a kind of recorder. Only it replays in the form of 3-D illusions. Slipe and the others got their breakthroughs out of this. Not directly. But from somebody who knew how to use it."

"And you know?"

"I do now."

Adam bent forward to study it. "Can you show me?"

"I can try. I don't know whether it'll work for you."

"Because I'm not clairvoyant?"

I shrugged. "Want to find out?"

"Is it safe?"

"Has been so far. But if it works—it's weird. You find yourself inside a 3-D video. Amusing more than unnerving. But it may shake you the first time."

"If there's more like the molecular inside, then I'll be shaken."

"Okay. I'll try. One thing—if we do get into the illusion, I'll be calling you a convert."

"Convert to what?"

"Forget the what for now. You'll just be a convert."

He shrugged. "Actually I'm an Episcopalian. That'll cover anything."

"You'll feel something tickle your mind. But don't worry." Before he had time to reconsider I called Bringer to say I was bringing an insensitive convert to see the City.

Transfer but not total immersion. We were still sitting in the library but an image of the City was floating before us. "God!" Adam was gasping. "This is sure some video."

"You can see okay? What do you see?"

"A city. Ocean. Forests. Distant hills." The image was zooming in and out. "Where is it, Richard?"

"I don't know. This is some kind of a recording. Realistic, isn't it?" The City was coming up toward us, panning beneath us, as we floated across it toward the agora. The same sensation of dream-flying as on my first visit. But not a word or a sign from Bringer. Evidently the arrival of an insensitive didn't warrant its attention.

"Sriking, isn't it?" I said, staring down.

"Striking's the word. Baroque Yale boxes. Bauhaus out of Disneyland. Whoever built this has abominable taste."

As the City below us represented my architectural ideal as modified by Alice, I could only say, "It's clean at any rate."

"Clean enough. No sign of industry."

"No smog."

"No smog over Calcutta. But hordes of vultures."

I bit back a remark that the only vultures over the City of the Word were Adam and myself, and we drifted on in silence until we were hovering over the agora with its central statue. "What the hell's that?" asked Adam. "War memorial or idol?"

"Easy." Bringer might be monitoring. "Remember you're a convert. Could be religious. It's called Truth Embracing Knowledge."

"Truth? Is there a recording of truth in this thing? That I must hear."

As though in answer, a deep voice came rolling from the tower at the corner of the agora. "Listen to the Word of Truth."

"What the hell is this?"

"I'm not sure. Just listen. I'll try to explain later."

The voice floating up to us was now launched into some kind of sermon. Across the table Adam, after his initial startle, began to listen with increasing interest. I listened also. Listened to the voice expounding, with impressive emphasis, the Cosmic Creed in Alice's exact words.

"That's real preaching," muttered Adam as the sermon ended with an injunction to spread the words of Truth and Knowledge. He stared at me. "Is this a new kind of video evangelist? Where is this place?"

"In our heads. Or inside that egg."

"In our heads—?" The City disappeared. "In my head? Of course. Mental images." He looked down at the egg. "That thing—it was projecting directly into my mind. And into yours?"

"Feels like it."

He picked the egg up. Studied it. "The sermon was good. Proclaiming wordy nothings—with the voice of a prophet and the authority of an archbishop." He looked at me. "That where you got the molecular—and Strongstik?"

"Essentially—yes." I was waiting for another gift from Bringer. Nothing. No flipped pages. Insensitive visitors evidently didn't rate an information reward. I stood up, put the egg in my briefcase. "Adam, that demonstration was just to show you what we've got. Better wait till Ebermann comes back, so I can tell both of you the whole story at the same time."

He jumped to his feet. "Then I'll have him on the plane pronto. Stay here for the night, Richard. Help to amuse the girls. You go back to the pool. I'll go and call Harold."

I did not find the girls particularly amusing, perhaps because I kept returning to thoughts of how Bringer had plagiarized Alice's Cosmic Creed for its sermon. When I finally got rid of the one trying to amuse me I whistled up Bringer, thanked it for allowing me to show the City of the Word to an insensitive sap, and congratulated it on the sermon. Theoretically a machine cannot be embarrassed but Bringer showed something close to it when I mentioned how well the words had matched what I had said to it several days before. As a gesture it gave me a gift as commercially useless as flat champagne—a proof of Fermat's Last Theorem.

* * *

Ebermann arrived at Talloaks the next afternoon, irritated at being dragged away from setting up Strongstik production. Adam took us into the library and I showed him the egg.

"What the hell is it?" Ebermann picked it up.

"I got the molecular and Strongstik out of that."

"It's some new kind of recorder?"

"Potentially—it's the most explosive thing on earth!"

"For God's sake." Ebermann put the egg down gently on the table.

"Not physically explosive." I picked it up, tossed it into the air, caught it and held it while I explained. "It's socially explosive. If mishandled it could blow the world's economy apart. We're the only ones with it and we've got to handle it safely. I think we're the only people on Earth who can."

Ebermann sat down slowly. "Ryan—what the hell are you talking about?"

"Adam—tell Harold about your trip yesterday."

Adam laughed, and gave a modified account of what he had seen and heard. He left Ebermann looking stunned and spoke to me. "Richard, you promised to tell us how it worked."

"I don't know how it works. I think I know what it is—a remote terminal." I paused. "A telepathic terminal. A terminal from an alien spaceship."

They both stared at me as if I was crazy. For a while they treated me as crazy. But they listened. After Strongstik, after the deal with Conray's, they'd have listened to a raving maniac, hoping for more spurts of deranged genius. And I sensed them starting to doubt my insanity as I gave them a resume of how I had come by the egg—and how I had learned about molecular computers. I finished my lecture by outlining Bringer's proof of Fermat's Last Theorem. That convinced Ebermann. He was readier to accept alien spaceships and telepathic remote terminals than believe that I was capable of mathematical genius. I did not mention Alice or Jean. Our partnership was on a need-to-know basis, and about those two they did not need to know.

"Telepathy." Adam stared at me, then at the egg. "And it's spilling its heart out to you, Richard. Why?"

"Since yesterday, I've been wondering. That sermon you heard gave me the clue. It thinks it's converted me."

"Converted you to what?"

"The Holy Word of Truth. That sermon you heard, Adam. Here's a summary of what it's saying." I put a copy of the Cosmic Creed on the table. "The religion of the people who made the machine. They made it to spread the Word. The thing calls itself 'Word Bringer.' Handing out technological goodies like superpure silicon and molecular memories is just its way of attracting attention—and converts."

"Rice Christians!" Adam swore. When Ebermann looked confused he explained, "A favorite method of my sainted grandfather for converting the heathen. Dish out sacks of rice along with the Bible. Converts got fed. My grandfather claimed he was saving both lives and souls. My father said it was more important to teach people to grow their own rice—and leave them with their own religion. That's when the fights started!" He laughed.

I found myself defending Bringer. "When you're starving, you take food wherever you can get it."

"It's not knowledge-starvation that's liable to kill us off," rumbled Ebermann in a sudden attack of social conscience. "We've plenty of home-grown knowledge we haven't digested yet. Are we likely to choke on what this damned thing tells us?"

"Molecular memories and a new adhesive?" I laughed. "But that's why I called it explosive. Not that it seems to be interested in weapons systems or anything that might involve us with Defense."

Ebermann was reassured and grew increasingly excited as he began to believe in the egg's potential. "Is it so naive that it thinks we'll fall for this religious con?"

"I've already convinced it we have. If I hadn't it would have sent out more remotes until it contacted some sensitive who did fall for it. Or headed on to another world inhabited by telepathic heathen. It's already visited several. So it told me. With success—in its view."

Ebermann filled his new pipe. "What do we do with it? Keep it to ourselves?"

"Maybe keep it convinced I'm making converts until we've extracted everything useful we can. That's what I hoped we'd discuss and decide. Want to visit the City yourself, Harold?"

"No thanks. I'll take Adam's word."

We sat around the egg considering our options. As is usual, thinking aroused caution. Presently Adam suggested, "Maybe we should pass this on—after we've taken our commission for finding it?"

"Pass it on to who?" grunted Ebermann. "Ryan was right in saying it's explosive. The first contact with an alien culture. A telepathic machine. A spaceship under the ocean. Christ, that would send the US economy—everybody's economy—into spasm. And how could we be sure we'd finish as winners? Also—what'll happen if the Commies get hold of it?" He brooded, contemplating the free-enterprise capitalist system foundering under a deluge of alien technology.

That reminded Adam of Metzler. "Is the Colonel onto this? You said he was at Slipe's lecture."

"Metzler's picked up some rumor about where Slipe got his silicon. That's all."

That worried them more than my news about an alien spaceship on Earth and hastened our agreement not to tell anybody at all about the egg until we had considered the problem further—and learned more from it and about it.

"Then we're into a holding pattern and we've got to keep it satisfied that I'm spreading the word effectively," I said. "Which means that I've got to convince it that I'm establishing the Terran diocese of the Cosmic Church. How can we do that?"

"With money," said Adam. "The craziest religions have been floated with money. And most of them have been profitable investments."

"For this kind of payoff I'd found a cathedral to the Devil," muttered Ebermann.

Adam was leafing through the Cosmic Creed. "Looks like we've got something to build on. Better than the guff put out by most gurus. Sold with skill we can pull converts away from those fundamentalist millionaire preachers— or I've no religious insight."

"We're already making more money than we can salt down." Ebermann regarded his partner with disfavor. "For God's sake Adam, don't get caught up on a religious kick. Fame isn't in our partnership agreement, remember?"

25

THE AEROSPACE GALLERIES at the Smithsonian are, for me, a source of strength. Some people renew their faith in God through touching the bones of saints, bits of wall, or chunks of basalt. Others turn to Nature for inspiration and refreshment. I use the Smithsonian to restore my confidence in man. Bringer's last gift was testing that confidence.

I wandered among some of the greatest achievements of our race, wondering what to do about Bringer and trying not to think about Jean, Alice, or Justine. Here was the scorched hull of an Apollo capsule. Somewhere under the Pacific was a spacecraft as far beyond that capsule as a nuclear attack sub is beyond a dugout canoe. But we had gone from the horse-buggy to the moon-lander in a lifetime. Had Bringer's builders advanced at such a hectic rate?

My impression was that conversion to the Cosmic Word had diverted them from high technology to elementary metaphysics. From faster-than-light travel to theorizing about the speed of thought. They had stopped trying to travel between the stars. They had sent their machines and imagons to do what we were aching to do, though for quite different reasons. I wondered about Bringer's builders to escape worry about Bringer's gifts.

I moved through the gallery among groups of chattering fellow-humans. My race might be a bunch of murderous fools, exploiting Nature in order to rule her, creating ways to do things better than she could. A patent-lawyer by trade; a romantic engineer at heart. The dreams which swirl beneath a surface of good sense. Dreams hidden beneath protective camouflage. Scientists can afford to be long-haired and wild-eyed. Engineers have to hold down jobs. They learn to keep their hopes hidden.

Crazy dreams like putting a man on the moon. Then they put one there. Newton had done the science they needed. It was Newton who, in Bacon's unpleasant legal metaphor, had put Nature on the rack and made her testify against herself.

Trying to forget Jean, Alice, and Justine, postponing thoughts about Bringer, my mind wandered with my feet. Bacon had been a lawyer. Lawyers plead a cause, scientists search for truth, engineers change the world. Bring into existence systems which never existed before. Engineers create—scientists translate. Translate what they extract from Nature. Statements put into Nature's mouth are false science—or science fiction.

Why was Nature always female? "Mother Nature is a bitch" the lab stick-ups used to say. Bet they didn't dare stick that up any more. Too many women were bitches—on purpose or by default. Jean for instance—I checked that line of thought and stared at a display showing the flight paths of *Apollo XI*, the beautiful curves from Earth to moon.

Ours is the first truly creative age in the history of mankind. In my own lifetime we have broken out of Earth's gravity-well, transcended the sun as a source of energy, kept a man alive after his heart had stopped, extended our reach beyond Pluto. Firsts which might be matched but could never be surpassed. No mean memorial to leave for the future. If we had a future. That's what should be worrying me. The problem raised by Bringer's latest gift. Not my mental meanderings about my first profession or the psychological nuances of three damned women!

Without a convert to produce I had doubted whether Bringer would give me even a handful of rice. But, when I asked, it had let me leaf through its catalog of gifts for saps. I had stopped at "Safe Efficient Energy Sources," and started to check them one by one. Fusion was among the first, but a glance at the plans for a fusion generator showed it too complex for building during the lifetime of a master patent. Flicking on through the catalog I had found a fission design and objected, "The by-products of fission are dangerous and hard to dump."

"Only in the cruder forms of fission generation. With more advanced fuels, waste disposal is not a problem."

"More advanced fuels? What fuels?"

"A semistable isotope you have not yet discovered. Its formula is as follows." And I had copied down the row of symbols floating in my mind. Symbols I hardly understood individually, far less when they were combined.

"How do you prepare this stuff?"

A set of instructions which I had more or less understood. I had been kept busy writing the several pages that followed. Too busy to appreciate properly what I was writing, and afterward in explaining why I had no new convert to introduce. Bringer had left me with the impression that if I wanted more rice I had better save more souls.

When we signed off I had smoked for several minutes before reading what I had written. And had started to sit up straighter and straighter. Bringer had presented me with a gift which could move us into a hydrogen economy. Could bring salvation, even wealth, to the poorest and most wretched of human societies. A cheap, clean, easily built and operated source of energy. The vast amounts of almost free energy needed to desalinate seawater, make the deserts bloom, provide power for rural farmers and cottage industries. That could help the have-not nations share some of the world's wealth. Safe, clean energy for all. For a moment I had not been a lawyer reaching for the big bucks. For a moment I had forgotten about fame, admiration, envy—all the things I thought I wanted. To hell with money and fame! Acknowledged or unacknowledged—I would be a true benefactor of mankind. I could make sure this gift was not preempted by greedy corporations or authoritarian governments.

Too great a gift to exploit until we had the capital to exploit it generously and wisely. It had lain in my safe until that morning when I had taken it out to check. And as I reread my heart had begun to sink. A cheap, safe, easy way of initiating fission. Obtainable raw materials, minimal engineering skills, about fifty kilowatts of electrical power. Everything needed to build a simple nuclear station—or a simple nuclear bomb.

It lay on my desk beside Alice's Cosmic Creed. The

lethal beside the banal. Knowledge that would turn every small nation, every terrorist gang, into a nuclear power. The nightmare the physicists had convinced themselves and us to be impossible. And probably was impossible with current Terran technology. Would be impossible through any Terran technology for generations. But probable if what I had on my desk became public knowledge. That was the problem I had brought with me to the Smithsonian in hope of spiritual guidance.

Despite Ebermann's gibes I am an ethical man in the general sense. The ethics of this were so contrary that I needed help to make any decision. To whom could I turn? The reactions of most people, if I could find any who believed me, would be so skewed with emotion as to be useless. So swayed by patriotism, or Luddism, or shortsighted selfishness as to be dangerous. Who could make a detached calculation of the pros and cons? Not when arguing an academic conundrum. When answering a question in reality, a question which would decide the future of them and their children.

I could think of nobody except Ebermann, Haskard, and myself. We alone could treat it as real and terrifying. My partners had plenty of proof that Bringer was real. They, at least, would accept the validity of the dilemma it had brought. I knew my partners. Ebermann and Haskard were devoid of any ethical constraints except those related to their own betterment. Their own long-term betterment. Because their continued prosperity depended on retaining their clients' absolute trust they could be trusted. I could turn to them for the most selfish, and therefore the most valuable, advice. I made a decision to dump the decision on them, left the Smithsonian, and took a taxi to their tower.

"It's a new reactor fuel. A fuel that leaves no radioactive waste. It can be used in most current reactors but reactors designed for it can be made far smaller and less expensive."

"Christ!" said Adam who is seldom blasphemous. "That sounds like a real winner!"

"Nuclear?" Ebermann's expression was a compound of hope and doubt. "A cheap safe nuclear fuel?"

"Yes. But there's one thing that worries me."

"The Feds? The Atomic Energy Act?"

"We could easily end-run those. Dozens of foreign governments would love to develop it. In fact, there's the problem. That's why we have to discuss this." I took a deep breath. "The technique's so simple that almost anybody could apply it. Any group with minimal knowledge and access to commercially obtainable materials. Any group with a small building and about fifty kilowatts of electrical power." I took another breath. "Fuel for a nuclear generator. Or an atom bomb."

They both stared at me.

I plunged ahead. "You see why I'm uncertain about patenting this?"

Ebermann said slowly, "Ryan, if I didn't trust your survival instincts I'd shoot you to make sure you don't. Probably shoot Adam too. Even shoot myself!"

His reaction was far more definite than any I expected. "Because of the danger of it getting into the wrong hands?"

"Because of the certainty of it getting into the wrong hands. Because any hands would be wrong. I don't fancy a world where every group of crazies can manufacture bombs in their back yards. It's bad enough with the big boys making them."

"It would be disaster for our business," added Adam with a forced smile. "Within ten years we'd have neither customers nor clients."

Ebermann exploded into fury. "Ryan, you bastard, you've got us into the biggest crunch in history! You've stuck us with a problem that's none of our business."

"I didn't know that machine was going to tell us things like this."

"Well—we know now," said Adam, recovering. "Harold—it's no good getting mad at Richard. Just because he's dumped the future of civilization on us."

"The future of civilization?" Ebermann chewed on his pipe. "Maybe this is all a scam? Maybe we've all got infected with Ryan's delusions of grandeur? History isn't made by individuals—especially individuals like us."

"I'm afraid history's been turned round on occasion by individuals with poorer talents and even weaker consciences." Adam gave another forced smile. "For example—"

Ebermann ignored his partner. "It's too dangerous to treat as a scam. This isn't a zero-sum game. Those moleculars and Strongstik work. Our optimum strategy is to assume this damned nuclear will. Ryan, you've sure exploded that egg."

"We could dump it on someone else," I suggested. "Metzler and the DIA for instance."

"For God's sake—no. He'd take it as a gift to the US from the Almighty Himself."

"Metzler's not like that. He may be a bastard but he is a sensible man."

"He's obsessed by righteousness and duty. His duty would force him to tell the brass. And you know what they'd do. Some of 'em at any rate. Reporting this as top secret would be as good as publishing it in the papers."

"Well—as you suggested—we could throw this thing in the Potomac and then all three of us could shoot ourselves."

"That doesn't appeal to me, Ryan. Even if you shot yourself first."

"Wouldn't work anyway," said Adam. "From what you told us Bringer would put out more probes until it snared a cooperative telepath. And we can't bet our futures on its catching one with your sensitive conscience. Only thing to do is to persuade it to move on to fresh mission fields. And that means convincing it that it's established a flourishing church here to leave behind."

"For that we need to convert other telepaths."

"Do you know of any, Richard?"

"One—or two."

"Well—you'd better start recruiting 'em. We can deprogram 'em later if necessary."

I finally told them about Alice.

A second period of disbelief, comprehension, and fury. "You mean all this started with a fourteen-year-old kid?"

"She's fifteen now."

"And she's the one who wrote up this Cosmic Creed?" Adam stared at me. "Richard—the child's a genius. Here's the basics for a new popular religion."

"Our problem at present," growled Ebermann, "is popular atom bombs." He looked at me. "Think you can get the kid to play the recycled convert again?"

"Maybe. If I can persuade Jean."

"Who's Jean?"

I told them. When I finished, Adam had his head in his hands and Harold was staring out of the window. "We agreed to exchange knowledge on a need-to-know basis," I reminded them. "And you didn't need to know about Jean and Alice before."

Ebermann answered slowly. "Ryan, you had better persuade her to persuade the kid. Or—" He left the alternative to my imagination.

I went to the telephone and got through to Jean. "Tell Alice I want her to tell you everything about Bringer."

"About who?"

"Bringer. That I say it's vital you know everything. Then call me back at this number after she's told you. And this is super-top priority." I took a deep breath. "Her life—your life—my life—we're all in danger."

26

THE TWO HOURS waiting for Jean to call back were long and unpleasant, the unpleasantness being directed at me. The partners insisted I stay in their office until I had done something to extract them from my mess. I sat silent by the window, staring out at Washington, wondering how I could. Adam stalked around the suite like a caged hawk, pausing at intervals to strike at me for having discovered the City. Ebermann sat at his desk like a fat rat trapped in a maze, tugging at his stuck pipe or glaring at the egg beside it.

Half-a-dozen times they decided to dump the whole problem on somebody else, to go public, to forget the whole business. Every time the prospect of what might happen afterward stopped them. Their exchanges suggested there were consciences where I had thought none existed. Of course their chief concern was what might happen to them. But they seemed just as worried about what might happen to humanity in general.

At intervals Adam's lovely secretary appeared with coffee—they rejected my pleas for bourbon. She smiled only on her first visit. Our expressions must be radiating disaster. When I suggested that I leave them for a private discussion Ebermann snarled, "You stay right here, Ryan. Until you've got us out of this shit!"

Eventually Jean did call back, sounding both furious and confused. "I've talked to Alice."

"Now will you let me talk to her?"

"No way! Not until I know a lot more."

"Jean—it's vital I tell her what's happening. And it's top secret."

"Tell me first."

I swallowed. "Then come to Washington tomorrow.

I've got two colleagues here who'll help explain. Men I can trust."

"Tomorrow? I have a departmental meeting."

"This is urgent, Jean."

"So's my meeting." She hesitated. "I suppose I can dodge it. Okay—silence and secrecy. I'll come to Washington on the train tomorrow. But you'd better have a damned good explanation for Alice's extraordinary story. And for fouling up my schedule. Where do these colleagues of yours hang out?"

"They've got an attic in Ford Towers. Ebermann and Haskard, Inc. Top floor. I'll explain everything when you arrive."

"Better explanations than you've produced in the past, I hope."

"Jean, I've got things to show you—!" But she had already hung up. I turned to Adam and Ebermann. "At least she'll listen to us."

When she did arrive, soon after three the next afternoon, her attitude was not warm. Nor was she impressed by the penthouse. "So these are the colleagues you trust." She inspected Ebermann and Haskard, who tried to look trustworthy. "Introduce me!"

"Adam Haskard—our lawyer."

"Another lawyer?" She nodded coldly to Adam.

"And Harold Ebermann. Harold's a mathematician—like yourself."

"Though without your achievements, Doctor Grayson," said Ebermann, attempting gallantry. "My field's Bayesian statistics."

"Bayesian statistics!" Jean's reaction was as close as she could come to a sneer. "I've offended a dozen mathematicians by missing a departmental meeting." She sat down and studied us. "Now, what's so urgent that I've had to interrupt my schedule to come to this beastly city." She looked out of the wall-window with distaste.

"It's about Alice," I ventured. "Where is she?"

"She's safe. And she's got enough problems without adding you to the list. Before you can talk to Alice you'll have to talk to me. And this time I want the truth—the whole truth."

"Richard always tells the truth, Doctor," said Adam, turning on the charm. "He has a reputation for telling the truth."

Jean was not charmed. She listened coldly as I protested that I had told her all the truth I had known at the time. "It's only now that I'm learning what we're really up against."

She pointed to chairs. "Then sit down and teach me. Alice let her imagination run wild. Some nonsense about an alien spaceship that talks to that egg thing."

"Everything she's told you is basically true." I took a deep breath and started to explain as well as I could, turning at intervals to my partners for confirmation.

Most people would have been incredulous; Jean was more furious than incredulous. Furious that I had misled her. Mathematicians are used to dealing with the incomprehensible and the unbelievable—impossibilities like the square roots of negative numbers, lesser infinities, and n-dimensional space. A telepathic machine and an alien spaceship seemed comparatively easy for her to accept. She must have been chewing on those incredibles ever since her interrogation of Alice.

After I had confessed as much as I thought relevant I stopped and she stared. "You mean—that object Alice kept in her teddy bear really is from outer space?"

"More or less."

"And it contacted Alice? Why Alice?"

"That research station of her father's was investigating ESP. My guess is that they succeeded better than they knew. Built some kind of an amplifier which radiated thought waves—or whatever brains radiate. Only there wasn't any input. Nobody with telepathic talent at the microphone, so to speak. The station was probably radiating only carrier—like a broadcast transmitter when nobody's talking. As Bringer was entering atmosphere it picked up the carrier, assumed the source was a telepathic-sapient center, and sent down its remote to establish contact."

"But why Alice?"

I hesitated. "She's a sensitive. She didn't know it then."

Jean considered my suggestion. "She could hear the

egg. You can hear the egg. Are you sensitive?'' Her laugh lacked humor.

"I guess so." I shrugged. "Never believed in such nonsense. Not until now.''

When she still seemed skeptical, Ebermann showed her my proof of Fermat's Last Theorem. She was more impressed by the fact that I understood what Fermat was proving than by Bringer's proof. "Fermat said he had discovered an elegant proof. I don't call this elegant. It's a machine-aided attempt at proof. You'd need hundreds of hours on a big number-cruncher to test it. And Fermat didn't have even a hand calculator.''

"Damn Fermat!" My exasperation broke through. "We're into something much bigger than any mathematician ever dreamed. We need Alice's cooperation to keep Bringer talking.''

"Saying what?" She rounded on me. "Richard, you're a patent lawyer. Have you been patenting what you've heard from that egg?''

"Well, just a couple of items. We need capital—"

"Capital? Money?" She looked at me with loathing. "You claim to have made the first alien contact. The first demonstration of telepathy. And you're keeping it secret so you can exploit it for your own greed. I'd never have believed that anyone—anyone—!" Her voice broke.

"In our society, Dr. Grayson, it is legitimate for a discoverer to be rewarded for a discovery," growled Ebermann. "We're industrialists—not academics.''

"The laborer is worthy of his hire," added Adam soothingly. "We need the capital for religious reasons. To spread the Cosmic Creed.''

"The Cosmic Creed." Jean went from reproach to fury. "Alice showed me that. It's beastly.''

"Silly perhaps—but why beastly?''

"It's the worst kind of political theocracy. Pure fascisto-communism. Ruthless technocracy. Is that what this Bringer's bringing?''

"Partly. But we don't have to take it seriously. We just have to set something up that'll convince Bringer we're on the job.''

"Listen, you greedy fool! A lot of people are liable to take this stuff seriously. And not just the lunatic fringe. It fits the preconceptions of every anti-democrat everywhere. Of every fundamentalist preacher. Christian, Moslem, Jew, or what have you. Back it up with technological goodies and you'll get converts by the millions.''

"I'm not going to let anybody but Alice and me listen to the egg.''

"That's what you think. Found a religion centered on a demonstrable oracle and you won't be able to hold 'em off.''

"Compared with some of our home-grown religions—it's not bad,'' I protested. "Mutual help. One for all. Rule by the best. Philosopher-Kings. Sounds a bit like Plato.''

"He was pure fascist.''

"More like communist propaganda,'' muttered Ebermann.

"Greatest good for the greatest number.''

"Fascistocommunist filth. Filth that leads to the suppression of minorities. Like women! Your preferred society, Richard?''

"Of course we'll edit it for Terran consumption,'' said Adam. "But it's a good guide to a way of life for the people for whom it's designed.''

"What kind of people would this fascist nonsense be good for?''

"Well—for example—a colony of intelligent ants. Each serving the whole colony. Each working at the job it does best.''

"Best for whom? For some queen? What would it do for the individual?''

"Everything—if each felt itself part of a thinking whole.'' Adam smiled. "It's the ideal creed for intelligent telepaths''

"Intelligent telepathic ants. Mister Haskard, you have a vivid imagination.''

"An asset in our business, Doctor.''

"Well, humans aren't telepathic ants. However you edit this cosmic filth you'll still be putting out fascist propaganda. And I'm not going to let Alice be a party to that. It's taken me weeks to clean out her mind after her stay with Richard.''

Adam shrugged. "Richard, why don't you try and show Dr. Grayson the City?''

"Well, I—''

"You mean, you can show me this place Alice talked about?"

"Perhaps. I don't know. If Bringer accepts you—?"

"It accepted me," murmured Adam.

Jean regarded him with acute dislike. "Then I certainly want to see for myself."

Reluctantly I took the egg from my pocket and placed it on Ebermann's desk. "I can't guarantee this will work." Then, struck by Jean's glare, "Okay, I'll try. Sure you want to see inside this?"

"If Mr. Haskard did—I must."

"Okay—it's your choice. But I'll only take you if you promise to do as I say." I sensed her rising protest. "That's not male chauvinism. It's necessary."

"I gave Richard the same promise," said Adam soothingly.

She glanced at him, then at me. "All right. I promise. As long as you don't tell me to do anything offensive."

"Oh God! Of course I won't. Ready?"

She nodded. I whistled the call-sign and asked Bringer to let me bring another insensitive sap convert to hear the Word. Hesitation, then assent. Jean flinched as she felt the mind-touch. The office faded into the periphery and the City expanded beneath us. We seemed to be floating together above it.

Jean, beside me, shuddered. "That's enough. I'm convinced."

"I'm afraid that, now I've brought you, we'll have to stay and hear the sermon. Or I won't be allowed to bring any more converts."

"I'm not a convert."

"Please act like one. That's the cost of the trip."

Disgust replaced alarm. "You con everyone, Richard! Including the machine who's faking all this."

"Pipe down. We're moving."

We had started to float across the City toward the agora. When we halted above the statue in the center of the square she asked, "What's that?"

"It's called Truth Embracing Knowledge."

"Truth? Here?" She stared down. "That crowd—they don't look like intelligent ants. They're just projected images, aren't they?"

"Recorded images of real people. They call themselves imagons."

"People? Alice talked some nonsense about them having six legs. That seemed to upset her."

"They look like people to us, because we're people. Back in the office, anyway. But they're actually the imagons of intelligent beings from Bringer's home world. And from other worlds it's visited. They talk and act human when you're among them. Too much like humans. Too much like us."

"Richard, you don't approve of them being like us?" For the moment she was less hostile.

"I've always had a childish hope that somewhere in the universe there are races wiser and kinder than we are. Sentimental bullshit of course. Any race with a high-tech civilization and space travel must be full of individuals looking out for themselves—or their race. Partly good—partly mean. Like us."

We hung in silence for a few minutes, then Jean muttered, "Enough! Back to Washington."

"Better wait to hear the Word. Bringer may be monitoring how my insensitive converts behave."

"Insensitive convert—!"

"Quiet! The sermon's starting." The voice was ringing out across the agora, across the waiting crowds, the opening injunction rising to us. "Hear the Word of Truth and Knowledge."

Once again I had to listen to the Alice edition of the Cosmic Word. It sounded even more impressive than before. I began to appreciate what Jean meant, what Adam hoped. It was the sort of creed that many people, floundering in permissive societies, would grab onto because it offerd a firm code of behavior, rules that told them how to act in invidious situations. A way of life for people who longed to be told what to do. A rigid framework to support an uncertain conscience. The dehumanizing attraction of all fundamentalist faiths. More sentimental, more logical, more humane, than many of those current on Earth. A creed which, when proclaimed by a powerful giver of real gifts, would drag converts from born-again Christianity, ayatollah Islam, over-reformed Judaism, and spineless churches.

Jean's reactions as she listened would have shown any monitor that Bringer had watching us that she was certainly not among the converted. As soon as the voice finished with its command to spread the Word of Truth and Knowledge, she snapped, "Get me out of here!"

"Seen enough?"

"I certainly have."

We flicked back to the penthouse suite. After Jean had recovered she walked over to the wall-window and stood staring across Washington. "This place looks almost good after that one." She swung around to us. "You don't really expect me to let Alice help you spread that Cosmic filth?"

"Jean—once we've persuaded Bringer to go and preach to some other planet we can dump the whole damned religion. But we still need Alice to persuade the thing to leave. It's too dangerous to ignore."

"What's so dangerous about it? According to you, what we saw was an illusion. And the thing itself is just a machine lying on the bottom of the ocean. You said it's no physical threat to anybody."

"It's a threat to the whole human race. No—not just an intellectual threat. A physical threat."

"How can it be?"

I glanced at my two companions. Ebermann looked unhappy but Adam nodded. I turned to Jean. "I'll tell you why—if you insist. But I warn you, you'll wish I hadn't after I have."

Her lips thinned. "All the more reason for me to know before I'll let Alice get involved."

"You've asked for it." And I told her the most cogent reason for persuading Bringer to continue on its way.

"Cut-price atom bombs!" Her fists clenched. "That damned machine told you how to make them?"

"I didn't realize what it was saying until it had finished."

"And where are the do-it-yourself instructions now?"

"We've destroyed them," growled Ebermann. "I wanted to destroy Ryan too. Only Adam didn't think that would help. The machine would only blab to some other sensitive. Someone even greedier than Ryan."

"It would be the same if we tried to destroy the egg," Adam nodded. "The machine would send out another.

The only hope we have is persuading it that it's done it's job here and can move on to spread its cosmic word among other unfortunate races.''

She stared at us. ''The future of civilization on Earth is sure in six grubby hands.''

''In eight hands, Dr. Grayson,'' grunted Ebermann. ''Knowing how to make the stuff would be fatal. Knowing that it can be made is almost as dangerous.''

Jean turned to him. ''Why?''

''Because once it's been shown a thing can be done human beings go on trying to do it until they can. If it wasn't for the birds we'd probably still be sitting on the ground. It's obvious that what's heavier than air can't fly.'' He tugged at his stuck pipe, filled the one in his hand, and looked at her. ''So, Doctor, you're in this mess with us now.''

''Oh my God!'' She stared at him, then started to walk up and down the office. ''We're talking about the future of mankind.''

''Not just talking about it.'' I caught her arm to stop her prowling. ''We've got to decide what to do about it. Let me tell Alice. It's her problem as much as ours.''

''Get the child involved?'' Jean jerked her arm free.

''She's not a child. She's got more sense than any of us.''

''Tell that kid?'' Ebermann scowled. ''Then five people will know. Five to keep a secret like this?''

''There's others who know something,'' I confessed. ''About the egg. Not about the nuclear.''

''Colonel Metzler?'' suggested Adam.

''Yes. And—and—'' I saw Jean's face and faltered.

''You mean that woman you kicked?'' she snapped.

''What woman?'' Ebermann heaved his bulk to his feet. ''You never mentioned any woman, Ryan.''

''A woman tried to kidnap Alice,'' explained Jean. ''A gangster woman. At least, she has a gang. What's her name, Richard?''

''Justine Ladrich.'' I tried looking out of the window.

''Justine Ladrich? That analyst who works for Loucher Freres?'' Ebermann clenched his hands as though they were on my throat.

''She doesn't work for Loucher Freres.'' I couldn't

resist shocking him further. "She *owns* Loucher Freres. And I think she's another sensitive."

Adam froze. Ebermann dropped back onto his seat with a thud. Jean passed from disbelief through horror into decision. "That woman a telepath too? It's bad enough us knowing. She certainly must not!" Jean started toward the door. "We've got to involve Alice. Damn you, Richard!" She stopped with her hand on the handle. "Are you coming?"

I slipped the egg into my pocket and tried to give my partners an encouraging smile. "Chins up! I'll phone. Tell you what happens. Pray for us."

They glared back with positive hatred, and I went after Jean. She was no friendlier. She sat beside me, tight-lipped and silent, as I drove slowly and with extra care through the rush-hour traffic. Only when I turned north on the beltway did she spit out, "Philadelphia's that direction."

"I know. I'm testing for tails. We're going via Frederick."

"Tailed by who? That woman? That Colonel?"

"By them. Maybe by others." I knew the rented car wasn't bugged and I was sure I hadn't been followed from Annandale. I circulated through several cloverleafs before I was convinced I wasn't being followed now, and headed away from Washington.

Jean was silent until we were passing Frederick, then her curiosity broke through. "This telepathy stuff—can you read minds?"

"Of course not. Alice and I—we can sense emotions." I hesitated. "But Bringer can communicate directly."

"Only with Alice and you?"

"Only with sensitives like us."

"Are there any others?"

"You heard me in the office. Justine Ladrich has a reputation for detecting deceit."

"I wish I had. Then I'd have seen through your lies in the beginning."

Driving toward Princeton in an attempt to save the human race, I exploded. "Me a liar? You didn't do so badly yourself, Mrs. Jensen. When it suited you. You caught on quicker than I did. Like Alice says—for such a nice person, you're real smart."

That quieted her for a while. Presently she asked, "Can you sense my emotions?"

"If I try. With you—I don't try."

"Why not? I've got emotions like everybody else."

"Not like anybody else. Anybody I've met. My specialty's detecting deceit. With you—there isn't any deceit to detect. You show how you really feel—always."

"You said I lied to Miss Lister."

"What you called white lies. For you—emotionally—those don't count as deceit. In women, ends justify means." I laughed. "Now you're mad."

"Not mad. Sad! Because you think like that." She paused, "Richard, whatever the rights and wrongs of all this, we can't afford to quarrel. After seeing the City I have to believe your crazy story. Are there other crazy things you haven't told me?"

"Yes—and I won't unless I must. Relax!" I touched her hand. "If I did tell you, you'd agree I shouldn't have."

27

THE COTTAGE WHICH Jean had borrowed from her friends was the amateur's idea of a "safe house." Standing alone at the end of a lane, surrounded by woods and fields, the nearest farm a mile away. Comfortable and safe if nobody suspected you were there; a trap if anybody did. So far nobody had.

Alice came bursting from the front door as I turned into the driveway just after ten, and flung herself into my arms as I got out of the car. "Oh Dick, you've come at last!"

"Good to see you, brat!" I patted the seat of her jeans. She was shaping up well.

"Alice—restrain your enthusiasm until you've heard the mess he's got us into." Jean led the girl back toward the cottage. "Come along, Richard."

"You explain. I'll hide the car." I was glad to let Jean describe the mess for which everybody was blaming me. Jean was honest and persuasive. She was now convinced that Bringer was a physical and political threat. And that Alice's cooperation was vital.

After I had parked the car I scouted the area as well as I could in the darkness. A city apartment with restricted admission and a second exit would have been safer than this isolated cottage. I was still unhappy about security when I returned to face Alice.

She and Jean were in the kitchen preparing a late supper and turned toward me when I came through the back door. "Jean's explained things, Richard. I know we've got to fool Bringer. If that explosive stuff gets out—the TV showed what would happen. Ugh!" She shivered.

"Then you'll pretend to be different new converts?"

She nodded. "Can't think of any other way of persuading Teddy to leave. He said he'd sail as soon as you'd converted a few more sensitives. I don't like fooling Teddy, but I guess I must. When do we start?''

"After supper," Jean cut in. "You'll both fake better with full stomachs."

"Good. I'll check the house." And I started on my rounds, still worrying about what might happen in this lonely place.

It was a well-built cottage, updated with the conveniences needed to support the life-style of a pair of professors. The locks on windows and doors were adequate, and after I had made everything as secure as possible I went to the living room. Jean was serving supper. "Richard's more paranoid than ever," she said.

"I've a lot to be paranoid about." I sat down at the table, discovering that I was also ravenous.

The last meal I had eaten with Jean and Alice had been more ordeal than pleasure. That evening we ate almost like a family—something I had not experienced for many years. Jean was an excellent cook. Alice chattered along, complaining about life alone in the country with Jean away at Princeton most days. For a while I forgot my guilt at having foisted the future of humanity onto a sensitive teenager and a sensible mathematician. Yet perhaps there was no pair on Earth better suited for such a task. Two intelligent, decent, and essentially honest young women. For, at times, I found myself looking at Alice as if she were a young woman rather than a girl. She was still at that age when kids oscillate between child and adult. Shifts which occur far more frequently in the female than in the male. As Alice had once reminded me, Juliet was only fourteen when Romeo got her into his mess.

After we had finished supper I lit a cigarette while the girls cleared away the dirty dishes. Then I put the egg on the table. Jean came in and sat on the couch. "That beastly thing!"

"It's not beastly," Alice protested, joining me at the table. "Teddy means no harm. He's just trying to help us. He doesn't understand what we are. He hasn't given us weapons or whiskey—as we used to give savages. He's a well-intentioned missionary."

"So were most of ours. And look at the mess they left!

You two have got to persuade your well-intentioned Teddy to leave before his presents destroy us.''

"Perhaps if we just explain—?''

"Too risky," I said. "He'd call us heretics and put out another probe, searching for true believers. And you know what he might find. Jean's right about your Cosmic Creed. That—plus free gifts—would be dynamite if planted among some fanatics. Read the newspapers!"

Alice sighed. "Okay—I wish it wasn't so. But his last present—we must con him into moving.'' She reached across the table and squeezed my fingers. "All systems go!"

Her touch warmed me. Then her grip tightened and my hand closed on hers under a sudden sense of imminent danger. Jean was on her feet. "What's with you two—?" Cut off by a dull thud from the kitchen.

The thud of a plastic charge. I let go of Alice and jumped for the door, drawing my gun. Flung back as it was thrown open. A man burst through, knocking me aside, taking me to the ground. Four more behind him. I glimpsed Alice diving for the bedroom. Jean started after Alice, was grabbed and pushed onto the couch.

Two of them were on me. A gloved hand clamped over my mouth, a muzzle struck my head. The room rocked. When it steadied two men were holding Jean flat on the couch, a cloth between her teeth. Another emerged from the bedroom dragging a struggling Alice. Sounds of a fifth searching the rest of the cottage.

Alice screamed. She was cuffed to silence. The man searching the cottage returned to the living room and went out through the kitchen. None of them had said a word. But I knew them. Justine's personal thugs.

Justine Ladrich herself came from the kitchen. She glanced at the three of us, then went to the table and picked up the egg. She stood examining it for a moment, then looked at me. "Richard—you had it all the time. I should have guessed." She knelt beside me. "Show me how it works."

The gloved hand was raised from my mouth. I snarled, "Go to hell."

Jean spat out her gag, struggled upright. "Who are you? What do you want?" A slap across the face knocked her onto her back.

"You bastard!" A burst of fury gave me strength to break free. I caught the gloved hand, pulled its owner forward over my shoulder, grabbed at Justine's ankle. A blow from the pistol knocked me silly. Raised again, then halted at Justine's sharp command. She was pointing at me, then at Jean.

Two held me while they taped my wrists and ankles. The other two pinned Jean flat. One caught her hair, holding her head, punching her face and body.

She screamed, "Richard—don't tell her!"

I croaked, "Justine—remember my credit! What I didn't do."

She glanced at me, laughed. "Richard—you've spent your credit." She said something and the man stopped punching Jean. Alice was dragged over to face her. "So you're the child who found this? Did Mister Ryan tell you about my generous offer?"

"It's not for sale." Alice kicked the man holding her. He slapped her and she started to sob.

"My offer's still good—if you show me how to work it. I'll find out for myself, sooner or later. Or you'll tell me—sooner or later. Save Dr. Grayson, Richard, and yourself a lot of discomfort by cooperating now. While all of you are in a state to bargain rationally. Later on—" she shrugged—"you won't be rational."

Alice continued to sob, playing the terrified teenager. Justine bent forward, looking into her face. "Child, you can't deceive me. You and Richard know why, don't you? I sense you do. Then you must know how much I'll hurt you and your friends if you don't cooperate."

Alice stopped sobbing, rubbed her eyes, and looked back at Justine. After a moment she muttered, "Okay, let's make a deal."

"Alice—no!" Jean was silenced by a blow.

"No deal if you hit my friends!" Alice straightened her shoulders, stared directed into Justine's eyes. "You know that, Miss Ladrich."

"You think that, child?" Justine laughed, shifting the egg from hand to hand. "If you show me how this thing works the offer I made to Richard is still good. And I promise to turn all of you loose, unharmed. After I'm back in Paris."

"How much?"

"He never gave a price. What do you suggest?"

Alice spoke calmly. "A hundred thousand cash and a cut in what you make. Twenty percent if I have to work it. Ten percent if you don't need me. And no harm to me or my friends."

"You'd trust me on that?"

"I know I can trust you, Miss Justine. Like you know you can trust me."

"Don't trust her!" Jean called before the cloth was pushed back into her mouth. She had not yet realized why Alice could take Justine's word. I knew, but was starting to distrust Alice herself.

"Then show me how to use this." Justine held up the egg.

"Listen to it first."

Justine put it to her ear. "Singing noises." She shivered. "And a feeling inside." Bringer had scanned her. "How do I get it on playback?" She was still thinking of the thing as some kind of recorder.

"You have to use the access code. I can't explain. You have to whistle it. Let me have the egg and I'll show you."

Justine smiled. "Remember child, I can smell deceit." She spoke to the man who was holding Alice, listening without understanding. He pulled the girl's wrists tight behind her back. Justine held the egg to her mouth. "Whistle the code now."

"Okay." Alice pursed her lips and began to whistle aloud the cadence running through her mind.

The room shivered. Then Alice, Justine, and I were standing in the courtyard, under the rose arbor.

28

JUSTINE'S SHOCK STRUCK like a blow and the courtyard shivered, the roses on the arbor fading as she stared wildly around. "Where are we?"

"Safe," said Alice. "Where you wanted to be."

"Where's that?" Justine was breathing fast but her voice steadied as she forced her fear deep. Jerked into the unknown, without warning or concept, most people would have retreated to hysterics or shock. Justine showed her quality by controlling her terror. "Where are we?"

"Inside the egg, I guess." Alice's smile was malicious.

"Where?"

I broke in. "Maybe like Alice said—inside the egg. Or through the egg."

"Through? To another universe or something?"

"Perhaps." I let her assume that. "The home of ultra-pure silicon et cetera." I caught her arm. "Don't panic and blow it now."

Her pride was stung. She jerked her arm free. "What's here?"

"What you're after."

"What we're after," said Alice. "Our cut—remember?"

"Some guide will arrive to show us round," I explained. "I'll introduce you as a convert. Understand?"

"Convert to what? Guide to what?"

"You'll see. We're quite safe. Keep quiet and don't argue."

She was starting to argue when the Doors of Perception opened and Edwina Bringer stepped into the courtyard, wearing her automatic smile. "Welcome, Richard. Welcome, converts. Welcome to the Holy City of the Word. You have come seeking truth and knowledge. Both will be given to you."

''Who's she?'' Justine hung back.

''The local guide. It's her job to show visitors around. Come on!'' I took one arm, Alice took the other, and between us we urged Justine after Edwina through the Doors of Perception.

She froze at her first sight of the City. She did not know this was all illusion. For Justine, this was reality. Even I, knowing what it was, found it close to real. The light breeze on my cheeks, the soft grass under my feet, birds singing among the trees on the slope down to the road. The scents of flowers. The impression of reality was greater than on any previous visit. Why? Of course! We were now three—including Justine who believed what she was seeing.

''Please take a few minutes to appreciate the traveler's view of our Holy City—the City of the Word—before we enter it to hear words of Truth and Knowledge.'' Edwina started her usual spiel but not with her usual smooth assurance. As she pointed out landmarks in the city ahead she hesitated at intervals, as if noticing things she hadn't noticed before.

Landmarks I hadn't noticed. The same beautiful city, but subtly changed. Grimmer, taller, grander, more Byzantine. Walls, battlements, and gates. Walled, not for ornament but for defense. Justine, unconsciously, was adding her contribution to our combined image of what a Holy City should look like. And the City had changed—was changing—to match our joint design.

Not only the City. The surroundings too. The woods were deeper and darker, the distant hills higher and shrouded in mist. The weather was changing. The light breeze from the land shifted to a fresh wind from the sea. White horses were charging across the bay to break in foam on rocks and sands. And now there were more rocks than sand.

The highway at the foot of the hill was broader and better paved. People were no longer sauntering toward the city in groups. They were crowding along, pushing each other in their haste. A squad of the soldiers I had seen on that side street came swinging past in measured step. And now there were passenger vehicles rolling along the hardtop, pedestrians jumping out of their way.

Bringer had evidently had to make some rapid restructuring to meet Justine's unconscious expectations. I glanced at Edwina, Bringer's embodiment, and saw her momentary confusion with her own creation. Then she recovered her poise. "Our car's down there. So if we're all ready?" She started down the hill toward a vehicle parked by the curb. Justine hesitated, then followed. Alice slipped beside me. "Richard, what's happening?"

"Justine's arrival has altered things. Let's find out how much."

"Do you think we can trap her here?"

"Her imagon, you mean? I doubt it. And whatever happens here, she herself's still in the cottage with her thugs. Try to think of something we can do when we go back."

"If we go back!"

"Of course we will. Nothing can happen to us here." I wished I was as confident as I tried to sound. "Just hang close to Edwina."

Our guide was getting into the waiting vehicle, an elegant wheeled shell. A vehicle that started to absorb Justine's attention. And mine. Silent, no noxious fumes, doors that opened for us, seats that adjusted to our curves. Justine muttered, "If we could get this home—it'd sell for a million."

"Too big. Watch for the small stuff. Like that door-sensor. Shipping costs from here must be out of this world."

"I'll check on costs later." My attempt at humor had failed. Justine's eyes were everywhere; judging, evaluating, calculating. The ability to direct the unexpected which had made her the owner of Loucher Freres. Sitting beside her, riding toward the city, her sense for the profitable fired my own. There were more extractables here than holy words and missionary handouts.

"What are those guards doing?" Alice was pointing to the city gates ahead. What the guards appeared to be doing was dragging selected men and women from the crowds pouring past, beating them with the shafts of their spears, then tossing them aside to crawl away. They were doing it with zest. "Why are they hitting those people?"

"It is the guards' duty to stop the faithless from entering the Holy City." Edwina spoke with less than her usual confidence. "I presume that's what they're doing now."

"There's Jerry! And Ada!" Alice was standing up in the vehicle. "They're hitting Jerry."

Jerry was hitting back, exchanging blows with one of the guards. Ada was scrambling to her feet from where she had been thrown. Alice screamed, "Jerry! Jerry!"

Jerry knocked down the guard, looked up, and waved. "Alice! Come for the action?"

Alice made to jump from the vehicle. I caught her arm, pushed her back into her seat, and snapped at Edwina, "Stop this thing!"

The vehicle stopped just short of the gate. Jerry came running over to us. "Jerry, what's going on?"

He looked up, smiling. "The Word knows! We were out in the woods when the snap came. We're trying to get into the City and find out."

Ada limped to join him. "I know!" She looked grim. "We've taken someone unpleasant aboard and something nasty's about to happen." She tugged at Jerry's sleeve. "Back to the woods, Jerry. Or back to electronics. I don't want to see what's in there. The Guards are out so it's sure to be bad."

"Come with us!" implored Alice as the pair moved away.

"It is unwise for converts to mix with confused citizens." Edwina looked as confused as any citizen. I remembered her early statements that anything that could happen might happen. Edwina—Bringer—was unprepared for whatever was happening now. The vehicle started forward toward the gates. Alice looked back, waving to Jerry and Ada.

"What was all that about?" demanded Justine, showing more interest than alarm.

"There is sometimes confusion during a switch," said Edwina, as though that was a complete explanation. "The Guards will not interfere with visitors."

We reached the gateway. The Guards were men and women in the same black Roman-type armor and short swords but with an incongruous addition—Luger automatic pistols. They ignored our vehicle when it rolled past into the City.

The streets to the agora were narrower, darker, more crowded than before. The people moving out of the path of our vehicle looked quarrelsome and sullen. The windows of the buildings were shuttered. There were clouds overhead. The whole character of the City and its people had changed. The influence of Justine had been very much for the worse. My alarm at what might happen increased. I whispered to Alice, "Perhaps we should pull out. I don't like the look of this."

"I don't like it either," she whispered back. "But I like the thought of the cottage even less. Everything's static there while we're here. We must fool that bitch somehow before we jump."

I turned on Edwina. "Bringer—this isn't the City you showed us before."

"It's the same City of the Word, modified to meet the expectations of your converts, Richard. You brought them here. I can only follow the program. I warned you that this was a stochastic non-deterministic system. In this recording the individual units act as individuals."

"Recording or not—this is total immersion. And we're in it. How do we get out of it?"

"Whenever you and your converts wish."

"Can't you snap the whole thing off?"

She glanced at me. "Not unless you want to stay here and become a citizen."

"But I'm back on Earth—not here."

"Your imagon is here. At the moment you are your imagon. If I snap now you—what you think is you—will stay here. Do you wish that?"

"No! For the Word's sake."

"Then stay and experience the whole of this interaction. When all three of you are satisfied you have learned what you came to learn, then you will agree to return and I will close down." Edwina-Bringer spoke with a worried authority.

"What's going to happen next?"

"Whatever the conjoint probabilities bring forth."

"In other words—you don't know?"

"Not in detail. But in terms of conditional probabilities—" She stopped and put her hand to her mouth. The vehicle had reached the edge of the agora. Truth still embraced Knowledge at the center of the square, but now beside the statue stood a scaffold and gallows.

A conjoint probability which evidently shocked Edwina as it shocked Alice and myself. I gripped her arm, shook her. She felt like a woman; I had forgotten for the moment she was an illusion. "What the hell's going on?"

"I—I don't know." She strove for her accustomed calm. "This is most unusual. Perhaps some rebel is about to pay the penalty for rebellion."

"Rebel? You have rebels and executions in your Holy City?"

"Error must be eradicated to keep the City holy. But never before—!" She checked herself.

"You've guided millions of converts around but you've never shown them a rebel being hanged. Is that it?"

"I explained—the recording is indeterminate. All possibilities are open." But Bringer had never imagined this one.

Our vehicle inched forward through the crowd. Justine was standing up, tense with excitement. She glanced at me, her lips moist and her eyes bright. "Execution coming up? We're just in time for the show."

This must be Justine's show. Who was her subconscious about to hang? Then the voice rang out from the tower. "Hear the Words of Truth and Knowledge!" The words were as before, the voice was harsher. And the crowds now packing the agora were not awed into silence. There were murmurs of approval and dissent now running among them.

"They're about to hang a heretic, aren't they?" I hissed at Edwina.

The voice spoke again. "Before you hear the Word of Truth, watch the fate of the Liar and the Lie!"

A commotion on the near side of the agora. A squad of black-armored guards were forcing their way toward the scaffold. And the crowd was starting to act more and more like a human mob; some people cheering the prisoner, others hurling curses.

I stood up in our vehicle to look over the heads of the crowd at the prisoner. A tall, well-built young man, naked to the waist, his arms tied behind his back, moving slowly with his escort toward the scaffold. A handsome young man, a smile on his face, showing no fear of the gallows ahead.

"Help me up. Let me look!" Justine was on tip-toe beside me, straining to see over the crowd. The procession and the prisoner was now level with us. I swung her up by her elbows.

She looked, saw, and gave an anguished cry. "Gamar!"

The prisoner turned his head. His brave smile changed to horror. "Justine!"

She gave a twist and was out of my grip, out of the vehicle, fighting her way through the mob toward the guards lining the approach to the scaffold. Without thought I plunged after her. Alice and Edwina shrieked for me to come back. I continued to fight my way forward.

I say fight, because that's what it was. This was not a popular execution. Public opinion seemed split halfway. The voice exhorting order and threatening death rolled across the agora and was ignored by the mob. I fear a mob with a dreadful fear. The rage and cruelty released by idealists rioting in support of their ideals. I would shoot down any mob which reached the lynching stage. I have seen mobs at work and helped clean up the results of their work. This mob was truly human. I forced my way through it against every impulse to stay out of it.

Fearful as I was, I was also larger and stronger than most of these illusions. Illusions? They were no longer illusions. They were men and women getting in my way, flailing at me, falling beneath my fists. All was real. It hurt when I was hit. I reached Justine as she reached the line of guards. Prisoner and escort were only feet away.

She lunged toward the prisoner. A guard held a crossed spear in her path. She dodged under it, grabbed the Luger from his holster, and shot him through the throat. He fell, spouting blood. The line of guards broke as the mob surged forward. Spears and swords thrusting and swinging. Justine's shot was the only one fired.

She dropped the Luger, pulled the sword from the dead guard's scabbard, and dodged spears to reach the prisoner. I followed. A guard's spear raked my side. In a gust of fury I caught the shaft, jerked it from him, knocked him down with the butt. Then I jumped to cover Justine's back as she bent to hack at the ropes round the prisoner's wrists.

"Richard—look right!" A teenage shriek of warning. I swung to block a sword-blow, lost my spear, grabbed my attacker's sword. Alice, slipping between fighting bodies, snatching up the short spear, was beside me. "For God's sake, let's leave. Now! Before we're killed."

To hell with Justine! This brat of fifteen shouldn't be in the middle of a bloody struggle—real or imagined. I caught my breath, concentrated, we tugged together. And did not shift. Justine was holding us with all the strength of her raw emotions. The prisoner was free, picking up a sword, fighting beside her. We forced our way to where she stood. The young man swung at me. Justine shouted, "Gamar!" and a word in her unknown tongue. He grinned and turned to cut down another guard.

We were four united people in the middle of a confused mob and scattered guards. Justine pushed back her hair, looked round, and called, "Follow me!" I glanced toward Edwina, standing horrified in the vehicle, helpless to affect a situation she did not understand. I followed Justine, Alice, and Gamar who were fighting their way through the crowd with vigor and enthusiasm. I became rearguard, holding off assorted attackers coming at us from behind.

Justine had a strategist's eye. She wound her way through the mob to a narrow alley on the rim of the agora. I had never seen a narrow alley in the city before, but I was seeing many new things that bloody day. We started up the alley, Justine leading. I paused at the entrance long enough to cut down two guards who rushed me, then ran to join the others, waiting at the next intersection.

"Good work, Richard!" Justine smiled a savage smile. "Anybody following?"

Breathless, I shook my head.

"Then come!" She took Gamar's hand and led us, running, down a side street.

I looked at Alice, her face and arms streaked with blood, dust, and sweat. "You okay?"

"Seem to be. You look like hell." She turned to follow Justine. "More action ahead, I'll bet." What for me was a ghastly killing was, for her, a fantasy come true. We might be hurt in this dream city, but we couldn't be killed. Or we'd surely have been back on the agora.

I panted after them, trailing blood. Justine was at the open door of an alley house, waving us in. I fell through the doorway after Alice. Justine slammed the door, shot the bolts and, ignoring us, threw herself into Gamar's arms.

The room was bare except for a bed. The door was stout but the only one. The window was small and shuttered. "We're in a trap," gasped Alice. "Might as well sit it out until we're murdered or rescued." She slumped onto the floor, her back against the wall, watching with interest as Justine and Gamar moved, still entwined, toward the bed. "She must have met him before."

I sank down beside her. There were dozens of questions to ask. Dozens of critical decisions to make. I was too exhausted to consider any. All Alice's attention was on the lovers. Justine disengaged her mouth from Gamar's long enough to shout, "Guard the door!" Then she went on her back across the bed, pulling at his belt.

"Looks like they're going to make love," said Alice, standing up to get a better view. I reached to pull her down. She shook off my hand. "This is part of my education."

This was madness. This was illusion. Hard to maintain that conviction with my shoulder throbbing from a sword-slash and the rest of me bruised and torn. Alice was oozing blood from a dozen cuts but for the moment interest outweighed pain. Justine was half-naked and on her way to becoming completely so. The streaks of blood on her white skin made her a true tigress.

A tigress mating. I am no voyeur but I pulled myself up to stand beside Alice, leaning against the wall, watching with awe the passions loosed on the bed. Passions as far above the pleasure she and I had shared as the eruptions of Mount St. Helens are above the spewing of Old Faithful. I stared, overwhelmed. Alice brought me back to the illusion of reality by punching the wound on my shoulder. "She's rising! When she goes flat—we pull out. But I can't sense—"

"She'll grunt first," I said without thinking.

Alice glanced at me. Justine grunted. Climax on the bed. We pulled. She came. All three of us went together.

29

BACK IN THE cottage. Justine swaying against the table, eyes closed, mouth part-open in the ecstasy of climax. Her men staring at her. I still on the floor at her feet.

Justine opened her eyes, looked around her, then down at me. "You tore us apart!"

"An illusion! A dream. Bringer creates illusions. It had to end."

"Take me back!"

"You can't go back into the same dream."

"We did as we promised!" shouted Alice, jerking against the man holding her wrists. "We took you into the egg."

"And you'll take me back." The passion in Justine's voice became icy with threat. "Now—or I'll start on your eyes." She crouched beside me, her nails hovering over my face.

"But we fought beside you. We fought beside you!" Alice screamed.

"Take me back and we'll fight again."

"But we can't! We can't!" wailed Alice.

"Don't try and fool me, child. You're no sniveling brat. I saw you swinging a sword." Justine stood up, her voice softer. "Maybe we can't make it—but we can try." She went to the table. "We couldn't save Gamar before. But we did rescue him there—wherever there is. I must go to him."

"He won't be there. He'll never be there. He never was there. You created him!"

"He was there!" Justine radiated hope, frustration, anger. Her passions swamping all logic. She snatched up the egg and pushed it against Alice's mouth. "The call-sign. Whistle it! Or I'll put out Richard's right eye."

She would! Alice knew that too. She shivered and pursed

209

her lips. For the second time that night she whistled a cadence. Quite a different cadence. Shrill and urgent, unlike any I had ever heard. An alien series of notes that carried a common message. I didn't hear an alien call. I heard calls I had never heard, calls from the human past. A cavalry trumpeter sounding the "Rally." Roland's horn, ringing down from the Pyrenees to echo across Europe. The archetypal call. The desperate cry for help.

A moment of silence. Then a wave of fear, rolling out from the egg. Terror flooding the room. The men holding Jean were on their feet, staring into vacancy, pupils dilated, expressions ghastly, stinking sweat, paralyzed with dread. Jean herself lying frozen, her eyes wide, released but unmoving.

The tableau broke. The man holding Alice's wrists let go as if they were red-hot. He squealed like a frantic horse, turned, and plunged for the door. His companions flung themselves after him. Their feet clattered down the hall, the front door crashed open, steps pounding along the garden path. The sound of a car starting.

Terror-stricken insensitives! We sensitives reeled but recovered. Alice dived for her bedroom. Justine grabbed at her, missed, and swung at me. Reaching beneath her skirt, pulling a Biretta from the holster on her thigh, pointing it at my groin. "What happened, Ryan? Tell me or I'll blow your balls off! You know I will."

I did. She was beyond reason. I had braced myself against pain—even death. But the threat to my testicles drove me to the verge of surrender. I was opening my mouth when Alice erupted from the bedroom, the flashgasgun in her hand. Justine, half-turning, took the jet in her face.

She clutched at Alice. The Biretta spat, plaster showered from the ceiling. Then her legs folded beneath her. She collapsed, gasping fury and hate. Alice was kneeling beside me, ripped away the tape round my wrists. Then she ran to Jean. The egg rolled from the table to the floor.

I caught it. "What did you do?"

"Repulsed an attack by subsaps."

"What—what did they see?"

"Whatever they feared most." Then a hint of criticism. "Your own defenses seemed inadequate."

"They took us by surprise."

"The price of security is eternal vigilance." Another catch-phrase from Alice's readings. "Hostile subsaps are best controlled by evoking their own fears."

"No sign of 'em anywhere." I had returned from searching the garden and the lane. "Their car's gone. They're gone."

"They'll be back to rescue her," whispered Jean through bruised lips, nodding toward the room where Justine was lying trussed on the bed. "Call the police, Richard."

"No cops!" Alice jumped up from bathing Jean's face. "Those goons won't be back. They'll never be back. And they'll never be able to come near any of us again."

"How do you know?"

"Teddy told me. At the very beginning he told me how to call for help if I was attacked by subsaps. When I didn't even know what subsaps were." She grimaced. "I do now."

"Why didn't you holler for help before?"

"I didn't know what Teddy would do. I might have—in that bus station. As soon as I got my bag. Might not. Afraid he might hurt somebody saving me. Should have known he wouldn't harm anyone—only scare the hell out of 'em. And you saved me—so I didn't have to." She stroked Jean's hair.

Jean sat up slowly, holding her head. "It scared hell out of me all right. I saw—I saw—!" She shuddered, as if waking from a nightmare, dropping her face into her hands. When Alice put an arm round her shoulders, squeezed her, she looked up. "Sorry—a private horror. What happened after you whistled at the egg the first time?"

"What did it look like?"

"Not much. You two and that woman stood staring at the thing."

"For how long?"

"Maybe fifteen seconds."

"A lot happened in fifteen seconds." Alice sat down, taking Jean's hand. "We went to the City. All three of us. I'll tell you later. It's quite a story. Richard was a hero. And she—she was on our side."

"We were on her side." I wanted the record straight.

"That guy—that Gamar she grunted under—who was he?"

"Grunted under?" Jean stared at Alice.

I cut in. "Gamar? Some figment of Justine's unhealthy imagination."

"We—well—we shared the same illusion. Kind of," added Alice.

Jean tried to stand up, dropped back onto the couch. "That evil woman—if you don't give her to the police— then what are you going to do?"

"She threatened to shoot off Dick's balls. And she meant it. I vote we do something equivalent."

"Alice—that's an appalling suggestion!" Jean straightened. "I'm ashamed of you. You must never say—never even think such things. Or you'll be as bad as her."

"I was only joking." Neither her mind nor her expression supported that.

Joking or not—best divert her from seeking vengeance. "Justine can wait. Our real problem's at the bottom of the Pacific. The sooner we can persuade Bringer that it's time to leave, the safer we'll all be." I picked up the egg, put it on the table, looked at Alice. "After that shambles, still ready to go back to the City? Act converted to get Bringer under way?"

"Go back? Back to the fighting?" Excitement rather than fear.

"Bringer should have snapped things back to normal after us visitors left. Without Justine—there shouldn't be any fighting." Or so I hoped.

Jean started to protest. "Richard—you can't take the child back into—into whatever was happening."

"She's no child, Jean. Not there, at any rate." There, Alice was a bloodied warrior.

"I must." Alice sat down at the table. "I just hope that Teddy's still the sucker he was."

My hope also, though I knew none of us would ever be the same after exposure to Justine's naked emotions. I sat down opposite Alice. Jean sat silent, watching us.

A whistle and we made contact, but no vision or total immersion. I faltered, "Here is another sapient who has accepted the Cosmic Word."

It was several seconds before Bringer answered and

there was censure even in its machine voice. "A short while ago I was in contact with one of your sapient converts. It did not scan me but I scanned it. A bad mind. Your race has many bad minds. Start revolt and disorder. Awaken primitive passions. Your last visit to the City of the Word brought destruction. My makers have evolved beyond such disunities. Your race is still far from truth."

Damn Justine! "That bad one's not typical. This new convert has a good mind. Soon I will have converted sufficient good minds to form a church."

"There is no longer need. I have contacted a much more responsive race than yours."

So Bringer had put out another probe. My heart sank. "Where?"

"In this ocean. A fully telepathic race. Aquatic, but with a philosophy suited to receive the Word. And they recognize my songs more readily than any of you. I am leaving the Word with them. You must learn from them."

"What—what are you going to do?"

"Continue my mission. I have planted the seed on this world. There are others waiting salvation. I am leaving now. Truth be with you." And the egg went silent.

Alice understood first. She put her hand at her mouth. "Teddy's converted the dolphins!"

"Dolphins?" Jean was on her feet, swaying but standing. "What dolphins?"

"Or perhaps the whales?" Alice's shock turned to laughter.

30

WE SAT STARING at each other. Whales and dolphins? Telepathic sapients? Could be. From what Bringer had said, seawater enhanced telepathic transmission. And being telepathic saps hadn't helped them much—in the past. Perhaps what Bringer had taught might help them survive in the future. I wished them well. Truth and Knowledge were safe with them. They were no threat to us—not in the foreseeable future. I tried to explain to Jean what had happened.

Alice cut me off. "What's important is that Teddy's done his job here. Better whales than us. They won't be able to make atom bombs under water. Probably won't want to. And he's off to convert other worlds. Wish I could have seen Jerry again!" She sighed, then picked up the egg. "This is just a dead toy now."

"What the hell shall we do with it?" I took it from her. My acute worry relieved, I reverted to earlier concerns.

"Let's give it to that Colonel? Dump it on him and get us off the hook?" Alice grinned. "Give him Justine too! Then he can take them both apart." She started for the bedroom door. "After I've had my turn at her."

"Alice—stop! Come here!" called Jean.

She already had the door open and was staring at Justine, tied on the bed. I jumped after her, pulled her back. "You stay with Jean. I'll talk to Madame Ladrich."

"Don't talk Richard. Kick! And kick her real hard this time."

I closed the door and walked across the room. Justine squirmed away, as though fearing I was about to follow Alice's suggestion. I stood over her. "Gassed with your own gun. Lucky it wasn't cyanide."

She glared up at me, radiating sorrow and fury. "You could have tried to take me back."

The sorrow swamped the fury; the agony of a lover restored only to be snatched away. Her pain hurt so much that I moved back from the bed. Alice, in the next room, must have felt it too. She burst through the door. "What are you doing to her?" Then she realized the cause of Justine's grief and stopped dead.

"That's what love does to you, kid."

"You don't know what love is," spat Justine.

"Who was he?" Alice moved to sit on the bed. "Come on! We're both supersaps. And we fought together. I may hate your guts but you can still tell me—and Richard."

"Then untie me." Justine rolled on her side, presenting her wrists.

Alice bent to the tapes. I touched her shoulder. "Just her hands."

Alice nodded, ripped the tapes free, and helped Justine to sit up. She swung her bound ankles over the side of the bed and sat rubbing her wrists.

"Who is he?" persisted Alice. "That guy Gamar?"

"My husband." Justine's face and mind quivered. "He was my husband. They shot him. The year after we were married."

"Who shot him?"

"One of the governments who've divided us up. Who knows which one? They fight each other. The only thing they agree on is tyrannizing us. Gamar was our leader." She paused. "He sent me to Paris to collect money for our cause. One government caught him and traded him to another. That one shot him." She tried to stand up, stumbled, and dropped back to the bed. "I'm still a fighter. I fight with money now. Money always wins in the end." She looked up at me. "You understand that well, Richard Ryan."

"So Gamar died for your cause. And we saw him fight like a hero." Perhaps we had only seen her idealized image of her dead husband, but that was beside the point. "You were luckier than most widows, Justine. You saw him again. Long enough to make love. Be thankful for that."

"You called it a dream. You said that egg-thing creates dreams."

"Illusions. Realistic illusions. Would you have known—if we hadn't told you?"

Slowly she shook her head.

I played a hunch. "Would you want a thing like that for your fighters? People mostly prefer dream fighting to real fighting. Fights when you don't wake up dead."

She took my meaning. "No—I'd give it to our enemies."

"Ever heard of a weapon staying on one side for long?"

She sat silent for a moment, then hissed, "It would seduce us all into illusions. It's the work of the devil. Destroy it!"

"You already have. One visit from you and the Holy City's gone to hell. No more visitors. No more dreams."

"The egg's fucked up," added Alice. "It doesn't work. Never will work again."

She believed us, of course. "Who made it?"

"Alice," I said. "Get out!"

"You're not going to hurt her? You mustn't! She's suffered—" Alice saw my face and retreated from the room, slamming the door.

I turned to Justine. "Who betrayed us? Come on. I've got to know that before we can talk business."

"You'll talk business if I tell you?"

I nodded.

"Who betrayed you? You betrayed yourself."

"How could I? I didn't know where Alice was until Jean brought me here."

"Fool! Your watch. The one you've got is bugged."

I looked at my wrist. "It can't be. I never take it off."

"You did once. When I asked you." She laughed, then flinched at my impulse to hit her. "I switched watches. Noted the one you wore when we went dancing. Had a duplicate bugged and switched on you that night when I was a Selected Escort. That's the one on your wrist. Not strong enough to monitor. But a strong enough signal to track. You led me here with a bugged watch."

I cursed. "Should have bugged you when I had the chance."

She flinched again. "What are you going to do with me now?"

"Make a deal of course—as usual." I sighed and sat down. "Those goons of yours won't be back. Jean wants to hand you over to the police."

"Charged with what? And by whom? A runaway kid and a lawyer with a shady reputation? You'll have trouble making anything stick. And I'll make plenty of trouble for you."

"I could do as you'd have done. Dump the body in some river."

"I wouldn't have and you won't. That woman—Jean—she won't let you." She stared at me. "And you haven't the guts anyway. Not to kill cold."

"Not if I can dodge it. So I'm going to give you—and that toy—to Colonel Metzler. And tell him you know how it works."

"But I don't."

"You may be able to convince him of that—in the end."

"You bastard! You call that a deal?"

"That's what'll happen if our negotiations fall through. If we do reach an understanding, then I'll still hand you and the toy over to Metzler. But only after I've told both of you what it really is. In return—"

"Yes?"

"In return for presenting Metzler with you and the egg I'll get his promise to leave Alice and Jean and me alone. In return for my not letting Metzler think you know more than you do—I'll want the same promise."

"You'd accept a promise? From him? From me?"

I shrugged. "The Colonel keeps his word—when he gives it. And—like you—I'm sensitive."

"You'll tell the truth about that toy? To both of us?"

"Yes. Metzler may not believe me. But you will."

"He won't be able to hold me. He's got nothing on me." She saw my face. "Has he?"

I shrugged. "Something outdated and unimportant. Co-operate with him and he'll turn you loose."

"Anything else?"

"Only that you don't tell Jean or Alice about my watch. Or mention Selected Escorts."

It was after three when I phoned the duty officer at the Unit and was surprised to be put through to the Colonel immediately. In his office at that hour of the morning? "Ryan—what is it?" He sounded weary.

"Colonel—I've got that egg thing for you. If you'll come and fetch it."

He was suddenly awake. "You've got it? Where?"

"I want immunity for the girl—Alice Drummond—and myself before I hand it over."

"Ryan, you know I can't guarantee immunity."

"Just tell me you'll leave the kid alone after you're satisfied she can't help. And hear what I have to say before you do anything. How's that?"

A pause. Then, "I'll come at first light. Where are you?"

I gave him directions. "And put the chopper down quietly. There's a field about half a mile away. I'll be there to meet you. You won't want to attract attention. I can tell you that much in advance."

"We'll come in muffled. Any shooting?" He sounded hopeful.

"Shooting's over. Situation secured."

I hung up and turned toward Jean and Alice. "He's coming by chopper. Jean, use my car. Take Alice back to your apartment and stay there. I'm pretty sure Metzler won't hassle either of you."

"There's one thing I want to know first," demanded Alice.

"What's that?"

"How did you know about the grunt?"

"Experience, kid, experience."

"But how—?"

"Enough questions," snapped Jean. "I've a lot that need answering myself. They can wait until we've recovered."

"But—?"

"Alice—get into the car!"

Alice glared, scowled, hesitated, then flung out of the room. The front door closed with a crash. I said, "You're going to have trouble with that girl."

"She's worth taking trouble over." Jean limped along the hall. "I'm going to try and adopt her."

"Fine. But that won't be easy for a single woman."

Jean laughed through swollen lips. "If we were married

then Alice would be your legal daughter. And the incest taboo might cramp your style.''

''Are you proposing—?''

She left without making clear exactly what she was proposing. I watched the tail-lights disappear down the lane, What had she meant? Not sure I liked the possible interpretations. Too confusing to consider for the moment. I sighed and went back into the cottage to prepare for Metzler's arrival.

It was just after dawn when the hum of an approaching chopper came from the southeast. I left the cottage and walked along the lane to the field as the command helicopter came muffled out of the morning mist. I waved it in and greeted Metzler when he jumped out, three agents in civilian clothes at his heels.

''Morning, Ryan. It's been a hell of a night. And you've picked a hell of a time to hand that thing over.''

''I called you first chance I had.'' I glanced at his face. He looked old. ''What's been going on?''

''Full alert. Didn't you know? I guess not. Stand-down just before you called. Well, where is that egg thing?'' He stood, rubbing his hands.

''You'll leave the kid alone? She's been through a rough time. And I can tell you everything she knows. More than she knows.''

''I may have to speak to her. I won't harrass her. If you're telling the truth.''

''Okay. An interview to quiet your conscience. But later. And only if you think it vital. After you've heard me out you may choose to let it go at that.'' I started down the lane beside him and stopped at the cottage gate. ''Colonel, you won't want your boys to see or hear any of this. Not until you've decided what to do.''

He looked at me sharply but told his escort to wait outside and stay out of sight. I led him up the front path, opened the front door, and waved him in. ''Come and get the egg. And a bonus.''

''Bonus?''

I opened the door to the living room. ''Her!''

Justine was sitting at the table with the egg at its center. She looked up and smiled. ''Colonel Metzler! This is an unsought pleasure.''

"Madame Ladrich?" He saw the egg. "Is that the thing?"

"That's it. Sit down while I tell you both about it."

"Tell her?"

"Yes, Colonel. Afterward—she's all yours. But please—hear me out first."

He objected, of course. To have a woman with Justine's reputation present while we discussed something that might be top secret with need to know. At one point he nearly had her lugged off. But with both Justine and myself reading his conflicting emotions we convinced him that I wouldn't say a damned thing unless she stayed. Justine's amusement at this example of sensitives cooperating did not show on her face but was clear in her mind.

"That thing's from an alien spaceship," I began.

Justine's amusement changed to horror. Horror which increased as I went on to give them both a laundered version of the egg's story. She knew I was telling the truth as I believed it to be. But if I believed what I was saying I must be mad. By the time I finished she was sure I was mad.

Metzler, after his initial spasm of disbelief, began to look increasingly thoughtful, and was finally looking at me as if he wasn't certain what I was. I said nothing about dreams, or cities, and only enough about the Word to make some sense of Bringer's purpose in visiting Earth at all. When I had finished my summary he sat silent for a moment, then asked, "That alien, where did it say it was?"

"It didn't say exactly. From the picture it showed me of its arrival I'd guess it was in the Pacific, about six hundred miles south of the Aleutians."

He cracked his knuckles and looked at me. "You heard anything yet?"

"About spaceships you mean? Only what you mentioned once. Somebody's satellite falling into the Pacific. Nobody knew whose."

"I didn't say where. Heard anything since then? No, you couldn't. You couldn't possibly have heard."

"Heard what?"

He glanced at Justine, then at me. "It'll be in the papers by this time tomorrow anyway. Those damned reporters."

He sighed. "What time did this missionary machine of yours say it was leaving?"

"One forty-seven."

"The same." He stared at the egg. "Exactly the time that missile went up from the Pacific. From under the Pacific. A thousand kilometers south of Kodiak."

"Missile? What missile?"

"They called it a missile. Because that's what everyone assumed it was. Only it went straight up. And kept going. We had an alert because the comps thought it was a missile fired by a submerged sub. But everybody—us, the Reds, the Brits, —everybody who might be able to fire anything denies they did. We went on alert. Everybody went on alert while the comps were calculating the target. They're still busy calculating the target. Somewhere between Mars and Venus was the last I heard." He clenched his fists. "The politicians—theirs, ours—are agreeing to call it a radar-computer error. So the public can blame the military for scaring the shit out of everybody. And the pacifists will have another lie to hit us with." Colonel Metzler tended to see every event in terms of its impact on the defense budget.

Justine had lost some of her skepticism on hearing Metzler's announcement. "Colonel, Richard Ryan thinks he's speaking the truth."

"Never known him to speak anything else, Madame." Metzler looked across the table as though suddenly remembering her presence and being shocked at the memory. "Never known him to tell all of it either. Tough story to swallow. But that thing leaving the Pacific and this toy going dead at the same time—could be coincidence. Also tough to swallow." He stood up. "Okay, Ryan. You've fulfilled your agreement. I'll want to talk to that girl. But later. In the meantime—don't talk to anyone."

"Nobody'd believe me if I did. That egg's all the proof there is. And you've got it. Maybe the boys will be able to take it apart. But my guess is there'll only be debris inside. Of course there's Slipe and his superpure silicon. Lean on him hard enough and he'd probably sing."

"Sing what? Slipe as an unwilling witness at an inquiry? Not if I can help it."

"You've got me." Justine smiled at the Colonel. "As a witness, I mean."

"You, Madame, are the last person I would want to give evidence—anywhere." He put his hands on the table and leaned toward her. "Tell me now and save yourself trouble. Who are you working for? I know your firm was once retained by the KGB."

"Years ago, Colonel. And against my enemies only. In this—I work only for Loucher Freres. No connection with any government of any kind. Against them all, you might say."

"She's telling the truth. She's working only for Loucher Freres." I paused. "She *is* Loucher Freres."

"She's—?" Metzler laughed. "That they won't swallow. I'll have to report—" He stopped, realizing what he might have to report. "They'll think I'm crazy too. You were right, Ryan. No publicity. Or they'll have us all hunting UFOs." He sighed. "Madame Ladrich, you'd better come with me. I'd like to hear your side of the story."

"You've no right to arrest me. I'm a citizen of France. The French Consul—"

"I'm not arresting. I'm inviting. If you don't accept the invitation—well, there's an old unsettled affair." He put the egg in his pocket. "Be sensible, Madame. Come with me to Washington." He sighed again, his conscience in conflict with his duty to protect the security of the United States. "Regard it as a business trip. There are certain potential operations due to be subcontracted which might interest a firm with Loucher Freres' facilities."

"On that basis—very well. But I've no more ideas about how that egg worked than you have."

"I believe you, Madame. I'll give you a lift in the chopper if you'll come with me now."

"I can't!" snarled Justine. "Richard's taped my ankles to this chair."

After I'd freed her and they'd walked to the door, Metzler turned. "The brass won't swallow this. Even if they open the egg without destroying it. They'll bury anything I write. Pity in a way."

"Pity?"

"Pity if our first ET contact isn't recorded. Richard, you're a kind of writer. Why don't you write all this up? As fiction of course."

And that is what I have tried to do.

AN OPEN LETTER
TO THE AMERICAN PEOPLE

Astronauts Francis (Dick) Scobee, Michael Smith, Judy Resnik, Ellison Onizuka, Ronald McNair, Gregory Jarvis, and Christa McAuliffe understood the risk, undertook the challenge, and in so doing embodied the dreams of us all.

Unlike so many of us, they did not take for granted the safety of riding a torch of fire to the stars.

For them the risk was real from the beginning. But some are already seizing upon their deaths as proof that America is unready for the challenge of manned space flight. *This is the last thing the seven would have wanted.*

Originally five orbiters were proposed; only four were built. This tragic reduction of the fleet places an added burden on the remaining three.

But the production facilities still exist. The assembly line can be reactivated. The experiments designed for the orbiter bay are waiting. We can recover a program which is one of our nation's greatest resources and mankind's proudest achievements.

Soon Congress will determine the immediate direction the space program must take. We must place at highest priority the restoration and enhancement of the shuttle fleet and resumption of a full launch schedule.

For the seven.

In keeping with their spirit of dedication to the future of space exploration and with the deepest respect for their memory, we are asking you to join us in urging the President and the Congress to build a new shuttle orbiter to carry on the work of these seven courageous men and women.

As long as their dream lives on, the seven live on in the dream.

SUPPORT SPACE EXPLORATION!

Write to the President at
1600 Pennsylvania Avenue,
Washington, D.C. 20500.

DAW
SCIENCE
FICTION

DAW'S NEW WONDER-WORLD
OF SCIENCE FICTION STARS